TANGLE

Arnold Peabody visits Madame Lily, a local medium, after his mother dies to see if he could obtain contact with her from beyond the grave. Before long, Arnold drowns himself.

Soon after, Mildred Hewitt from Avenbridge falls to her death at a local beauty spot on a snowy night. Her son Gilbert decides to visit the medium too and he goes off the rails while the community watches in fascination.

Henry Beaumont, who had frequently visited Avenridge since he had been evacuated there, knows many people in the area and was sure that murder had been committed . . .

TANGLE

Meg Elizabeth Atkins

First published 1988
by
Marion Boyars Publishers

This edition 2005 by BBC Audiobooks Ltd
published by arrangement with
the author

ISBN 1 4056 8507 7

British Library Cataloguing in Publication Data available

To Clare
for Veronica,
and much more

Printed and bound in Great Britain by
Antony Rowe Ltd., Chippenham, Wiltshire

ONE

The room was crammed with ponderous furniture, lit by dim bulbs in shades shaped like the trumpets of lilies. It had its own smell: incense, dust, the creeping persistence of boiled sprouts. It had its own density, the residue of bewilderment and yearning and fear. With curtains muffling doors and windows, shadowy and pungent, it hung in the nowhere of the night, itself a nowhere — if the medium could be believed: a meeting place of dead and living.

The medium, short and very fat, wore a wig, raven black against her white dumpling face, her mouth was a primped rosebud. She looked unhealthy, like something kept too long from the light, her expression passive with the satisfaction of one who feeds on admiration. There was much self-regard in her, and the surging, obdurate strength of stupidity.

She sat in a grandly carved chair, her legs dangling, her feet bulging over her patent leather shoes. She seldom exerted herself physically. Her gift, she was careful to point out, drained her, took everything out of her, she had to be careful not to overtax her strength. She said, 'We'll have a few minutes silence to start, the spirits like me to sit and wait.' Her voice was soft-toned, with a faint, slovenly whine.

There were four people in the room: two young women sitting close together on a sofa, an elderly woman in a severe hat on a straight-backed chair — and Arnold Peabody, trapped in the depths of a gigantic armchair like half-swallowed prey in the mouth of a monster.

The medium said, 'There's a very recent loss here, very recent.' Her eyes, shiny as the beads that swathed her bosom, moved slowly round the room, rested on Arnold. 'The sea. I'm getting the sea very strong. Waves, sand, a sort of beach. The tide coming in and out.'

He had winced backwards, involuntarily reacting to the exposed nerve of his grief. But with her eyes on him, her voice reaching out, he was drawn forward: images filled the space between them.

'Was it the sea, dear?'

He responded at once, as if retrieving his place in an interrupted conversation. 'We went every year. The Isle of Wight. Our summer holiday. Mother loved it.'

The medium closed her eyes. 'Sun and sand. Buckets and spades. A really happy place, really happy.'

'She always said, she'd like to retire. There. But. Her illness.'

'I can feel the sea breeze on my face, sand in my shoes, a really happy place. It's never too late.' Her eyes snapped open, fastened on Arnold. 'It's never too late.'

He was frowning. *I shall be all right, he said, after her death to anyone who asked. I shall be all right. His wretchedness, with nowhere to go, congealed on his feature, making them bland. No one noticed the desperation in his eyes.*

It's never too late.

He struggled. 'What? It was only. Last week. Do you mean? I couldn't understand. What she said.'

'That's right, it's not too late, it'll always be a happy place. You're not to grieve. Plenty of time. She understands.'

For an instant there was repose on his face. 'She always understood. Everything. But. It's being alone. Wondering.'

'We're never alone. Our dear ones are always with us.'

He blinked. That was not right. His mother was not with him anywhere. Except, perhaps, here?

'Always watching over us,' the medium said, on an inflection of finality. She turned her attention to the women. She had comfort from souls at peace: your friend says not to worry about Beryl, he can see a way through the trouble. Messages: your father's here, he doesn't want you to do anything about the boarding house yet. Occasionally her button eyes flickered towards Arnold, who sat bemused in the maw of the armchair.

Abruptly, she stopped speaking, raised a plump hand to her brow, said 'Aaah . . .' and on that single exclamation, more like a sigh, the atmosphere in the room shifted, thickened. A turbulence quaked through her body, set the beaded bodice aquiver, the jowls wobbling. Her voice, devoid now of professional consolation, began with a gasping emphasis. 'There's a lady here. Not a young lady. She wants to speak particular — ' The gaze riveted Arnold. 'She worked so hard, all the years in the shop. A sensible, careful lady. She knew you'd never be able to manage the business without her, that's right, isn't it?'

Arnold, mesmerized, nodded wordlessly.

'She did what was best for you. You mustn't blame her. She felt you blamed her. You never said it, but she knew, knew you wanted things your way, so you blamed her.'

'No,' Arnold whispered, pleading.

'You were so close, always. And she was ill for such a long time. She needed you to look after her, you couldn't have managed the business as well. She's come to bring you comfort, she's here, oh, yes, she's very strong here now . . .'

Did the lights flicker? The curtains stir? Arnold's hand went forward as if to grasp an impalpable presence; yearning broke open his features. 'Where? Where?'

'She says you're going to be all right, you'll do what's right, you always have.'

'I've tried. I've always tried. But. Now. I can't manage. I don't know. What to do — ' Overwrought, he was unaware that he spoke aloud, that the words were wrenched upon a sob.

The three women politely averted their eyes from this naked indication of his grief, submitting to embarrassed scrutiny some hideous ornament or piece of furniture.

The medium said, 'You must let go. You'll be all right. Time heals all. She needs peace.' Again the pudgy hand went to the brow, the tone slackened. 'She's gone now.'

'No,' he whispered.

But the medium was stirring, gathering herself, her business in the next world concluded. 'That's all for this evening.'

The women made restrained motions of departure, opening handbags, pulling on gloves. In a dazed way, Arnold became part of the general movement, the inhibitions of a lifetime reinstated themselves: in unfamiliar situations — there were few in his life — he did what everyone else did.

The woman in the hat, frowning and shaking her head to add weight to her words, spoke to him in an undertone. 'She's marvellous, is Madame Lily, marvellous. I always take her advice. Always.' She had a large, worn purse in her hand. The two young women also had their purses out, depositing something — it was impossible to tell how much — into a black velvet bag. In an atmosphere of such furtive gentility no one mentioned money.

'For the flowers, dear,' the medium said, smiling.

He fumbled a £5 note into the bag. There were no flowers in

evidence except plastic lilies stabbed into urns. In the dim hallway there were more, fashioned into the shape of a cross that hung on the wall by the coat stand. 'Can I come again?' he asked.

The front door stood open, the women were leaving, uttering hushed goodnights. In the narrow hallway the sharp-cornered coat stand thrust him into physical intimacy with the surge of the medium's bosom, an intimacy that in normal circumstances would have terrified him. But his distress clung to him, giving him an uncharacteristic tenacity; and the brief display of her powers, amazing him, placed her in a category where conventional social responses did not operate.

'Of course, Monday nights, dear. You don't need to phone again, just come along Monday.'

Monday. A whole week. He did not know if there were such things as private sessions, how to ask for one.

The sound of the women's footsteps faded. The lamplit street was quiet. A current of air drifted, carrying from a window box somewhere the swooning scent of the first wallflowers of Spring.

'I think Mother wanted me to come here. She used to have . . . A friend . . . Mrs Parkwright . . . She was interested in . . . She used to visit you.'

'Oh, yes, dear. I can't call the name to mind. So many people consult me.'

'She died. Some years ago. Mrs Parkwright.'

'Ah, she'll be at peace now.' Assuming personal responsibility for this, the medium gave a satisfied nod. 'Your mother came to me, did she?'

'Oh, no. No.'

'I thought not. I'd have known her.'

Overwhelmed by such competence, he stood in silence,

twisting the brim of his trilby hat in his hands. He looked reluctantly at the door opening to the night, to the emptiness of the street, the loneliness of everywhere.

The medium peered up at him. 'You're greatly troubled, aren't you?

She spoke on the moment he prepared to mutter goodnight, turn and go. A nervous reflex seized him, he stammered. 'You see. There's no one.' No one who was the least interested in him: he had always been a man talked at, not listened to.

'I can always tell. But you've relatives?'

'Well. They're not. I can't.'

Sympathy enveloped him on the gust of her sigh. 'It's not always easy to talk to them as should be nearest us. But we are greatly loved by our departed ones, of that we can be sure. And they're in a lovely place. Lovely. Eventually.'

'Eventually?'

'There's what we call a period of transition, dear. If they went unexpected, or have some unfinished business, they need us to help them through.'

Questions crowded, stunning his features.

She shifted wearily from one foot to the other, put her hand on the door. 'I'll tell you what, would you like to come Thursday afternoon? I'm fresher in the afternoons and we'll have time to talk.'

'Yes, thank you. I would.'

Her bulk, remorselessly inclined towards him, dislodged him from the coat stand, eased him across the threshold.

'What time?' he asked the closing door.

'Three o'clock, dear.'

'Thank you. Thank you,' he stammered.

A woman stood in the bay window of the front room, looking along the row of tall Victorian terraces. She watched the three women leave, go down the steps that gave directly on to the pavement, pass beneath the window and walk off in a huddle.

From the hall came the indistinct sound of voices. Then the door closed. Arnold emerged, his figure smudging as he stepped from the lamp-light and crossed the piece of waste ground beside the house. He got in his car and drove away.

Had any of the visitors looked back they would not have seen the woman. Thick net curtains of a dingy yellow-white hung at the window, and the room was in darkness. It had the mustily dank air of a place seldom used, the smell of accumulated sootfalls from the open fireplace, and the furniture was chill to the woman's touch as she felt her way back to the corner where she had been sitting for the past hour.

The door in the corner stood open a crack, she pulled it wider, jerked aside the curtain and stepped into the back room.

The medium was sitting on the sofa, eating sugared jellies from a box. Wariness glimmered for an instant, submerged in the fat of her face. She said, on an ingratiating note, 'Make us a cup of tea. I'm wore out.'

The other woman did not answer. She turned up the gas fire and stood over it, warming her hands. Then she began to prowl about the room; something feral had entered it with her. 'What was all that gasping business? "There's a lady here, she wants to speak to someone." Your voice changes.'

'It's my gift. It comes over me suddenly. I'm just sitting there, talking, picking up vibrations. You have to apply a bit of psychology, insight.'

'Psychology. Insight,' the soft voice repeated in contemptuous amusement. 'And they pay you for the privilege.'

''Course. Why not?'

The woman sat at the table before the curtained window, emptying the contents of the velvet bag. 'Are they usually as generous as this?' She held up the £5 note.

The medium glanced at it indifferently. 'Must be that new chap.'

'Pathetic little twerp. Who is he? Where does he come from?'

'I don't know. Manchester, I think he said.'

'But you must have known his mother had just died. Known beforehand.'

'No. I can tell when they come in. There's something about the recently bereaved, something sort of grey all round them. That's why they come. They want me to tell them things, and I do. Somehow I know what they want me to say. Then it comes over me suddenly, my gift.'

'How? What happens?'

'I don't know. I can't explain. Something sort of looms round me. Then it's inside me. I'm like — like — a vessel.'

'A sacred vessel, I suppose.'

The medium, seeking out jellies in the box, missed the glance that raked her pitilessly from head to foot. 'Yes. A sacred vessel.'

'Holy shit,' the other woman breathed. Then, 'Go on. Tell me.'

On a defensive note, the medium began to explain herself. She was singled out by fate, blessed with a power both precious and dangerous, to be used only for the good of others. Soon, however, she was caught up in the drama of herself, and her account of her extraordinary talent — conjectures confirmed, pronouncements revered — gathered momentum. She grew excited, gabbled, repeated herself: her bulging eyes lost focus, a dribble of saliva coursed from the side of her rosebud mouth. Eventually, her squat body quaked to its climax, she lay back, gorged on self-admiration; her panting breath steadied, slipped into normal rhythm.

The gas fire hissed and popped.

The woman at the table had not uttered a word. She had sat

with her face half turned away in disgust, but her sidelong gaze never wavered.

The medium, stirring, wheezing, responding to a silence suddenly chill in the stuffy room, roused herself and saw that the woman was smiling. She looked away, quickly, her gaze seeking the safety of familiar objects.

'Go on, make us a cup of tea,' she whined at last. As if nothing had happened. As if she had not seen, in the shape of that smile, the outline of a menace against which all her powers were futile.

Arnold drove home, an hour's journey along steep, twisting roads. At the south Lancashire border the suburbs began, increasing in density until they merged with the fringe of the city, where his red-brick bungalow stood beside a roaring dual carriageway. A high privet hedge, grimy with exhaust fumes, shielded the long front garden; gloomy conifers grew at the side.

The bungalow was full of dark, ugly furniture. Nothing had changed in it since his parents bought it in 1937, the year before his father died. Now, after all those years of familiarity, Arnold lived in it like an intruder, making his meals and tidying up in an apologetic fashion. Sometimes he just sat for hours, unmoving, while time opened up endlessly about him, great desolate tracts strewn with the wreckage of routine.

There was no one he could talk to. His relatives, despising his devotion to his mother, offered bracing condolences with the advice that this was his chance to lead his own life. But for so long had he existed as an adjunct to his mother he ceased, for them, on her death, to exist at all. And he had never had friends, shyness kept him from a social life, his mother kept him from women.

But her narrow virtues were his. In place of pleasure he had always had the satisfaction of work: the hardware shop where, neat in his overall, safe behind the counter, he was also secure in expectation — 'one day all this will be yours'. But the scheme of things faltered, his mother became ill. When she sold the shop he stifled a regret close to bitterness; she needed him to look after her, times were changing, family businesses were no longer secure investments . . .

He agreed with her, because she was always right. He had his duty and he loved her, although that was not a word they ever used. And they could not speak of the future, which had become a blank wall rearing before them both. Instead, she made reference to some dimension where her existence continued unquestioned, her authority undiminished, and with her failing physical strength took on a grotesque power, assuring him that whatever happened she would never leave him, they would always be together.

The only relative with whom Arnold had much contact was his cousin Edith, a grimly meddling woman who lived on a vast Council estate where she exercised her energies making ends meet and looking down on her neighbours. At her insistence, he occasionally walked round to her house for a meal; he would have liked to refuse but her invitations had such indignant undertones he did not dare. Edith was never going to let it be said she failed in her duty towards him.

The visits were an ordeal. Edith's husband was a morose man, persistently out of work; her three children, reared in her tradition of despising Arnold, were embarrassed by his bereavement. He never knew how to speak to them and they never had anything to say to him, except at Christmas when he gave them generous gifts of money. Then they shuffled and went red and could not meet his eyes. He would have preferred to buy presents for them, to discover with great cunning what they most desired, make his purchases in secret, watch them take the lavishly wrapped parcels from beneath the tree, open them with shining eyes . . .

But Edith was unyielding. Money was sensible, it always 'came in', and it was her duty to provide for her family where she could. As the Peabodys' closest relative, and the only one to take the trouble to keep up a show of interest in them, she had nursed hopes of something coming her way at the sale of the shop. She received nothing and was again disappointed when Mrs Peabody died. Her mouth set then in a harder line: only Arnold stood between her and the modest Peabody capital. She lived in unspoken expectation of something sudden and painless happening to him and waited for the moment to tackle him about his will.

Whenever Arnold mentioned his mother, Edith's stock response, 'Well, she's gone now', converted the reminiscences that trembled on his lips to a sigh of agreement. His grief was burdened by confusion — he had not understood, at the end, what his mother had been trying to tell him, what her instructions were. There had to be instructions, there always had been, without them the last prop of his sanity would give way.

With guilt at work in him, the sense that he had failed in some vital requirement, he tried to talk to Edith of Mrs Parkwright, his mother's old friend, and of the medium. In Edith's rigid view such matters were not merely bizarre, they were unhealthy. A long-submerged outrage surfaced, she was at last able to refer to Mrs Parkwright as a daft old woman who had given her the creeps. 'I'm surprised your mother ever listened to such nasty nonsense.' And disposing of them both with an adamant, 'Well, they've both gone now,' she thrust Arnold back into silence.

Arnold drove over to Avenridge to make his second visit to the medium. She opened the door and regarded him without any sign of recognition. Her wig was askew.

At a loss, he took off his hat and stood mute until she uttered, 'Yes?' when he stammered apologetically that she was expecting him.

'Was it for a reading?'

He had no idea what that meant and said, 'Well,' helplessly.

'You're not from Social Security, are you?'

'No. Oh, no. You said. To come this afternoon. Arnold Peabody.'

The name plainly meant nothing to her. 'You'll have to excuse me, I'm not myself today. Just a minute.' She waddled away on the flap of carpet slippers, her bulk disappearing into the murky reaches of the hall. After a while she returned, indicating he should come in. She had put on her patent shoes and straightened her wig.

The zest of the afternoon could not penetrate the back room. The heavy curtains were partially drawn over several layers of obscuring net; the gas fire hissed, the air was close and frowsty.

She sat on the sofa, put her feet up. 'You don't mind, do you, dear? Only, I'm not myself today,' she said again. 'Now, what was it about?'

He did not know, he had come to be told.

Her eyes slid about the room uneasily. 'I've had an upset,' she said as if to herself.

They sat in silence for a while. Somewhere in the house there was movement, a door closed, a shape occurred and vanished in the back yard, beyond the curtains. She sighed, mouth quivering, then reached for a box of jellies, offering one to Arnold. He shook his head. 'They're good for you, the sugar gives you energy.' She began to consume them. 'You've been here before, haven't you, dear?' she said vaguely.

'Yes. Monday. I came about. It was my mother.'

She nodded. 'I recollect now. She had a message for you.'

'I didn't quite. Understand it.'

'No, well, it's often the way. And it's no good me trying now. There's some days I'm drained, drained, I haven't the strength to get through to the other side. I don't like to disappoint you, dear, especially as you're so troubled in your mind. Did I bring you comfort last time?'

'Yes. It's so. Amazing. How you knew. About the Isle of Wight.'

'It is amazing. It's because I'm what they call a sensitive, you see, dear.' Admiration had a restorative effect on her.

'I wondered. Why you chose that. Particularly.'

'Choose? Oh, I don't *choose*, I'm at the mercy of forces beyond myself. Whatever's important to you communicates itself to me. It was a place that meant a great deal to you.'

'Our holiday. Every year.'

Every year. They always stayed at the most expensive hotel, scarcely ever relaxed for fear of doing the wrong thing, but their secret pleasure was the unaccustomed luxury and their ability to afford it. They wore their best clothes every day, went to variety performances, sat on promenades listening to brass bands while the sun burnt their pallid city flesh. The colour and light and freedom of those days shone through gloomy winters and drab springs. Treasuring the smallest detail in recollections and holiday snaps, they talked of retiring there, as if they were of an age, husband and wife, not mother and son.

His memories were so vivid he could not be sure how many spilled into speech, how many stayed in his head: he knew that he talked, and she listened. Then she told him of her triumphs, her infallibility, and he in his turn listened, filled with awe. She made tea. The afternoon passed. At last she said, 'You'll have to be off now, I suppose.'

He had nothing to do, no one claimed his time, but he stood up obediently, took out his wallet. The black velvet bag was nowhere in sight, he was too embarrassed to search for it in the clutter of the room. He folded a £5 note and put it under his saucer.

They made another appointment. She asked him to bring something of his mother's — a glove, a scarf. 'It helps, you see. I can get much closer then.'

His expression indicated that this was something he yearned to do, and could not.

'There's a veil between this world and the next. The way is clear for them as can read the signs,' she said as she waddled with him to the door.

'Is it? I don't think I . . .'

'No. Ordinary people can't.'

'Ah.' He was ordinary. He was content to leave the phenomenal, the fateful, to her.

TWO

The suburb Arnold had known since childhood, the shops and pubs, tall dusty trees and homely sidestreets, had been swallowed by a mammoth development of roads and tower blocks. He continued to shop there, anonymous in the supermarkets of a precinct of insane grandeur that overwhelmed him, made him fumble and forget things. Away from its garish lights and fountains and balconies were areas of sudden silence, deadened, depopulated underpasses and multi-storey car parks. Gangs of youths roamed these dangerous places, lifts were permanently out of order and light bulbs smashed, there were alarming stories of assault.

It was in the enclosed shaft of a concrete staircase that Arnold suffered the terror of pursuit by a crowd of hooligans. They thundered on booted feet down from the level above, whooping and jeering, while he fled, skidding through rubbish, throwing himself round the sharp-angled turns. On the final flight they surrounded him, hard, furious bodies, the smell of sweat and beer, foul language yelled into his ears. A violent thrust in the small of his back sent him lurching. He tried to cling to the handrail but it had long since been wrenched from its moorings and swung out wildly. With a faint mew of despair he pitched down the remaining steps.

He never recalled more than a few details of the incident, although the memory of its panic remained with him. What happened immediately afterwards was a blur of faces, voices, hands. When he found himself sitting in an antiseptic room, the taste of vomit in his mouth, his left wrist securely strapped, he was too stupid with shock to take in anything the crisp, buxom sister said. She handed him a card. 'Off you go, Mr Peabody. Your friend's waiting to take you home.'

He had no friend. He went dazedly out into a corridor.

A young woman sat waiting, she held his shopping bag, his smashed watch and his wallet. 'You left this behind when you went off in the ambulance. I thought I'd better come after you.' She handed him his wallet. 'It must have fallen out of your pocket. Unless it was what those vandals were after and they dropped it when they ran off. Aren't you going to look in it? See there's nothing missing?'

But he stuffed the wallet awkwardly away in his pocket. As he did so he looked down, made a strangled sound of disgust. His clothes were stained, fouled with smears; he shrank inside himself, violated by contact.

She studied him, her head on one side. 'Pity, it's a good suit. It'll clean. I suppose you could get the tears mended.'

He would throw the suit away, remove all trace, all memory, all madness.

'Lost your voice?'

'What?'

'You had enough to say when we were waiting for the ambulance.'

He did not believe her. He had never set eyes on her before. 'Oh.'

'You don't remember. You do look rather dreadful. Come on.'

She led him along corridors, down steps. He heard nothing of what she said. In her car she asked his address. He told her, then closed his eyes.

In the kitchen she made tea while he sat at the table waiting for her to go away. He had suffered too much shock to react to the presence of a strange woman opening cupboards, touching things.

She sat opposite him. 'You talked to me while we were waiting for the ambulance. Told me about your mother. I'm sorry.' She spoke softly. 'And your shop. I remember your shop. It's empty now, they're going to pull that whole row down. Sad.' She gave him two aspirins. 'When you've had those I think you should go to bed.'

He sipped his tea. His mind moved sluggishly towards the conclusion that she was some kind of social worker from the hospital.

'Is there anyone I can phone for you? To come round?'

Only Edith. Edith, with her loud, hard voice, bullying him, and making him feel everything was his own fault. And she was not on the telephone. 'No. No one.'

She repeated, 'No one,' and looked at him gently as he sat there in his torn suit, his shiny shoes scuffed, his hand trembling at his tea cup. She chattered for a while about the new building programme, the way things changed. He said nothing, nodded occasionally, did not notice the way she looked round at the neatness of the kitchen, the depressing, cared-for, lifeless look of things that had stood in the same place for forty years. At last she got up to go. Something jolted inside him, touched his stunned senses. He looked at her in alarm. 'My car.'

'What?'

'It's. Still there.' Cars left overnight in the multi-storey car park were vandalized, stolen.

'Well, I'm afraid you can't do anything about it, can you?' She looked pointedly at his strapped wrist.

'But. It might be. You see.' He had a new car every two years, as an investment, his mother had insisted. He washed and polished it himself, every week; she had crocheted little covers for the cushions on the back seat. His desperation expanded.

But the young woman was busy. It would take too long for her to go all the way to the shopping precinct by bus, drive his car back. And it would be dark by the time she got there.

He looked towards the window. The looming conifers screened off light, but he had lived in the house so long he automatically registered the time of day by infinitesimal alterations in the gloom. She was right: unnoticed by him the day had fled, unreal, catastrophic. 'But. You must. Do something,' he said.

She stood by the door, thinking. Eventually, she said, 'Tomorrow.' Tomorrow she would call for him, they would take a taxi, collect his car, she would drive it back for him. He had to be satisfied with that, he had to rely on her. There was no one else.

The next morning he had recovered sufficiently to thank her for her trouble. He was too embarrassed to look at her, he had never known how to behave with women. Accident had placed her in his life, he had no curiosity about her, knew nothing except her name, which was Meena. At least, that was what she told him.

Edith's visits had grown less frequent. She was satisfied she had, as she termed it, 'put him back on his feet', and her truculent invitations had given way to equally truculent reminders that he knew where to find her if he wanted her. When he did not appear, making a nuisance of himself, she grew resentful; she would have suspected him of getting up to something if she had believed him capable of getting up to anything at all. She knew nothing of his visits to the medium in Avenridge.

She went round to see him and found him in the garden, weeding with his good hand. She was outraged to discover he had broken his wrist without telling her. She glared at the bungalow. His conscientious housekeeping had always prevented her interfering there, now he would have no excuse. 'It must be like a pigsty,' she said, with satisfaction.

He murmured that it was all right. Really.

'All right? How can it be? You can't keep down dirt while you're in that state.' She was obsessed with dirt. 'And what about shopping? Cooking?'

He said inadequately that he was managing. He could not begin to explain Meena.

'I leave you alone for five minutes and look what you do to yourself.'

'I didn't. It wasn't me.'

She insisted on details. He stammered the little he could recall of the incident, panic uncoiling within him. Meena had told him that forgetting was a natural defence mechanism, but Edith had an appetite for disaster, her questions bored into his brain, reviving terror and humiliation. 'You never get over that sort of thing. Never. It's probably affected your brain. Look at you, you're in a pathetic state. Pathetic.'

'I'm all right,' he said, trembling. Beyond Edith's aggressive shoulder he had a view of the side entrance to the bungalow. Meena was driving in, in his car.

Edith turned. Stared. 'Who's that woman?'

'That's Meena.'

'What's she doing here?'

Arnold struggled. He could not account for Meena, even to himself, it had not occurred to him to try. Edith was glaring at him, waiting for him to say something. 'She helps me.'

'What?' Usurped, Edith went red in the face.

Meena got out of the car and stood in a patch of sunlight. She wore a silk blouse and the full-length skirt and ankle-breaking platform soles that were the fashion of the day. With her exotic and dangerous air she was out of place in the dusty garden. She made no effort to approach but posed elegantly against the side of the car, looked straight into Edith's glare and raised her eyebrows in amusement.

'Helps you,' Edith hissed venomously. 'Why?'

Arnold said the first thing that came into his head. 'She's my friend.'

'We'll see about that,' Edith said.

Edith's visit was short. She barged about the bungalow, ignoring Meena and talking loudly at Arnold about seeing he was properly looked after. She left carrying a bundle of his washing, triumphantly shrilling it was filthy. Filthy. Piles of it.

'Good. I hate doing the washing. But it's given her an excuse to come back,' Meena said as she and Arnold stood at the window, watching Edith stamp down the garden path. 'God, what a cow.'

Arnold looked haunted.

'Don't worry, I'll protect you,' Meena said.

But she was not always there. He never knew what she did for a living, although she explained herself in various ways. Her presence was neither an intrusion nor a comfort, she merely occupied the corners of his life for which he had no use. Sometimes she took his car and went off for days. Even if he had the capacity to object, he did not; he had no use for it with his strapped-up wrist and whenever he wanted to go anywhere she drove him. Her own car disappeared mysteriously at a time she described as financially inconvenient, so he made her a loan to buy another one. And there were other loans, intricate investments on which she assured him he would get a good return; money had little significance for him, his mother had always been in control of it.

He talked to Meena about his mother, and she talked to him about herself, whether he listened or not. Her manner and her accent placed her in a social realm that had always daunted him, and what she told him of her background was in the improbable language of privilege — private schools, dancing classes, a mother who sat on committees, a famous sister. This world was so remote from his it might just as well as have been fiction, and he had never understood stories. The only thing he grasped was the occasional, distant echo of yearning for a lost happiness; something obscure had occurred to separate her from her family. If he had thought about that at all it would have seemed to him appropriate: Meena, having come out of nowhere, remained for him a creature of nowhere — until one day when she said: 'Avenridge,' and by locating herself so precisely, she penetrated his unspoken anxiety.

He had telephoned the medium, trying to explain his accident, his absence. 'Pity,' she said, 'just when we were really beginning to make contact.' It would be all right, she added, sounding doubtful, provided he didn't leave it too long. 'They fade, you see, retreat farther over the Other Side.' He could scarcely form the words to entreat — 'Could you. Somehow. Manage to tell her.' Madame Lily was adamant, 'Oh, no, she's a particularly demanding spirit, your mother, she'll only come if you're here. And then it takes all my powers, as you know.'

He was so filled with dread he began to relapse into the condition that had afflicted him immediately following his mother's death; sitting motionless in the parlour, unconscious of time passing. Sometimes, when he came to himself, Meena would be in the bungalow. She never said anything to him and he never knew how long she had been there, what she had been doing. Eventually, when she mentioned Avenridge, she unlocked his silence; he told her about the medium.

She listened, watched him carefully, asked questions. 'Well, it all sounds harmless enough to me, if it makes you happy, Arnold. But how on earth did you find this — woman?'

He told her about Mrs Parkwright and showed her a book Mrs Parkwright had long ago given his mother. It was called *The Eternal Beyond* and had grainy, appalling photographs of mediums entangled in ectoplasm. On the flyleaf, written in pencil, was a Manchester address, it had been crossed out and an Avenridge address written beneath it. 'Mrs Parkwright used to visit her when she lived here. Then she moved. Mother was always interested. Edith thinks it's. Well . . .'

'Ha, she would.' Meena enjoyed anything that enraged Edith, she treated her with a burlesque civility that brought Edith almost, but not quite, to boiling point. From such encounters Arnold crept away and hid, he was terrified of scenes.

'Never mind,' Meena said. 'You're having the strapping off your wrist this week, you'll be able to go and see your friend again.'

Arnold did not think of the medium as his friend, she was too extraordinary to have a place in the structure of mundane relationships. In the dusty back room where the sun never shone, she held the delicate link that joined him to his mother, at great cost to herself she sought to discover and interpret his mother's last wishes. He had seen her white face pearled with sweat, her eyes starting, her body shaken by spasms, as the words tumbled out, a babble of sound, urgent, incoherent. The curtains stirred and the lamps flickered as he strained forward, strained to hear, to understand what he had to do.

Edith called at all times; if Arnold was alone he tried standing still, in the hope she would go away. But she took to prowling round the bungalow until she caught sight of him through a window, or she came at night, knocking and calling, 'I know you're in, the light's on.' Her stealthy footsteps, her rappings, her voice, began to haunt his sleep. At last she bullied a key from him and after that he was helpless. She questioned him relentlessly about Meena and said vicious things about women who preyed on men with money, older men, who needed watching for their own good.

When Meena was there Edith spoke self-righteously into the air about a solemn vow she had made to Arnold's mother to look after Arnold and not let him get himself into all sorts of trouble. Arnold dared not accuse her of making this up, for all he knew it could be true. He spoke to the medium, who consulted the cards. Oh, yes, it was there plain enough — an unscrupulous woman trying to come between him and his mother, but her power was only in this world.

What was to be done?

She shook her head gravely. The cards foretold the future, they did not offer specific advice. There was a crisis looming. And beyond that? All would be resolved, suffering healed, effort rewarded — 'You'll know what to do. You have the comfort of the eternal.'

But while Arnold tried to contemplate the eternal, his domestic life grew increasingly wretched. Edith fumed about the bungalow, meddling, bullying, determined to get rid of Meena. Meena stayed put, enjoying the drama of Edith's suppressed rage. They were too engrossed in each other to notice the change in Arnold, he might have been no more than a shadow falling between them. He ate little and seldom spoke, neglected his appearance, his responses slowed to a fumbling lethargy. His gaze was turned inwards towards his grief, to the revelation — Madame Lily assured him — of the stupendous certainty it contained. But no matter how intently he regarded this inner vision, how frequently he fled to Avenridge, he could not escape the two women. Their squabbles grew louder and uglier until they erupted into scenes: Edith uncontrolled and screeching, scarlet-faced — Meena, goaded out of her self-possession, screeching back. Arnold crept away and put his hands over his ears so that he could not hear what they were yelling about each other, himself, his mother, and — with headlong inevitability — Madame Lily.

His distress was acute. He had never warned Meena not to tell Edith, it had simply not occurred to him that she might. Edith pounced. She had the inexorable memory of all busybodies; it was months since she had demolished Arnold's timid interest in Mrs Parkwright and the medium, but during that time he had defied and deceived her. Galvanically outraged, she restated her opinion: the whole business was disgusting, she would put a stop to it.

'He can do what he likes, you interfering cow,' Meena said, making matters worse.

Edith could afford to ignore her, she had a temporary triumph. Fortified by the prospect of doing something destructive she stamped away to consider her course of action.

Meena paced, overwrought. It was uncharacteristic of her, normally she shed Edith with glee. Perhaps she felt regret at having unintentionally betrayed Arnold. 'Oh, God, it's not worth it,' she burst out. Then, with exasperation and urgency, 'Listen, you can do whatever you like. Don't forget that. Don't let her stop you.'

Was she going? Going as unaccountably as she had arrived, and stayed?

White faced and shabby, Arnold stared at her without words. The crisis had come.

They left him alone while days passed, uncounted by him — or, if they appeared, he did not comprehend them. Astonishingly, he found he was prepared, he knew what to do. He attended to the few, necessary arrangements, then, one evening, locked himself securely in the bungalow, made himself very spruce, shining his shoes and putting on his best suit. When he was dressed he went into the gloomy little parlour with its lumpy three-piece suite, its souvenirs of the Isle of Wight, its glass-fronted cabinet containing the best china and the urn with his mother's ashes.

He sat there all night until the first pale light of day seeped through the net curtains. Then he stirred, picked up the urn very carefully and went out.

'You stupid old bag,' the voice said furiously over the telephone.

'It's not my fault. I didn't know he'd do that,' the medium's jowls wobbled. 'He was grateful. People are grateful to me. I bring them comfort — '

'You'll bring a load of trouble.' The voice had a great deal to say about legal proceedings and scandal and Madame Lily's cretinous inability to manage her own affairs.

'I thought you'd be pleased. It's money,' Madame Lily whined.

'*Pleased. Money*. It's peanuts. You could have ruined everything.'

The medium shifted from one foot to the other. 'I'm going off me legs. The doctor says it's bad for me to stand about.'

'Get yourself a chair, then.'

She laid the receiver on its side and waddled off down the hall to the back room, where she would have a spasm, or a fit, or a trance, anything that would mislay the memory of the phone lying off the hook.

Much later, she replaced it. Later still, it rang again. This time the voice was deliberately restrained. Not conciliatory, never that, but more reasonable. 'Listen, I know it's not your fault . . .'

In their rolls of fat the medium's eyes glinted with momentary satisfaction. Her stupidity and sloth had worked on the situation and brought about a change. She was not capable of analyzing the method but she recognized the result, it was something that had been happening to her all her life. 'I came over queer — ' she began to go into details about her spasm.

'Shut up. I've been thinking. Things might not be so bad. You're not responsible. There was no pressure on him. You didn't even know what he had in mind. Just stick to that if anyone turns up asking questions.'

'Who?'

'How should I know? Not the police, they're not likely to be concerned. But someone might, family.'

'Well, that cousin — '

'Oh, for God's sake don't inflict the boring little sod's relatives on me. I'm out of it, completely. As far as you're concerned I don't exist. There's the future to think of.'

Madame Lily never thought of the future. Or the past. 'None of it's anything to do with me,' she said comprehensively.

'For once you're right. Stick to that. No one's going to believe you're capable of influencing anyone, they've only got to talk to you for two minutes.' There was a nasty laugh.

'Are you coming round?'

'Oh, God, don't you understand anything? I'm keeping away from you till this blows over.'

'No one sees you. The back way. And you haven't done anything.'

'That's not the point.'

The medium sighed but said nothing. The point had always eluded her. It always would. She would make sure of that.

THREE

Mrs Carter was early. She organized her cleaning jobs with variations in routine, but always conscientiously, and everyone left her to it. Sometimes she did not see Chief Inspector Henry Beaumont for weeks, sometimes they waved in passing — he pulling out of the driveway in his Triumph Stag, she rounding the corner, a tiny, intrepid, bicycling figure.

There were occasions when her unexpectedly early arrival called for discretion: a strange car parked by the front steps, scent lingering in the hallway, the murmur of voices. On these occasions, by a combination of natural tact and fast footwork, she managed to be occupied in the kitchen while Henry's visitor left. The first time, after high heels had tapped across the porch and the strange car driven away, Henry came to stand in the kitchen doorway, a lean, broadshouldered man with glints of grey in his dark hair and the wary strength of experience on his face. 'Mrs Carter, I don't want you to be embarrassed. Or the lady. Or me,' he said deliberately, with every appearance of calm.

'No one is, these days, Mr Beaumont,' Mrs Carter answered.

'Thank God for that,' Henry said, relieved.

He never guessed the romantic notions she cherished on his behalf, her wistful hope that *this* time his visitor would turn out to be the nice, refined lady he would marry and settle down with: by Mrs Carter's conventions he was well past marrying age.

That morning there was no strange car in the drive. Mrs Carter let herself in, hung her coat in the hall cupboard and went into the kitchen.

'Am I late?' Henry asked.

'No, Mr Beaumont, I'm early.' She found it difficult to explain why and began to assemble her dusters and polishes and cleaners in a flurried way, unlike her usual self.

Henry was busy finishing his breakfast, getting himself ready, but he was a man who noticed things. 'What is it?' he asked.

She said at once, before the moment was lost. 'It's my neighbour, Mrs Blore. Her cousin was Arnold Peabody. You remember Peabody's, the ironmongers. Off Barlow Street.'

'Ah, yes. It's pulled down now. But then, what isn't?' Henry said fatalistically.

The Cyclopean development that had obliterated the landscape of his childhood did have its limits. Some old property remained, guarded by playing fields and the vast spread of the cemetery. He had the ground floor of a Victorian house in a tree-lined road that wound past the playing fields, down to the river. As a boy he had delivered newspapers along the road, overawed by its stateliness, never dreaming that one day he would own a small part of it. Peabody's belonged in his memory from those days: a bell that jangled dementedly above the shop door, minutely arranged displays of homely and sensible articles, the smell of paraffin and creosote.

Mrs Carter's memory was longer than Henry's, but she regretted none of the lost landmarks. She thought the new shopping precinct was lovely. It was a puzzle to her why a man of Henry's elegance did not move into one of the smart new blocks of flats. But her mind was on immediate problems, she said what a dreadful thing it was, Arnold Peabody going off and drowning himself. 'There was an inquest. And it was all in the papers. It's been terrible for Edith Blore, everyone talking.' She spoke with genuine pity, a fellow feeling for a woman very much like herself, wrenched from the shelter of obscurity into a brief and shameful notoriety. 'Only, you see, Mr Beaumont, she's asked me . . .' Mrs Carter paused, in difficulties.

'Yes?' Henry prompted gently.

Mrs Carter made a confused attempt to convey something she did not herself understand: Edith Blore had information about her cousin Arnold's death she felt it her duty to pass on.

'Information,' Henry said. 'Look, tell her to telephone the station, they'll send someone to talk to her — '

But that was Going To The Police, Mrs Carter intervened, rather desperately, and Edith Blore couldn't do that. Respectable people had nothing to do with the Law, Mrs Carter added, separating Henry from the capital letter of his professional role. 'But she said that if it could be unofficial. She knows I clean for you, Mr Beaumont, and she's been asking if I — well, I hate to bother you. I don't think it's the sort of thing that would concern you, seeing as you sit behind a desk and don't go about detecting. And I've told her you're very high up — ' Unaware of irony, Mrs Carter directed her anxious gaze up at Henry's six foot two. 'She won't say what it's really all about and I'd rather she didn't. It's not my business and we're not friends, only neighbours. That's it, you see. She sees me from her window as I go past, or else she keeps calling round . . .'

Out of this incomplete conversation the absent Edith Blore took shape as an unpleasant woman determined to make anyone's life wretched in pursuit of her own ends — although kind little Mrs Carter would never bring herself to say so. 'I hate asking favours,' she said unhappily.

'You never do, for yourself,' Henry pointed out. 'Tell her I'll have a word with her, unofficially, if that's what she wants.'

It was an angry evening. A battering wind hurled litter about the streets, rush hour traffic and the diversions that were an inescapable, maddening concomitant of the new development made long work of the detour to the Peabody bungalow that Henry took on his way home.

'Another minute and I'd have gone. I thought you weren't going to bother coming.' Edith made a brandishing motion with the door key. She wore a baggy coat of harsh black material and shapeless shoes; a bulging shopping bag stood in the hall.

Absorbing the impact of her rudeness without visible sign, Henry said pointedly, 'Mrs Carter phoned me at lunch time to make this arrangement. I wouldn't let her down after the trouble she's gone to for you.'

'That's what neighbours are for,' Edith snapped. There was nothing in her manner to indicate she had, or ever would, put herself out to assist Mrs Carter in a similar fashion.

She led him to the parlour, poky and chill, enduringly ugly beneath a harsh overhead light. She was belligerent yet ill at ease, planting herself on the extreme edge of a chair where she could glare at Henry. He was much too elegant to be a policeman, but he represented authority, for which she had a resentful, immovable respect. She held her own against him, and against her own prejudices, by brushing aside his warrant card as if it was something worthless he was trying to sell; but for an instant there was a tremor in her harshness, a hint of uncertainty.

Henry sat down on a hard armchair. Wind gusted against the windows, traffic on the dual carriageway formed a distant, never-ceasing background noise.

'Now, I understand this is about your cousin, Arnold Peabody.'

She made a sound, 'Huh — ' and began to talk of Arnold, his helplessness, his ingratitude. She had a great deal to say, in a voice charged with contempt: there was no suggestion of grief, or even sympathy. Having demolished Arnold's character, what there was of it — and Henry felt the pity of Arnold's colourless, unfulfilled existence — she disposed of his death. 'Going off and — doing *that*. I had to identify him, you know. All that way, the inconvenience. And the shame of it, I can't hold up my head. It's not as if he had cause, no cause at all.'

'According to the coroner's verdict he killed himself while the balance of his mind was impaired. He was depressed after his mother's death.'

'I don't know why. He knew she had to go some time. He just couldn't take it. Spineless. I was in and out of here, doing for him. He *insisted* I have a key.' She waved it aggressively, tucked it tightly back into her fist. It proved something, to her, at least. 'But it was all mother-said-this and mother-did-that. "She's gone now," I used to say. It was a kindness, making him face up to it. But would he, oh, no, not Master Arnold. He goes sneaking off, behind my back, getting his head filled with rubbish about *mother* watching over him. Waiting for him. Downright disgusting, I call it. Dangerous, too.'

'Dangerous?' Henry selected a word with possibilities of enlightenment.

'Well, of course it's dangerous,' Edith became strident. 'I told him, I *told* him to have nothing to do with her — that medium. Calls herself Madame Lily. Did you ever hear the like? Lives at Avenridge. I suppose you know where *that* is.'

'Yes,' Henry said, and suddenly the ugly room was full of its reality: woodsmoke, misty rain, the yellow stars of winter jasmine against faded fences, dense, shining shrubberies, the dark, passionate colours of clematis and the house that was part of his growing up. But on his dismissive, 'Yes, I know it,' these charmed memories fled like fugitives. Nothing would have induced him to part with one scrap of them to this rancorous woman.

'Well, there you are, shows what a hold she'd got on him. Had the poor fool driving over there, all that way, twice a week. Oh, I got it out of him, but by then it was too late. And *she'd* been egging him on, this woman he'd got himself involved with. *Girlfriend.*' Distaste crimped Edith's features. 'His poor mother would have turned in her grave. He'd never had a girlfriend in his life. Not that he'd have known what to do with one, anyway. It was his money, of course, he'd nothing else to recommend him, I can tell you. She knew he had a bit put by, she'd weighed it up, all right. Used to be here all hours. Disgusting. I don't know what the neighbours thought.'

They probably thought good old Arnold, finding out what it's for at last, Henry responded inwardly.

'She feathered her nest, all right. Hundreds he must have given her. Hundreds. Presents. Huh. Making out she came from this posh family, that was in Avenridge, too.' Clearly, in Edith's view, packed to its boundaries with thieves and charlatans. Henry wondered if she had ever been there. 'So she *said*, but you couldn't believe a word. Had liar written all over her. Not that he could see it. I put a stop to it, though. We had a stand-up row, right here, and she got the worst of it, I can tell you. Cleared off. Don't ask me where, no one knew where she came from in the first place. Good riddance. And then, scarce a week after, he goes and does that — that terrible thing. I don't know how he could.'

Because for lonely, driven Arnold, there was nothing else left to do. Hoping to bring Edith to the point, Henry asked, 'So, this girlfriend had nothing to do with Arnold's suicide?'

'Well, no,' Edith admitted grudgingly. Her eyes hunted, furiously, for some confirmation of her views. 'You're not saying it's right, her getting all that money out of him?'

'I'm not saying it's illegal. It was his, he could do what he liked with it,' Henry answered, in the sincere hope that Arnold had enjoyed what ever it was he had got for it.

'But if she hadn't egged him on things would have been different.' Frustrated, Edith grew shrill. 'I'd have found out a lot sooner about this Madame Whatever and put a stop to it. Look what it led to. He'd never have done himself in if she hadn't put the idea into his head.'

'Even if that's true, you're not going to be able to prove it.'

Edith's mouth snapped shut. She sat in bitter silence.

'I'm sure you know the facts as well as I do, Mrs Blore —' A phone call to the police station near where Arnold's death occurred had provided Henry with them, the details were fresh in his mind. 'Your cousin drove down to the Isle of Wight. There he drove to Windy Cove, left his car on the road and walked on to the beach and into the sea. The beach was deserted, but a group of young chaps hang gliding from the cliff top noticed him and realized what he was doing. One of them even flew over him and shouted, to get his attention, but he took no notice. One of the men ran for the nearest telephone; two ran in the other direction — for the Coast Guard, two tried to get down the cliff path in time to do something. They all acted promptly and sensibly, but they were too late. Arnold drowned himself quite deliberately and he was quite alone. You didn't dispute this at the inquest.

Now, do you have any information that contradicts that?'

'Of course not.' Edith swept it aside with a clenched hand, the brutality of the gesture suggesting she would have helped Arnold get on with it. 'I know all that. I've had my nose rubbed in the *facts*. But there's another fact that proves Madame was involved. And that's the two thousand pounds.'

'What two thousand pounds?' Henry asked.

'There, not all that clever after all, are you? He left it her in his will. You see, she stood to gain. Don't tell me that's legal, cheating honest folks of their money.'

'If Arnold — '

'I'm not talking about *him*. I'm talking about me. It was mine by rights. She's got to be made to pay it back.'

'Mrs Blore, is this the reason you asked to see me. The money.'

'Well, of course it is. You don't think I'd be bothered otherwise.'

'With your cousin's death?'

'No.'

'I see.'

There was a silence. Edith's face blotched with red. She dragged together the skirts of her coat, stared around the room. 'It's the principle. It's my duty, as a citizen. We're always being told to help the police. If I didn't say anything, she'd get away with it.'

'It's not a police matter, Mrs Blore. I did point out to you a moment ago, your cousin was entitled to do anything he liked with his money.'

'Squander it on a slut? Give it away to some old cow who filled his head with rubbish?'

'If that was what he wanted.'

'He wanted to spite me, that's what. I never got a penny when his mother sold the shop, the old battle axe. Not a penny. I should have tackled him when she died but I had too much decency. I thought he'd know his obligations after all I've done for him. He should have left me the lot, I was entitled. But what does he do? Fritters most of it, leaves all that to *her*, and the rest shared out in the family. All of them. There's dozens, folks as never did a hand's turn for him. Even this, shared out.' She thrust her arm out in a chopping gesture, distributing the bungalow amongst the distant and undeserving. Her eyes hunted, greedily despairing. 'It should have come to me. I've waited all these years for it. They say we'll have to buy the others out but we'll never have enough, we'll never have a decent place now.'

The ferocity with which Edith laid claim to her decent place had nothing to do with its value as property. It was gerry-built, like all the bungalows in the row, thrown together in the days when at least it had been possible to cross the road in safety; it was cramped and shoddy and thoroughly depressing, but it was what Edith wanted. For years she had hugged to herself the expectation of it, of being able to say, 'We live in a detached bungalow on the Didsbury Road.' And she had been cheated.

Henry said, 'These are personal matters, Mrs Blore, we can't intervene. It's your solicitor you want to see if you intend to contest the will.'

'Solicitors,' Edith muttered. 'What do I know about solicitors except they're out to line their own pockets.'

'It could be an expensive business, and you've no guarantee of success. If I were you, I'd give it a lot of thought before you do anything.'

'Is that all you've got to say? D'you mean I've been wasting my time hanging about here waiting for you to turn up when you feel like it, and when you do it's to tell me I can't do nothing?'

'Look, Mrs Blore, you're not disputing the circumstances of Arnold's death, are you? Right. Your complaint is that others have benefited from his will in a way you didn't anticipate. There's nothing we can do about that. I didn't say there was nothing you can do, you can take action, as a private individual, to claim whatever you think you're entitled to, but that's no concern of ours.'

'I might have known,' Edith said unspecifically, with bitter satisfaction. An imperceptible change in her bludgeoning attitude indicated that defeat was no more than she expected; as one of life's victims, always wronged, never in the wrong, it was perhaps *all* she had expected. Because there were always people with power or luck or sheer indifference, people who were better informed, better off, who would keep her in her place. Henry was one, and she hated him for it. 'I don't know why you bothered to come,' she said, deliberately insulting.

He did not remind her she had asked him, she was looking for a fight and he had nothing to fight about. He stood up.

She remained where she was, clutching the key, her big, square body rigid. He opened the door. In the cramped hallway the overloaded shopping bag squatted. He looked back. 'Can I give you a lift?'

'Oh, get out. Bugger off, will you,' she shouted.

Her voice followed him as he let himself out of the bungalow; for a respectable woman she could swear with remarkable crudity. Henry did not react, he had been sworn at far too often in the course of his profession and, although he might be the immediate target of her rage, it was Arnold who was the cause. It would not occur to her that if she had behaved decently she would not be sitting there, clutching the key of her dispossessed dream and shrieking obscenities into the empty air. And Arnold had left her something. Was that unmourned, sad little man capable of irony? Because, in treating her with scrupulous fairness he had, for once in his life, at the end of his life, got the better of Edith.

He had been home little more than an hour when Mrs Carter rang his doorbell. She had walked through the harsh night, in her best coat and hat, to apologise to him. She was close to tears. 'Mrs Blore came round shouting terrible things. It's all my fault.'

'No it isn't,' Henry said, trying not to smile. She looked like a distressed mouse. He took her into his living room. 'You really shouldn't have come out on a night like this.'

'Oh, but I had to. I was the one asked you to see her. I don't know what you must think of me.'

'I can tell you what I think of Mrs Blore. I could kill her for picking on you. I thought she'd just go home and give her family hell.'

'She did. I heard them yelling. Then she came round to me. She said all sorts of things. And it wasn't about Arnold's death at all, it was his money, and him leaving it to other people as well as her. If I'd known I'd never, never have bothered you. And she said you insulted her. I knew that couldn't be true.'

'Don't bet on it,' Henry said. He made Mrs Carter sit down, gave her a sherry, talked to her and let her talk until she had calmed down, reassured he did not hold her responsible for any aspect of the appalling Edith. Then she said she must go. She was out of her element, mornings were her time for his flat; by night, it was the transformed territory of his private life. She was fearful of intruding, it had taken a desperate state of mind to bring her there, and he knew that.

She wanted to walk back, but he put her firmly in his car and drove her home to the council estate, where acres of houses went on bleakly, street after street, exactly the same. It had been on his beat when he was a young bobby, he'd never mastered its geography, even then.

He said, 'I was in and out of that shop, over the years. I remember Mrs Peabody, but not Arnold.'

'Such a quiet little man. Always polite. It was terrible how lost he was without his mother. And, you know, Edith Blore wasn't much help. If you ask me,' the unaccustomed sherry made Mrs Carter reckless, 'She's only got what she deserved.'

'Agreed. She'll never see it like that, though. Do you want me to go and have another word with her, tell her not to bother you — '

'Oh, no. Best leave well alone. It's all over now, isn't it? The girl's gone off somewhere. And Arnold, poor Arnold, he's gone, too. Do you know, he took his mother's ashes with him, so they were together at the end.'

FOUR

Six months later, on a bitter Saturday in January, darkness
came early to Avenridge, and finally to Mildred Hewitt.
When the manner of her death became known, it sent
shock waves through the town; there was gossip, speculation,
bewilderment. Mildred Hewitt was a widow of excellent
reputation and social prominence, strenuous in charitable
work, a devoted mother, a scrupulous business woman and a
nerve-racking snob. The name of Hewitt stood well in
Avenridge, they had lived there for four generations,
establishing their business — Hewitt's High Class Printers —
going about their respectable, mundane affairs, consolidating
their modest fortune. Mildred Hewitt's pride in them, in her
status, gave her charm its ruthless quality and set an edge of
arrogance to her genteel resolution.

But Mildred Hewitt had a secret, and it was because of the
secret that she died.

The past clung gently to Avenridge, the grey stone town of
haphazard levels set in the scoop of the valley. Its origins
passed beyond measurable time and beyond the interest of the
industrious, spa-building Victorians, who gave it graceful,

tree-filled squares and handsome houses, a Pavilion, a pump room, ornamental walks and shops with wrought-iron and glass verandahs. But when the fashion for medicinal waters gave way to other fashions, Avenridge stopped growing, although it continued to prosper, and its greatest charm, its out-of-season air, enveloped it completely. Creeping mists and shrouds of winter snows blurred the definition of its ponderous, occasionally eccentric architecture until at some point in its later history it confounded time itself and grew, uncannily, to resemble the faded photographs of its own past.

To the south the town teetered decorously but, as it rose, ever more giddily, on the brink of a wooded chasm known as the Ridge. Nature having obligingly provided this dramatic landslip in conjunction with the gentle river Aven, public benefactors had improved upon it, planting and sculpting its slopes, transforming its ruggedness into an enchanted tangle of foliage and paths and tiny, tilted clearings. A narrow, tree-lined road climbed steeply out of the town beside the Ridge, on a hairpin bend it touched a rocky platform where the trees broke open and the lip of the Ridge jutted out, four hundred feet above the Aven. The angle of the road and the flat expanse of rock provided just enough space for two or three cars to park while their occupants admired the view across the Derbyshire hills; the road was little used and spiked with warning signs. In winter it was particularly dangerous.

It was from here, the highest point of the Ridge, that Mildred Hewitt fell to her death.

Her body wheeled crazily through the darkness, past shrubs and skeletal, rock-clinging trees on which the first thick snowflakes had begun to settle. At such a time of year, on such a night, the steep walks, the grottoes and arbours, were deserted, and the big houses that stood closest to the Ridge were too far away for anyone within to hear her last, despairing cry.

But up on the road, where Mildred Hewitt's Rover was drawn into the switchback turn, someone moved.

Along the edge of the tarmac surfaced road, no more than a shadow against the denser clustered shadows of the trees, the figure walked rapidly and silently down to the town.

On the morning of that Saturday Mildred Hewitt had received a letter. It did not come with the daily post but preceded it, unstamped and bearing no address, merely her name: MRS MILDRED HEWITT, printed in block capitals and followed by the word CONFIDENTIAL.

That weekend Gilbert Hewitt was away, an unusual circumstance, as he seldom went anywhere without his mother. Their inseparability, which operated not only in their domestic but their social and business lives as well — and was regarded by some as an ideal relationship and by others as a form of emotional vampirism — lightened Mildred's widowhood and extended Gilbert's bachelor state indefinitely.

No one who knew her ever accused Mildred Hewitt of selfishness, her strength and intelligence were used as much on Gilbert's behalf as her own; she was tireless in her encouragement of his interests, even his friendships were, in some manner, contrived by her. That these, like his interests, were shortlived, never deterred her from cultivating some other group in which to insinuate him and so maintain the fiction of his popularity.

It was one of his enthusiasms that accounted for his absence: he had left by the Friday afternoon train (he did not drive) to spend the Saturday hunting in Leicestershire. She packaged him tenderly in his winter underwear and expensive clothes and saw him off at the station. At the very last moment he said, 'I wish you were coming, too, Mother.' 'My dear, you know I can't, I have the charity dinner tomorrow evening. And what would I do while you're dashing about being so brave and clever with all those nice young people.' Having established him in this unlikely vision of himself, which they both desired to be true and which would recede from him as time and distance lengthened between them, she kissed him goodbye, and with her assiduous poise stood waving until his pallid face, yearning from the window of the first class carriage, passed from view.

Without him, in the high, handsome rooms of the house where the clocks ticked into emptiness, all the familiar things — the heavy, polished furniture, the paintings and ornaments, the velvets and brocades — underwent a subtle alteration, as if her knowledge of his absence had reached out and touched them. She was too sensible to give way to self-pity, too resolute to abandon routine and indulge in anxiety — but anxiety functioned beyond her will, the Saturday routine had point only when Gilbert was there to share it with her. More and more frequently her inner vision was startled by unwilling, quickly suppressed images of Gilbert amongst strangers, Gilbert daring the hazards of hurtling hooves, flying mud and vicious blackthorn hedges.

The letter came as a distraction, the manner of its delivery causing her momentary surmise she discounted as unimportant even as it occurred. It was unlikely — with the angle of the staircase and the size of the hall — she would have noticed the envelope lying by the door when she came down for breakfast at nine o'clock. But had it been there then? Since early morning? Or the previous evening? She would hear no footsteps in the porch, no flap of the letterbox unless she was in the hall. See no one on the drive unless she was in the dining room and she was never in there on a Saturday morning . . .

These queries and possibilities, seemingly trivial, encompassed the pattern of her days, the geography of the house and, most significantly, the uncommon circumstances of her being alone. It seemed to her mere chance that the letter arrived for her that day; but that was not so. And when she understood, it was too late.

The letter itself, brief and unsigned, was typed on one side of a sheet of cheap writing paper. It concerned Gilbert. There was an instruction to her to be at home at a certain time later that day to receive a telephone call; the final words were: All evidence will be destroyed at the appropriate time, until then it is vital you keep this safely about you. Failure to do so will result in tragic consequences.

A paralysis of the will gripped her. She did not register the passage of time or the meaning of her movements — pacing, sitting, senselessly reading and re-reading the letter — until at last fissures of rage and loathing broke open her stupor and she glimpsed chaos.

Her mind began to work, but in such disjointed fashion every attempt to order her thoughts gave way before the compulsion to do something. At once seizing upon the only possibility of action that occurred to her, she readied herself hastily, took her dark green Rover from the garage and drove across Avenridge to the northern edge of the town.

She parked her car outside the bingo hall and walked down Kitchener Terrace. There were no front gardens, the houses opened directly on to the pavement: she stood before one, knocking, waiting. There was no reply. She tried again, clutching her mink coat to her against the bitter wind. Eventually she gave up, and went away.

Mildred Hewitt drove home, too engrossed to be aware of anything but the frustration of her one attempt at action. But the frustration itself checked the progress of her panic, bringing her to the realization that in this one small incident chance had prevented her from behaving foolishly. With that she saw, with unrelenting starkness, how helpless she was, how she could trust no one, approach no one, until she knew her enemy. Suspicion consumed her, distorting every single person it touched upon — from those she called her closest friends to those with whom she had the briefest contact. She had a gregarious nature, her life had always been filled with people. She did not ask herself who had cause to hate her — she knew that well enough — but who, amongst the tumult of faces and names, had the means to thrust such menace into the stronghold of her existence?

The Hewitt's house stood on the inclines of the south west of Avenridge, a corner formed by the loop of the river and the lower slopes of the Ridge. Here long-vanished men, philoprogenitive, prosperous, had built their houses amongst tree-shaded roads and curving lanes. All the houses were large and most of graceful proportions; some grew outwards with bays and verandahs and conservatories, some upwards, grandiosely, with turrets and crenellations; but the passing of the years had brought coherence to them all — the grimmest garden wall hung thick with creepers, the maddest Gothic lurked, in inoffensive curio, behind glossy-leaved shrubs. And the people who could afford to live in the houses could afford to maintain them with discretion: a renovation here, an improvement there, did so little to interrupt the continuity that a century and a half of domestic architecture stood preserved in all its minutely recorded evolutions, in an atmosphere of tender melancholy.

The drive of The Laurels was short and wide, curving through its rim of trees and bushes in a manner that shielded the lower part of the house from the road. Beyond the bend in the drive, in front of the porch steps, Wilfred Hewitt's car was parked. All the patience, all the ponderous good nature that characterized Wilfred, was expressed by the way he sat relaxed in the driver's seat, waiting.

As Mildred pulled up at the turn that led beside the house to the garage he emerged from his car, saying, 'Hello, Aunt Mildred,' his resonant, amiable voice carrying across the drive and in through the closed windows of her car. During business hours he was obliged, like any other employee, to address her as Mrs Hewitt — but some tenuous family connection (on her late husband's side, the second marriage of a scarcely traceable cousin) also entitled him — and, obscurely, his wife and children — to call her aunt. She held out, it was her nature, her fastidious reaction to his loud, blundering cheeriness. She had her strategies for keeping him out of her social life — most of them too subtle to bring criticism on herself — and in response to the question, *Related?* the fine modulation of her tone: *only very distantly*, rendered him virtually invisible as a Hewitt. But still the accident, the fact of their relationship, remaining indisputable, brought his voice booming 'Aunt' at her with all the confident assumption of mutual goodwill.

He crossed the drive to her, a big man, soft-moving in spite of his bulk. He was dressed, as always, in obtrusively fashionable clothes, too young and too smart for his slackening, middle-aged body. He smiled at her through the car window, catching her expression, the wrenched look that fixed her features vacantly in the hiatus between one thought and the next. It would never have occurred to him that he was intruding, he was as kindly disposed towards others as he believed they were towards him, minutely observant of details and endlessly interested in the most mundane and trivial aspects of everyone's life. He began to talk even before she wound down the window, telling her how he had called earlier with his daughter Amabel, taking her to her friend Deirdre — 'she's staying overnight with her, some teenage party.' He was constantly in motion with the sixteen-year-old Amabel, driving her to or from somewhere. Bulky as her father and without a hint of her mother's glamour, the impassive Amabel went wherever she was invited, because she was invited, rather like Wilfred himself. Unlike Wilfred, she never gave any sign of enjoying herself.

Mildred, unresponsive, struggled with the transition from inner tumult to self command while Wilfred, opening the car door, helping her out, continued to shred around her the particles of his family's doings. His wife Linda would be out that evening at a meeting of the dramatic society committee, his son Wayne was also occupied in some way too meaningless to engage Mildred's attention. For her, the fragmented day was beginning to consolidate in familiar responses of resistance, irritation. Wilfred expected to be invited in for coffee; she stood her ground, hugged into her fur. 'Really, Wilfred, I'm rather occupied at present, was there — '

'So it seemed to me the best thing I could do was offer myself as escort to you tonight.'

She repeated blankly, 'Escort. Tonight.'

'The dinner. At the Pavilion. You can't have forgotten.'

'Oh — no. I — er — thank you, but — '

'Not at all, I'll enjoy it. Gilbert would have gone with you anyway, wouldn't he?'

This was undeniable, Gilbert went everywhere with her: on those grounds alone she knew her protest would be futile.

He bent his head, anxiety narrowing his gaze. 'Aunt Mildred, are you all right?'

'Of course I'm all right.'

'You're so pale and — fraught. Has anything happened?'

Her expanding annoyance shrank to the pinpoint of defence. 'Happened? What could have happened? What are you talking about?' But the broad, craggy face hung over her like a landslide and before his insistence that she was not herself, not at all her usual self, her spirit flagged. She resorted to invention, making a fretful admission she might be getting a chill.

'You'd better get inside in the warm, it's not the weather to be out if you're off colour.' He took her arm, unnecessarily, but such misdirected gallantry was typical of him. She shrank from the grasp of his large, softly padded hands: any uninvited touch — except Gilbert's — outraged her notions of seemliness. Her involuntary recoil merely made Wilfred tighten his grip, proving to her that if she wished to free herself she would be forced to conduct a wrestling match on the drive — to which the discrepancy in their sizes would lend an element of farce appropriate to Wilfred but unendurable to her. She resigned herself to being supported up the steps to the porch where Wilfred fussed over the finding of her key in her handbag and, in the house, the removal of her coat. She did not ask him to remove his but he did so, revealing an outfit of such relentless nonchalance he could only have constructed an image of himself from an advertisement in a colour supplement: 'this trendily casual weekend look is for you . . .' It was part of Wilfred's great innocence that he believed such things.

As always, when he was in the house, he generated disruption. He padded about, picked things up and put them down, sagged at ease in elegant chairs. Soon, Mildred knew with a flagging of the spirit, he would telephone Linda. As a family they were fanatically given to telephoning each other: she could never understand why, there was never urgency or point to their conversations and Wilfred constantly complained of the size of his telephone bill.

He followed her into the kitchen, saying, 'Why did you have to go out, anyway? Not to get your hair done. I said to Am when we called earlier, you always have your hair done on a Friday, I said. Besides, you've not been gone long enough. Just a little errand, I'd have done it for you.'

She diverted him by allowing him to make coffee. He

busied himself efficiently, knowing where everything was. She went to the worktop by the sink where bunches of flowers, evergreens and half-finished arrangements stood.

'Don't you usually do those first thing on a Saturday?' he asked.

'No.' But she did, assisted by Gilbert, who had an eye for colour, and perfect taste.

'Of course, you're bound to be upset, Gilbert being away,' he said with unbearable sympathy, carrying her cup across to her.

'Really, Wilfred, I'm not in the least upset. Nothing could please me more than the thought of Gilbert enjoying himself. And it's only two days, he'll be back tomorrow.'

'Still, you must worry. Dangerous business, hunting. Well, it can be, not that you could call Gilbert the reckless type.'

Gilbert's ineptitude on a horse was the marvel of all who witnessed it, although it was unrecognized by Gilbert himself, who never admitted fear but discerned it readily, and with scorn, in others. Those who knew, who were familiar with his pusillanimous strategies for staying upright and unbruised, waited for the day when he would run out of excuses and find himself on a decent horse and break his neck.

'I would be unnatural, Wilfred, if I didn't worry a little.' She spoke from a preoccupation that had nothing to do with Gilbert's immediate safety. Her mind was divided, Wilfred's presence pressed itself on her attention, it was impossible to ignore someone so loquacious, so amiably immovable, although she tried.

Eventually, he began to make arrangements for the evening, at least on an intonation of finality. What time should he call? Was she expected anywhere for drinks first? They would go in her car, he knew she preferred that. Then, inevitably, he said he would phone Linda.

'Really, must you?' she said, her mechanical objection stung by the desire to get rid of him, to think — if not in peace, at least in solitude. 'You'll be home in 15 minutes if you go now. Surely it will wait.'

'Ah, I've got one or two errands first. I'd better give Lin a buzz. Just in case.'

He always said *just in case*. When challenged, 'In case of what?' he would answer, 'Well, you never know.' Mysterious possibilities thronged around such lack of specification.

He went out of the kitchen and left her staring bleakly after him.

What did the evening matter to her? Her day had begun with the letter — that letter — and every menaced hour progressed towards the telephone call. She had given no thought to anything beyond that and but for his intervention she would have continued in the same state of frozen dismay. She had a sudden, appalled thought: could her enemy know of her plans for the evening? Assume a craven submission on her part if she cancelled them?

The humiliation of this thought was so intense it had the effect of jolting her back into the rhythm of her life: the duties, the obligations, the interests, that defined the woman she was. In that instant she believed that if she did not accept the challenge in terms of her true self, she would have no hope, and although in a sense he had made the decision for her, she came to it for herself, in a gathering wave of vigour. Of course she would go. She would demonstrate her strength — by behaving as if nothing out of the ordinary had happened.

At nine-thirty that evening Gilbert returned home. He travelled by taxi from the station and ordered the driver, who was prepared to pull up at the gate, to take him up the drive to the front steps of The Laurels. The house was in darkness but for the porch light, under which Gilbert stood counting out the fare and the tip. His fine-skinned face was patchy with cold, its expression tremulous yet seething: behind his jam-jar spectacles his eyes were rimmed with the angry pink of emotional stress.

Had his mother been there to greet him when he entered the house, she would have recognized these signs. Gilbert's weekend had been a failure. It was not his fault, it never was. He was ingenuous, misled by appearances *deliberately contrived* to deceive him, finding himself among social inferiors who were incapable of appreciating his qualities. There was a point beyond which he could not compromise his standards — he had made an excuse, left them to their vulgar entertainment. No one had the courtesy to consult a timetable for him. He had muddled arrivals and departures, missed connections, spent hours in deplorable waiting rooms with rude things written on the walls . . . So he would have told her, had she been there, his eyelids flaring pink and his moist, rosy mouth loosening and primping as he recounted in paranoid detail the inconveniences, the slights, the treacheries.

But she was not there. He had to make himself supper, eat alone and, with brandy and cigar, retrieve his threatened, desperate vanity. He was tall and had his mother's attenuated frame; his hair was colourless, fine as silk, his small head arrogant. Built for elegance, he was elegant only in repose: with his incompetent movements and his epicene hauteur, he had an air of incongruence that had once prompted someone, unkindly, to say he looked as if he had been cloned. Someone else, even more unkindly, asked who would want a clone of Gilbert Hewitt, and what for? The question was unanswerable.

Shortly after midnight, the telephone rang. Gilbert, flushed from a bath, went downstairs in pyjamas and dressing gown to answer it.

'Gilbert,' Wilfred said, loud and surprised. 'What are you doing home? I thought you weren't due back till tomorrow.'

'I came home today instead. What do you want, Wilfred?'

'Is your mother there?'

'Of course not. She's at the Pavilion.'

'No, I'm at the Pavilion. I came with your mother, as you were away.'

'Then if you're with her why on earth are you asking me if she's here?'

'Hang on, Gilbert, you sound a bit edgy.'

'I'm tired. It's late. You're not making sense.'

'I will if you give me a chance,' Wilfred said, with stentorian patience, but there was a hint of perplexity in his voice as he continued. 'It's a bit odd, what's happened. I'd been chatting for a while, at the bar, then I went to look for your mother and I couldn't find her. I thought perhaps she was having a dance with someone, or gone to the committee room to discuss something. So I went back to the bar — '

'Where else?' Gilbert breathed. Wilfred could drink quantities of beer without noticeable effect. In all things — drink, food, company — his appetite was large and uncritical; Gilbert found this lack of discrimination disgusting.

' — then I still couldn't find her. I asked around and no one had seen her, people were beginning to get their coats and everything, so it occurred to me to go and see if her car was there. And it wasn't — it isn't.'

Gilbert, bemused, said, 'I don't understand.'

'Neither do I.' Wilfred answered cheerfully. 'But there's bound to be an explanation. Perhaps she decided to go home, bit tired, or a headache coming on.'

'Then she'd have told you to bring her back if you *took* her.'

'Yes . . . yes, that's what's odd. Her car's not there, is it?'

'I don't see how it could be. Wait.' In the cloakroom Gilbert fumbled into overcoat and shoes and went outside. The night had taken on a weird, whirling radiance; blots of snow spread on his spectacles; he saw what he had earlier been too engrossed to notice and returned petulantly to the telephone. '*Your* car's here,' he said accusingly, and had to have the evening's arrangements explained to him, slowly, in detail.

After that they argued: she had taken a taxi, been offered a lift, set out to drive herself and had a puncture on the way. But to none of these possibilities did they give serious consideration; Mildred Hewitt's sense of duty was too strong to permit her to walk out of a social event without a word of explanation, and they both knew it.

Wilfred said doubtfully, 'Perhaps she had an errand and she's been delayed coming back.'

'My mother would *not* drive anywhere on a night like this.' Gilbert's voice was rising. 'Have you *seen* it? It's snowing. She *hates* driving in the snow, you know she does. Wilfred, *do* something.'

'It's difficult to know what. I've asked around.'

'If I'd been there this wouldn't have happened.'

'If you'd been here, I wouldn't,' Wilfred said, without irony. Then, disconcerting Gilbert with a loud wuff of laughter, 'Bloody hell, it's years since a date walked out on me.'

'This is no time for jokes.'

''Course not, just trying to relieve the pressure. You're building up quite a head of steam, old man. Listen, I'll get a lift and come round to you — '

'Is that your idea of action? Just leaving?' Gilbert said sarcastically.

'I can't do anything here, nearly everyone's gone, they'll be shutting up the place soon. There are two likely routes from here to you. I'll get someone to drive me along both of them in case she got into difficulties with the car and is parked somewhere.'

'If she had, she'd have phoned by now, to let me know.'

There was a slight pause before Wilfred said in a puzzled voice, 'But she doesn't know you're here. Does she? You haven't been in touch with her earlier, have you? To tell her you were coming home today instead of—'

'No, no, I wasn't thinking straight, you've got me so confused. Listen, how was mother? Was she all right — her usual self?'

'Bang on form, you know how she enjoys a good do.' To Wilfred pleasure was pleasure, he was incapable of making any distinction between Mildred Hewitt's gracious affability and the gusto of a fat lady on a seaside postcard.

Gilbert, closing his eyes for an anguished instant, said, 'How long is it since you saw her?'

'Must be — what? Hard to say, you don't notice the time when you're chatting and so on. Mmm, it's quite late now, isn't it? Must have been half nine, tennish.'

'What?' Gilbert said weakly. 'That's over two hours.'

'Doesn't mean to say she's been gone all that time, though. I never thought to look for her car till a little while ago. Look, I'd better get moving. I'll be with you in half an hour.'

'Supposing — supposing you don't see her car?'

'Then we'll have to think of something else.'

They stood in the hall, facing each other. The spangle of snowflakes gave Wilfred's bulky, battered masculinity an absurd air. Gilbert, in pyjamas and dressing gown, was overstrung as a child allowed to stay up too late. Waiting for Wilfred, he had had time to think — not constructively, that was not Gilbert's way. In his cossetted life his own incompetence had been kept from him, but its distant outlines shaped his attitudes: faced with crisis his first line of thought was to find someone to blame, his second to excuse himself from responsibility. After they had exchanged no more than a few words he said, 'Why did she have her car keys if you drove her there?'

'Because she wanted to drive herself, you know she likes to. And it wasn't bad out then.' To demonstrate the treachery of the weather, Wilfred shook himself, sending a cascade of snowflakes to glisten and melt on the richly subdued pattern of the carpet.

Gilbert's mouth primped. 'And why did you go, anyway?'

'You know your mum, she likes an escort. Quite right, too. A woman should have a bloke around, help her into her coat, choose the wine, dance with her. She's used to you being with her. I might be second best, but I'm better than nothing.'

'Did she ask you?'

'No, I offered. She seemed glad of it.'

'I can't think why, since you've managed to lose her.'

'Gilbert, calm down. Have a brandy or do some breathing exercises or something.' Gilbert's breathing exercises belonged in the past, to the rejected, unmastered yoga lessons. Wilfred too often tactlessly overlooked the brevity of Gilbert's enthusiasms.

'I'm perfectly calm.' Gilbert turned and marched into the drawing room. He had a moment to arrange himself haughtily beside the fireplace, one fine, faintly trembling hand laid upon the polished marble, before Wilfred, following more slowly, entered.

'I think it's all most peculiar,' Gilbert said, giving his words weight. But whatever accusation he intended to direct at Wilfred rebounded on him as Wilfred, in all his relentless patience, nodded agreement.

'Too right. It's got me stumped as well. I've been thinking. Supposing she had to go to the office for something.'

'What? On a Saturday? There's no earthly reason.'

'No . . . but just suppose. And if she did, she might have — slipped, twisted her ankle, been taken ill — I don't know. It's worth a try, I ought to go and see. If I don't find her, I'll do something else. On the way back, I'll call in at the police station.'

Gilbert's mouth opened and shut. Alarm vibrated around him, at the same time his attitude took on the amazed scorn of one who refuses to contemplate bad news; all he managed was one word: 'Police?'

'Yes,' Wilfred said firmly. 'Her car's *got* to be somewhere. One of the blokes out on patrol might see it, he'd report it if he knew there'd been an enquiry.'

'You mean it might be parked at the side of the road somewhere? Why should it?'

'Perhaps — perhaps she had engine trouble. Perhaps — oh, I don't know, Gilbert, I'm as much in the dark as you are.'

'I don't like this,' Gilbert said tightly, accusation in his tone.

'I can't say I'm mad about it myself.' Wilfred was forthright; he, after all, was the one who was going out into the bitter night.

Peevishly, Gilbert followed him across the hall. It did not occur to him that Wilfred might be moved to unaccustomed bluntness because he was tired and worried. 'Aren't you going to phone Linda?' he said to Wilfred's large back. 'I mean don't you think you should?' he added swiftly as Wilfred turned and almost caught the tremor of spite that crossed his features.

'Your mother wouldn't be with Linda.'

'It does seem unthinkable. I mean, at this time of night. But . . . just in case.'

'There'd be no point in disturbing her as late as this.'

The most naively honest of men, Wilfred could, on occasion, dissemble effortlessly. Gilbert knew the occasions and their cause, and out of Wilfred's hearing gossiped with satisfaction: someone ought to tell Wilfred we all know about Linda, tell him for his own good. Gilbert would not do it, he lacked nerve. He had other ways.

After Wilfred had gone, Gilbert remained in the hall, hovering over the telephone, his indecision measured in the resonant tick-tock of the grandfather clock. Suddenly he picked up the receiver and dialled Wilfred's number. After some moments the ringing-out tone ceased and a sleepy voice said, 'Hello?'

'Wayne. It's Gilbert.'

A humming silence on the line indicated that Wayne required to be instructed or informed. He was a weedy youth, impassive as his sister, and very nearly speechless.

'My mother isn't there by any chance, is she?' Gilbert asked. 'No.'

'Ah, no, I suppose not. I just wondered.' Gilbert, accustomed to Wayne's monosyllables, did not trouble to explain. And Wayne would never ask why anyone should expect his Aunt Mildred to be there at that hour. He had a blighting lack of interest in the doings of any generation but his own.

'I'd better speak to Linda — your mother,' Gilbert said. The phone was put down with a clatter, thumping footsteps receded and, after an interval, returned.

'She's not in,' Wayne said.

'Not in? Good heavens, isn't she?' Gilbert disguised his lack of surprise by speaking with strenuous astonishment. 'Do you know where she is?'

'No.'

'Not with your father, I've just seen him. The drama committee, perhaps? I'd no idea their meetings went on so late.'

As this was an observation and not a direct question, Wayne had nothing to say.

After a pause Gilbert said brightly, 'Oh, well. Never mind. Cheerio, Wayne.'

It was not long before Wilfred returned. He had no news, there was no trace of Mildred or of her car, no sign that anyone had been in the works office. They took a glass of brandy each and sat talking in a repetitive, helpless way, their speculations growing emptier as their perplexity increased. Every so often Gilbert erupted into a fidget and said, 'We must do something,' and Wilfred answered 'What? We've done all we can.' In the intervals between speech the stillness of the house closed about them, they were aware of the outside world, of the profound and transforming quiet that came with the snow. 'Where can she be on a night like this?'

They could only look at each other hopelessly and begin again: perhaps . . . perhaps . . .

Eventually, Gilbert said, 'I phoned Linda.'

'Why?'

'I had to do something while you were out. I couldn't just sit here. She wasn't in.' Gilbert pressed his pink lips together and studied Wilfred.

'I told you not to ring.'

'You didn't. You said you wouldn't. That's different.'

'What I meant was I wouldn't get Wayne out of bed at this hour.'

'Well, if you'd known she wouldn't be in, you should have said. I wouldn't have needed to ring up then, I just thought there was a poss — '

'She's always late back from those meetings.' Wilfred's expression was unreadable.

'Late.' Gilbert smiled, revealing long gums and very small, pointed teeth. He was enjoying himself. '*Late*. They never went on *this late* when I was on the committee.'

The Hewitt Silver Trophy, presented yearly, was not unconnected with Gilbert's position on the committee. He had never appeared in a production but the belief that the right leading part would come his way sustained him through several seasons of bravura off-stage behaviour and gleeful back-stabbing. The society, of decent reputation and long standing, thrived on the inner tensions of scandal, intrigue and exhibitionism; when Gilbert left — his talent untried, his vanity intact — it was on the point of disbanding. Surviving members shuddered at his name and said 'Oh, God' . . . in anguish and relief.

Much the same thing had happened with the Literary Society, the Historical Society and the Folklore Group, all of which had their silver trophies and distracted memories.

Gilbert said, 'Where is it tonight? The meeting? Whose house?'

'I don't know.'

'But suppose you wanted to phone her? She might get snowed up, wherever she is. It could be — ' Gilbert paused. 'Awkward.'

'Phoning up won't dig her out.' Wilfred got up to pour more brandy, he looked suddenly tired, his movements lumbered. 'How was your weekend? Wasn't there some kind of do on tonight? A dance or something. Why didn't you stay?'

Pointedly, Gilbert picked up a magazine and gave his attention to it. 'The sport wasn't up to much at all. I got bored.'

Wilfred, sitting opposite, studying him, said, 'Bit of a let-down, was it? Didn't quite come up to expectations?' Behind his polite expression there glimmered, and was lost, a sardonic knowledge.

From a lifetime of cheated expectations, Gilbert murmured, 'It's really of no importance.'

For some time they did not speak. There was nothing to say that had not been said again and again and the questions to which there were answers had temporarily exhausted themselves. No sound came from beyond the thickly curtained windows, the warmth of the room crept drowsily on the two men until, eventually, not even the chimes of the grandfather clock in the hall woke them from their doze.

Then the doorbell rang, nerve-starting, confusing Gilbert into knocking over his brandy glass and dropping his magazine. Wilfred collected himself at once and left the room: when Gilbert followed there was a murmur of strange voices and two uniformed policemen standing in the hall.

Wilfred said, 'Gilbert, you'd better get dressed.'

Gilbert looked at the policemen, his half uttered dismay breaking feebly on the rock of their professional calm. 'What . . .? Is it . . . Mother? What . . .'

'There's been an accident,' someone said.

FIVE

The inquest on Mildred Hewitt returned an open verdict. In spite of extensive enquiries the police could find no one who knew of her intention to go to the Ridge that night, no one who could offer the least suggestion why she should.

Wilfred, and two close friends who had been much in her company during her last evening, gave evidence — such as it was. Her manner had been completely normal. Her abrupt departure, without a word to anyone, had been the only aspect of her behaviour in any way extraordinary — and no one had witnessed that. She had not left her mink coat in the cloakroom but in the Committee Room, which was unattended. A corridor led from the Committee Room to a side entrance, it was assumed she had left that way as she had not been seen going out through the lobby. No one had noticed her driving her Rover out of the car park. When her body was discovered she was fully clothed and wearing her mink coat and jewellery. This was described by Wilfred who automatically registered such details. Her handbag was on the passenger seat of her unlocked car, it contained credit cards and forty pounds in cash; she had not been robbed. Suicide, everyone agreed, was out of the question, although as a matter of routine the police searched her house and her office for a suicide note but found none.

The snowfall was light by Avenridge standards, and by the time the funeral took place only a thin white crust remained; later on, there was a memorial service. Wilfred saw to all the arrangements. His wife Linda, seizing the chance to equip herself with an entire new wardrobe and a glamorously grieving air, conspicuously supported Gilbert. Even people who disliked Gilbert were stirred to sympathy by his blighted look and precarious dignity; there had been fears that he would not get through the public obsequies without breaking down and embarrassing everyone.

But Gilbert's grief had ravaged him instantly, and privately; only Wilfred and Linda knew of the bursts of noisy weeping, the gulping cries, the hours spent in his mother's room, her immaculate clothes crushed in his hands, his sobs echoing through the house. He had no memory of this frenzy which so enervated him that, when it was over, he appeared calm and in command. But he commanded nothing, least of all himself. An appalling event had occurred, its reality verified by a sequence of formalities that were directed and administered by others but he, the violence of his loss all about him, was incapable of understanding anything.

The pressures of the commonplace exerted themselves and he responded because he had no will to do otherwise. He made himself presentable, went for walks, watched television, and people began to say, 'Isn't it remarkable the way Gilbert's standing up to it, the way he's adjusting?' He was not adjusting, he was listening, distracted by the whispers that crept to him through the crevices of shock: what was she doing at the Ridge? Why did she go there that night? Why did she die there? These whispers occurred intermittently, on the thin, high babble of nightmares; he could not quite grasp them, not quite ignore them, they trembled behind his lips when he was speaking of other things and the confusion of their urgency was in the numb, appealing gaze he directed outward, looking for someone to help, someone to tell him what to do.

As a temporary measure, Wilfred and Linda moved in with Gilbert the day after Mildred's death. It was inconvenient but their duty, and there was no one else. Wilfred was busy with the firm; Linda, left to the boredom of Gilbert's company, occupied herself with distant, venal schemes, until she learnt about Mildred's will.

It was uncompromising. Several sums to charities, one thousand pounds to Mrs Blunt, the excellent daily woman who had been with the Hewitts for so many years, everything else was Gilbert's. No one had expected otherwise, except Linda, who seethed, cheated. 'It's an insult,' she said to Wilfred. 'We've been demeaned. Do you realize? Demeaned. The whole of Avenridge will know what she thought of us.' It was Wilfred's opinion that anyone who was interested had a good idea already. He had always been realistic about his Aunt Mildred.

Linda was not concerned with realism, she fed upon the show of things, the jealousy, admiration or desire they provoked in others. She had felt nothing for Mildred beyond a racking envy of her possessions; her expectation of a share of those possessions snatched away, she saw scorn in every sidelong glance of Mrs Blunt. She decided it was time to reassess her duty to Gilbert.

One grey, vaporous day, edged with hoar frost, she invited friends round to The Laurels. Gilbert, returning from a walk, found cars parked in the driveway. Linda had not told him she was entertaining, or if she had, he had mislaid the information in the stunned spaces of his mind. The drawing room was full of young women. With their scent and their chatter wafting round him as softly as the cooing of doves, they drank his coffee or his sherry and picked at his helplessness with hushed voices and glossy-lipped, soothing smiles. Time was a great healer . . . there was the future . . . he would marry, have a family of his own . . . his mother would have wanted that . . .

Would she? A woman in her place? Concerned with his own pain he missed the interchanged glances, the amused horror: who'd have him?

In other circumstances he would have judged these young women as he judged Linda: common, empty-headed and deceitful. But in other circumstances they would not be there, stalking him with their curiosity. It was the mystery of his mother's death that engrossed them, they relished possibilities: suicide, an assignation. Only Gilbert, it was generally believed, could supply answers, but no one dared ask him the questions, not directly. Innuendoes, ambiguous statements designed to draw information from him, deepened his confusion and turned his dazed attention inwards to the whispers inside his skull, while he murmured, a broken sound, 'I don't know . . . I can't grasp it yet . . .'

When they left, snuggled into warm coats, their faces framed prettily in fur, they pressed his hand gently, urged him to call, or if they could do anything, anything, not to hesitate, any time. Gilbert, plundered, his eyes moist, was visited by the fleeting reassurance that in each of these women — in every woman — there resided some small measure of the woman who had cherished him so long.

Afterwards Linda relaxed, her feet up on the sofa. She had a voluptuous body, sublimely indolent: she tried every new diet fad, but not for long, and every new fashion, no matter how unsuitable. Her wardrobe was full of cheap, bright clothes with broken zips and sundered seams. Very little in the way of expression troubled her face, her flamboyant good looks registered everything that was necessary; her mouth had its own mechanism for smiling, to dazzling effect, she expended no energy on it. Her exertions were vocal, prattle issued from her, generated by an animation that, disconcertingly, never quite reached her face. She gave dramatic emphasis to the most trivial statements and had an air of being special in some secret way. Like Wilfred's suits, she was too young and too smart for Wilfred, he was unsatisfactory to her in many respects, yet she perched in the crevices of the life he provided for her, a gaudy, sheltered bird, too secure to be dislodged.

In his normal state, Gilbert responded to Linda's sexuality with a terrified lust. His mother had once said, 'I know what it is that's so ghastly about Linda. She sucks everything in, like a vacuum cleaner. She doesn't *do* anything. She just sits. Look at all those photographs she has taken of herself, sitting. Smiling. That smile. It makes you wonder what's *fed* it.' The notion, gruesomely accurate, disturbed Gilbert's sleep for many nights afterwards. He dreamt he was being dragged into Linda by way of her slippery, rapacious vagina, a horrific reversal of the birth process; just as he was about to be engulfed he found his voice and shrieked, and woke.

Now he regarded her apathetically. The cumulative effects of his tranquillizers, his walk and the effort of being sociable, had reduced him to lethargy and he sat fishy-eyed, his long limbs sagging. Her voice rattled senselessly about him, he might have nodded, agreed. A word, a question, persisting, penetrated his indifference.

'Sunday,' he said. 'I'm going to lunch with the Dashes.'

'You never said.' She paused, leaning forward to pick up her sherry glass.

'I met Emmeline when I was in town. She invited me.'

'You never said. I wish you'd said. When you came in.' The

name of Dash had prestige, she had missed the chance of impressing her friends with it.

Olivia Dash, a successful actress, was seldom at home. Her younger sister Emmeline, dreamy, dishevelled and clever, had a workshop in a shut-down hotel that had once been one of the glories of Avenridge. 'You've got to admit Emmeline's peculiar,' Linda said, although Gilbert was not disputing the point. No one could. 'She's taken up this new hang gliding sport. Do you know what Will says? He says she always looked as if she's been dragged through a hedge and she probably is now, regularly.'

Gilbert said nothing. He knew how Linda longed to cultivate the Dashes, but her pretensions and strivings belonged to a section of his life that had become so meaningless he could take no pleasure in malice.

Put out, Linda sipped her sherry and, after a silence, said, 'Well, that's what I mean, you see. Picking up the threads. I said to Will only yesterday, I said we can't be selfish, stand in Gilbert's way. And he agreed. And with him having to devote so much time to the business now . . .' She always had a great deal to say about the business.

Gilbert stopped listening. It had always been his view — and his mother's — that Wilfred's place in their life depended entirely on his usefulness to them: what they had never acknowledged, even between themselves, was that Wilfred was efficient and popular with the staff and customers. He had ideas about modernization which they made a point of listening to, with polite attention, questioning, agreeing — and then ignoring, as if he had never spoken. It was their way of dealing with him, allowing him to define, for himself, his subservient position.

'Good, that's settled.' Linda stood up, smoothed her skirt over her hips. 'I'd better phone Will, tell him. Then I'll go up and get our things together.'

'Things . . . together?' Gilbert stammered.

She nodded and, with her devastating smile, left the room.

He sat staring after her. The short winter day had drawn to its close, spreading shadows in the corners of the room. He moved about switching on lamps, then went to the window where the lights from distant houses gleamed through the grey velvet dusk; frost glinted on the stark trees and massive, shrouded ranges of shrubs.

He could hear her voice from the hall. '. . . thinks it by far the best thing. Yes. He's quite sure, we've just had a long talk about . . . Of course, we're always *there* if he wants us, he knows he just has to say and we're *there* . . . You'd better go straight home after work and see to the kids' tea, then come on here for supper. Or perhaps the three of us could go out, I could do with a break . . . Am's dancing class tomorrow, and Way has to go to the optician's, and I have to organize my tupperware party . . .' She rattled on, filling the silence with the minutiae of their weekend arrangements. Later they would go over them and change them, the next day change them again. They were a restless, ramshackle family, always blaming one another for things forgotten, or late, or not done.

Gilbert drew the curtains and went to stand helplessly in the middle of the room. Its grace was despoiled by cups and glasses, overflowing ashtrays, magazines scattered, ornaments picked up, put down in the wrong place. Linda never tidied up; dividing her time between her own home and Gilbert's made too many demands on her, she said. She left everything to Mrs Blunt, the cleaning, the laundry, even the washing-up — unless Wilfred did it. She ordered the groceries by phone and had them delivered. It suddenly occurred to Gilbert to wonder what they were, what became of them, because Linda never cooked anything, her culinary range did not extend beyond Chinese takeaways, fish and chips, or instant dinners from the freezer. She did not sew or read or

arrange flowers or do any of the restful things that were part of
the structure of his life; she spent hours on the telephone and
went out quite often, giving him his tranquillizers, settling
him for what she called 'a nice lay down' and disappearing on
some business he never quite understood. When she was in she
sometimes mooched about the house, leaving a tell-tale trail of
musky scent and half open doors and cupboards. When he
asked her why she had been in the spare bedrooms or down the
back staircase, she said it was not her, it was Mrs Blunt.
'Snooping, I suppose. Those working class types love
snooping.' She and Mrs Blunt had never got on: Mildred
Hewitt's will ensured they never would.

Linda finished her call and went upstairs. Gilbert followed
her to the guest room and entered without knocking. The
room was wildly untidy; Linda sat at the dressing table,
making up her face. She said, 'Will thinks it's a good idea if we
eat out tonight.'

Gilbert said, 'Mrs Blunt only comes in the mornings.'

Linda said, 'Mmm?' studying her reflection minutely.

'Well. I can't manage.'

'No, of course not. You'll have to tell her to come more
often. I don't see how she can refuse.' It was the general view
— shared by Linda and in some instances propagated by her —
that Mrs Blunt's legacy was nothing less than a bribe, planted
with forethought by Mildred Hewitt to ensure some domestic
order in Gilbert's life.

'But she goes to other places,' Gilbert said, having only the
vaguest notion where. It was not his habit to hold
conversations with Mrs Blunt on the subject.

'Well, she'll have to make other arrangements. To tide you
over. Till you get a housekeeper.'

Gilbert sat down on the edge of the bed. It was littered with
frilly knickers and aggressively large brassieres. 'Housekeeper?'

'You certainly can't cope by yourself, not in a house this size. Remember that old boy down the road who lived by himself after his wife died? The house just rotted round him. They say there were even rats in it when they found him dead. No, you'll have to get somebody.'

'I've never been alone. Stayed in a house by myself.'

'Most people have to, sooner or later,' Linda said casually, although she never had. She had left her parental home at seventeen, and pregnant, to marry Wilfred. 'I think I'll wear my blue tonight. I wonder if this eye shadow will go with it? You'll have to get someone who can drive, be such a shame to have that car just standing there. Why don't you let Will use it sometimes, keep it running.'

'But I can't think of things like — a stranger in the house. It's too soon. You and Wilfred have to stay for a while, till I feel more like it.' His voice had a desperate edge.

'I have children, Gilbert, they need me at home. Oh, I know they're old enough to be by themselves, but not *so* much, and they're still *very* young, and the place gets in such a state, they don't — '

'Let Wilfred go home, then. You stay here.'

She gave a shocked, delighted laugh. 'I'm a respectable married woman, think of the talk. You wouldn't want our reputations ruined, would you? The two of us. Alone. Here.' The spurious drama of the situation absorbed her. When at last she had exhausted it, she began to apply her lipstick, tilting her chin and pouting at herself in the mirror, directing glances of wicked complicity at Gilbert.

He sat unresponsive. 'Well, not just now, suddenly. You can't go just now. There are things to talk about.'

She put down her lipstick. 'What things?'

He could think of none. 'I'll speak to Wilfred.'

'You can if you like. I already have. Don't you think it's time you took one of your pills?'

'I don't want pills,' he shouted.

'You'd better. I'll tell you what, I'll see what Will has to say about staying till morning.'

'Telephone him now.'

'Oh, no, I can't bother him with little things, he's far too busy. With him standing in for you *and* Aunt Mildred, he's absolutely snowed under. Anyone would think he was a partner, the amount of time he has to spend — '

Gilbert stood up and walked out.

The following morning they breakfasted in the kitchen. The atmosphere was strained. 'Why don't you come round to us this evening?' Linda said. 'We're going to have a lovely family evening together. Just the four of us. It's been ages since we did, with Will and me being here so long.'

Gilbert stared out of the window. In the grip of hoar frost, the garden was stiff and motionless and shining. On Saturday mornings he went out with gloves and secateurs to choose foliage to go with the flowers that were ordered and delivered on Friday. But no flowers had been delivered, no one had ordered them. All that was essential to his existence had been sheared away in a single, brutal moment, leaving this: a garden unvisited, a house without flowers, Linda's blithe, relentless voice.

'Why don't you, Gilbert? Will can cook us one of his specials.'

They would eat it on trays, in the glaring room Linda called the lounge, which always had something new in it, or had just been redecorated.

'I shall be busy,' Gilbert said.

'Mind you, the kids will have created havoc,' Linda said proudly. 'Every time I've managed to pop back home, there's been more havoc. Am broke the waffle maker yesterday.'

'Oh God,' Wilfred said patiently. 'Will it mend?'

'I don't know. You can get bigger ones now, anyway.'

'Can you?' Wilfred was interested, he shared Linda's passion for the latest gadget; the more garish and complicated it was the more he was amazed they had managed so long without it. Then someone broke it and it was put in a cupboard and forgotten.

Linda began to talk about having ornamental shutters for their windows. Wilfred objected to the expense. Linda said everyone had them, they increased the value of the house, so they'd have to afford it. They lived on the western outskirts of Avenridge, in what was called an executive cottage home on an estate where the houses, exercises in architectural savagery, had steep gables, Georgian bow windows and columned porches. Indoors, the sound proofing was minimal, but Wilfred and Linda did not notice, they lived with noise. Radio, stereo, musical toilet roll holders and cigarette boxes, alarm clocks that erupted into pop music: the television was always on, the telephone always ringing. On the few occasions Gilbert had been there he had left with a violent headache.

Their wrangling voices penetrated his lethargy. He picked up his coffee cup and took it into the drawing room. Someone, probably Wilfred, had tidied up the detritus of Linda's entertaining. It was not as Gilbert would have wished but if it had been left to Linda it would not have been done at all. Things were in the wrong place; the magazines and tabloid newspapers that seemed to multiply round Linda were roughly stacked on one of the exquisite occasional tables, on top of them the mess of scrap papers that were her 'reminder' lists. Wilfred had cleared out and relaid the fire. Gilbert put a match to it and sat staring as the kindling caught. After a while he got up, opened the door softly and crept down the hall to stand outside the kitchen door. It was ajar. He listened.

Linda was saying, '*Honestly*. In my bedroom. Getting, you

know, worked up. Suggestive. We can't stay, not if he's going to be like *that*.'

Wilfred's amusement boomed. 'Come off it, Lin, you're safe enough. All he's ever done with it is pee. I'd be surprised if he wanked.'

'You make me sick with your dirty talk.'

'All right. Masturbated.'

'That's just as dirty. Don't you ever think of anything except sex?'

Wilfred sounded hurt. 'You started it.'

Gilbert went back to the drawing room and sat by the fire again. When Linda came in he picked up the morning paper and stared at it blindly.

She had one of her silly lists, things he must do or remember: her manner was bright, brisk. 'I'll tell you what, as you're having your Sunday dinner with the Dash's, why don't you ask Mrs Dash to speak to Mrs Blunt for you. She's always ordering people about, and Mrs Blunt cleans for her.'

Gilbert did not reply. He lifted his eyes from the paper and gave her a look of hatred. She went away.

SIX

Henry drew back the curtain from the wide landing window. It was first light, houses and trees and the tops of shrubs rising from the icy breath of mist, the distant Ridge faint against the skyline.

He went quietly down the stairs. No matter how seldom he visited the house now, there was scarcely a detail he did not remember . . . in the shadowy hall the crinolined lady standing on a polished table. Her elaborately flounced skirts covered the telephone, the top half of her body was made of porcelain, one slender, lustrous arm crooked to hold a fan. On her right cheekbone was a beauty patch. She was ornamental in the fashion of the 1930's, the years had fled around her and still she smiled, the sweet smile of their first encounter, when he had never seen such an object and himself not been much taller than the telephone table.

In the kitchen he put the kettle on and gave his attention to the two wire-haired fox terriers. Elderly and quiet and set in their ways, they knew it was not time to go outside but they got out of their baskets and went to Henry, sniffing and nudging. He crouched down to stroke them, talked to them softly. 'I knew your parents — and your grandparents, too. In the war.'

Because he loved dogs, and there was no one to see him making a fool of himself, he put them back in their baskets and told them about it: the house full of relations from bomb-threatened towns, young servicemen convalescing . . . So many people who came and went while he stayed on, growing up, with no sense of the remorselessness of time, of irretrievable summers.

The kettle boiled and he began to make tea. In the breathless quiet of the morning there moved the memory of other mornings, when he was a small boy, helping Mr Dash. *It's very good of you to give me a hand Henry, I usually have to manage this on my own* . . .

The routine never varied. Mr Dash warmed the cups with boiling water, set them on a tray. Henry opened the biscuit barrel and put one Rich Tea biscuit on every saucer. Mr Dash poured a little milk in the cups and filled them with tea while Henry went to the fridge for the small jug of cream from the top of the milk. Mr Dash measured out the cream, with scrupulous fairness, a little to each cup.

At first, only Mr Dash talked; Henry had nothing to say. Shut inside his homesickness, he was intimidated by the big house in which he unaccountably found himself, where strangers with calm, high-English voices held conversations far above his head. He was conditioned to alarm, his parents had been tearing their marriage apart for years, then the whole world began to disintegrate with sirens and bombs and craters in the streets; but that was all he understood, he ached for what was lost and every night, before he slept, plotted the means to run away, find his way back. Yet every morning, when he crept down to the kitchen, there, with a persistence that dumbfounded him, were Mr Dash and the dogs and the Rich Tea biscuits. So he put off running away that day, or the next, and never at the time knew why, any more than he knew the moment when confidence replaced amazement, when some notion of stability took root in his consciousness. It was later, years later, he understood how his comfort began there, with the kindest of men, those mornings before the household woke.

The dogs pricked up their ears and looked towards the door. Henry went out to the hall. Emmeline was coming down the stairs, barefoot, her soft, mousy hair sticking out all over the place. She wore a bedlam nightshirt and a feather boa. She used her arms theatrically, draping herself over the bannisters: when she reached the hall she looked up at Henry and said, 'I am big. It's the movies that got small.'

'Gloria Swanson. *Sunset Boulevard.*'

She turned away without comment, she had expected him to know. 'I'm going to phone the met office.'

'Shall I take your mother some tea?'

'No, it's too early. She's got her tea-maker.'

Henry went back to the kitchen. After a moment Emmeline drifted in, the feather boa discarded, clutching a large photograph album. She said hello to the dogs and went to sit at the kitchen table, watching Henry pour tea. 'Mummy once found out you'd been pinching things from Woolworth's. For a dare. Your punishment was not to help Daddy with the morning tea. For a week.'

'Five days,' Henry said. 'Yes, your mother never wasted effort on threats. A straight chop to the vitals, and she never missed, you know that.' He carried the mugs of tea across and sat beside her. 'I didn't even want the stuff, I was just delighted to find out the nicely brought up little boys round here had the same criminal tendencies as the boys at home. I didn't even think of your mother till I'd done it. Then I did. God, she frightened me.'

Emmeline gave him the smile that moved occasionally like a whisper across her face, then her expression was composed again to its inwardness. Her father's fine bones, her mother's plainness, made her face vulnerable, always interesting. She was unusually pale, recovering from a bout of flu.

Henry said, 'Then she made me go to dancing lessons, I couldn't think what I'd done to deserve that. It wasn't a punishment, though — everyone else went and your mother wasn't going to have me left out. But, dancing lessons. The shame of it.'

'You went though.'

'Well. I found out you could get to hold girls.'

Emmeline smiled again, opened the album at a studio portrait of Mrs Dash, dating from the 1930's when Mrs Dash was what was then called a young matron. She wore an ankle length tea gown and strands of pearls across her stately bosom, her hair was Marcel-waved. No matter how fashions changed or the years accumulated, Mrs Dash remained in shape, in style, in essence, a lady of the 30's. She was built on the unyielding lines of a dressmaker's dummy; Henry, who now towered above her, remembered how at first sight she had seemed immense . . .

Avenridge railway station, a steam shrouded autumn afternoon, and he was an evacuee. Evacuee. The word still pitilessly defined a bewildered boy clutching his belongings in a brown paper parcel — in homes like his there were no such things as spare suitcases. A label with his name and destination printed in capitals threaded through the buttonhole of his cheap, outgrown raincoat. 'Henry,' Mrs Dash read, considering him from her height, her authority, her fox furs. 'We must see about getting you a good winter coat.' He was from that moment, and for a very long time, speechlessly in awe of her. It was Mr Dash who smiled, said, 'You'll be feeling a bit uprooted, won't you? Come along, old chap.' Who held his hand as they walked along the platform and talked to him of trains.

Thirty-five years ago. A war. A childhood. Mr Dash was

dead. Peacefully and unaware, looking out on the summer rain on the garden from his favourite chair, he closed his eyes. When Henry was told of it he wept, very privately.

Emmeline touched the portrait of her mother. 'You said Mummy looked like the drawings of Mrs Brown in the William books. Well, you said it in your diary and Olivia read it.'

'Olivia started as a bitch early in life. I hope she never told your mother.'

'She might have, if she thought it would please her,' Emmeline murmured.

Contained by Mrs Dash's discipline, both girls strove for her love, treasuring the least evidence of it. Mrs Dash had never been comfortably maternal, she was a busy woman, the world of childhood bored her; Henry had once heard her say that the best thing she could do for her girls was make sure they developed strength of character. As they grew up she grew closer to them, holding them in a fondness no one ever dared intrude upon by pointing out they had developed enough strength of character to demolish buildings, which was perhaps not quite what she had in mind.

Emmeline turned the pages of the album. The photographs were all black and white, taken in the 1940's and '50's. 'You and Olivia had all the fun during the war,' she said in her sweet, vague voice. She had been born towards the end of the war and remembered nothing of it.

'Fun? Gas masks and blackout. Sweet rationing,' Henry said.

'That's not the point.'

The point was that she was fascinated by a period of family history from which she was excluded, a time that belonged to Henry and Olivia: Emmeline could experience it only vicariously, by way of photographs and the conversations of her elders. Dressed in Olivia's clothes, she haunted the edges of fading memories, insinuating herself into them until she established a shadow of her presence. She took over the family album and, like a mad archivist, rearranged chronology according to what she wished it to be. Amongst photographs of Henry and Olivia as schoolchildren, she placed photographs of herself at the same age. Henry, skinny, with the tension of a young animal, fiercely attractive; Olivia, elegant even then, even in the unflattering school uniform; Emmeline, in the same uniform, looked wrecked — her huge, dream-darkened eyes stared out of the face of a Victorian orphan, her hair stuck out of its plaits, one knicker leg, minus elastic, descended beneath the hem of her gymslip. Someone would have tried to tidy her up, but in the moment it took to stand back, to focus the camera, to say, 'Emmeline, don't move' — Emmeline had accomplished her own demolition. Over the years her mother and sister had tried to do something about her indifference to appearances but eventually were forced to give up, to leave her as she was, concerned with her schemes, her gentle manias, the dramas that occurred inside her head.

Henry glanced sideways at her as she studied the photographs, absorbed. She had taken to wearing her hair cut very short, uncannily reproducing his boy's cut in the photographs. She seldom wore make-up; small boned and lithe, she could have been a boy. He wondered if she ever got confused about it herself. Then he thought, no, not confused. She had the equilibrium of the true eccentric, she would regard gender as a matter of choice.

He turned back to the album. There was a photograph of Emmeline in her teens, dressed in the outfit of a Land Girl; it looked as if she had taken it straight out of a trunk in the attic. Henry did not ask, she probably had. Beside this was a photograph of Mr Dash in his Home Guard uniform. Then a kaleidoscope: summer picnics, Christmas parties, bicycle excursions, Olivia in amateur dramatic productions; there were groups, faces captured so long ago Henry had forgotten most of the names. Studying one, Emmeline gave a low, disconcerted wail. 'Gilbert. Dammit. I invited him to Sunday lunch. We won't be here if it's a decent day, Mummy will have to manage on her own. It went right out of my head.'

Too many things went out of Emmeline's head to cause surprise, or offence, in those who knew her. 'And you haven't told your mother? Gilbert who? Can't you put him off?'

'No, that would be unkind, he's so lost. Gilbert Hewitt. You know.'

She pointed to a crowded garden party snapshot. Next to Olivia, who could not then have been more than sixteen and now admitted to thirty something, stood a pallid, well dressed boy. An unspecified dislike stirred in Henry. Rivalry? He had returned home to Manchester after the war, but the ties were never broken and with every visit Olivia grew more glorious, youths exhausted themselves striving for her attention. She had never been beautiful, she was not beautiful now, but she had grace, a high style that provoked desire and despised it. Her cool elegance made its own statement: she was available, but only on her own terms. He should know.

'Gilbert Hewitt,' Emmeline said again, nudging him.

'Oh, yes. Hewitts. The printers.'

'They fall from heights. Mummy will cope with him, she's good with people like Gilbert. And he'll just want to talk about his mother. But I should have *told* her, I shouldn't have forgotten. God, I am a fool.' Remorse accumulated in her. She got up and stood, agitated, wondering what to do, her toes pointing together, her hair wild.

'Emmeline, you're not going to wake your mother up now to tell her you forgot to tell her yesterday that Gilbert's coming to lunch tomorrow,' Henry said patiently.

Emmeline pondered this, then agreed, 'Daft.'

'Yes. We'll tell her before we go out, she should be stirring by then.'

'You have a decent pair of boots, haven't you?' Emmeline said, diverted by the thought of going out. 'We can lend you a crash helmet, but you do need good boots. You'll have to run a lot, there's not much wind today.'

'I have impeccable boots,' Henry said, not liking to admit that his heart was already in them. Why did he want to learn to hang glide? 'Come and finish your tea and tell me why Gilbert's lost and only wants to talk about his mother.'

'Because he is bereft.' Emmeline sat down again and told Henry about Mildred Hewitt's death. As she talked, he recalled a sharply handsome woman who had patronized him because he was *unfortunate*. He was not disposed to be much interested in her.

'Odd, though,' Emmeline finished. 'Why she was there, of all places.'

'Unaccountable things happen,' he said inattentively.

'Not to Mildred Hewitt, if she could help it.'

'Presumably she couldn't then. Is it time we were moving?'

'Mmmm?'

'Come on. Cut along now, young shaver.'

She giggled. '*Boy's Own Paper*.' He had discovered bound copies of them in the attic and read them hour after hour, fascinated. She had read them all, too.

The next morning, Sunday, swathes of rain billowed over Avenridge, obscuring the surrounding hills. Henry counted his bruises with a childish mixture of relief and disappointment that there would be no hang gliding instruction that day. 'We can go over the theory,' Emmeline said helpfully. She took it for granted he had enjoyed himself. After a day spent pounding down the nursery slopes, trying to take off in a nil wind, he was not so sure. 'At least you got in the air,' she said, 'not everyone does first time.' He had, it was true, not more than fifteen feet, his senses galvanized; it was the landings that were so punishing. He marvelled that someone as small and weightless as Emmeline had not long ago been carried home in pieces, but she flew with astonishing grace a kite she had built herself.

After a late breakfast they took the dogs and went out, walking through the rain to the old hotel where Emmeline had her workshop. Henry wore his hooded anorak, Emmeline something that looked like a groundsheet, her hair pushed under a W.A.A.F. officer's cap. Scarcely anyone was about, rivulets rushed along the gutters of the up and down streets and the greyness of Avenridge, its changing textures, came back with love and wonder to Henry. The sky phosphorescent before snow; the chiffon veils of mist; the autumn grey of woodsmoke, and, in this downpour, the stone buildings shining like old pewter.

On the edge of the town the residential area merged into genteel tea rooms and antique shops and tailoring establishments that sold sturdy, subfusc clothes that never wore out. Here, marking a boundary in preoccupations and in time, stood Dash's hotel: creeper-clad turrets and lancet windows, an endearing and insane survivor of the Gothic revival.

There were old people living in Avenridge who had spent their lives in service there as maids and porters and bootboys. During the war it had been a convalescent home for servicemen and afterwards reverted to a hotel. Henry could just remember tea dances there, in the gilt and red velvet lounge, but its grand days were over, it began to lose money and was closed down. It was owned by a confusing number of Dash relatives, Emmeline amongst them, who could not decide what to do with it. The dispute was amicable, there were vague plans for modernization, or conversion, but no one was in a hurry, and Emmeline said to Henry that somehow it wouldn't be right, breaking into its time capsule 'Give it a little while,' he said, 'and it'll be fashionable again, just as it is.'

They went in by one of the side entrances, through a door in the wall surmounted by an arched, weather-beaten wooden sign: Dash's Tea Gardens. The paths were cracked and mossgrown, in the wilderness of the lawn a summerhouse was collapsing gently, gracefully; the dogs ran about, happily searching out familiar scents, finding new ones.

Emmeline's workshop, once the dining room, was full of the soft pearl light of the drenched morning. Its long windows looked out on the tangled garden and even on busy days no sound of traffic reached it. In all its elements, in the machinery and tools it contained and in its beautiful havoc, it reflected the state of Emmeline's mind: practical, daring, inspired and cluttered. She could make anything, even as a child her talent was exceptional; after refining it at Technical College and Art School, she returned to Avenridge and established her business. She worked in wood, making models of old houses and shops; every architectural detail was exquisitely reproduced and faithful to its period, the shops had stalls outside with their wares displayed. She worked from old photos or prints or sketches, from the actual building if it still existed, and exhibited in the big craft fairs all over the country.

Henry was fascinated by these models, by something beyond shape and proportion and artistry. They conveyed a reality so eerie, so persistent, the flavour of the age to which they belonged clung about them. When he stood before them his own sense of reality dissolved, he was drawn into their atmosphere, to smell, to sense, to hear: it was evening, always evening, the cobbled street gaslit; the muffin man rang his bell; a tired horse drew its last load home; in the distance, a forlorn thread of sound, a train hooted on the soot-smelling air . . .

The first time he had seen her work, Emmeline had watched his face and knew he understood. He said, 'They're memories, aren't they? Not yours, or mine. The generation before us. That's why it's evening, they're going into the dark.' It had troubled him once that she should choose to mislay her place in time and had the skill to seduce others into following her. 'But, Emmeline, it's the 1970's. It's *now*.' — 'Not necessarily,' she answered, the great reasonableness.

In the corner of the workshop stood a vast old sewing machine. Emmeline was making herself a harness that would enable her to fly her hang glider prone instead of seated. 'Everyone will, eventually, stands to reason. Less wind resistance,' she explained.

The theory made sense to Henry, the application made him nervous. 'It's a different flying technique, isn't it? And you don't know that thing will work till you get in the air. It'll be a bit late then.'

Emmeline had thought of that. She had a friend who was a builder, he was going to let her use his crane, hoisting her into the air while she practised getting into position. 'You know why your schemes succeed?' Henry said. 'Because they're absurd. No one else would think of them. You're like the Giant Rat of Sumatra.'

'I know, the world isn't ready for me yet. Keep hold of this piece while I machine it,' Emmeline said, engrossed in a complicated arrangement of webbing, rope and nylon.

When she no longer needed his assistance, Henry made coffee, then went out to wander about the hotel. His reflection slid across the surfaces of enormous, mottled mirrors, his footsteps broke the silence of grand rooms full of huge pieces of furniture and ecclesiastical fireplaces.

Emmeline's share in the hotel had come to her through Grandmother Dash, an alarming lady who had once been a suffragette and of whom Henry, as a boy, had been prepared to believe anything. She suffered a stroke in her later years and lived with the Dash's. Emmeline called her the Ancient of Days, she had always loved her dearly and devoted herself to the old lady. No one else could understand the tortured attempts at conversation, but Emmeline claimed to, and they spent hours together, looking at old photographs, talking of the past. Sometimes Emmeline would mention an incident, and her mother would say, 'Emmeline, how can you possibly know that? I couldn't have told you, it was fifty years ago. Everyone's forgotten.' — 'Grandmother hasn't, she remembers everything.' Many old scandals were revived, with relish; Grandmother Dash had never believed in shielding girls from the more interesting aberrations.

The Dash family was large, many of them were wealthy, they lived long and, for the most part, joyfully; as they died off inheritances cropped up, to be received with grace or, with equal grace, to be diverted to any member felt to be more in need. To Henry it was entirely appropriate that out of those mild and loving eccentrics Emmeline should be one to receive a share in the hotel. Mad and forlorn, with its velvet curtained recesses and twisting turret stairs, its echoing corridors and creeper-twined windows, it mouldered all around her while she worked, full of whispers she understood.

The day lowered, grey at the windows; the standard lamps were switched on. Emmeline and the dogs sat in an armchair in front of the fire. The dogs were not allowed on chairs but they were allowed on people, a distinction they understood and exploited.

Mrs Dash said, 'Henry. Sherry. I think we should fortify ourselves before Gilbert arrives. Not that I wish to be unkind.'

Mrs Dash was kindness itself, her sympathy genuine, but she saw no reason, in the intimacy of the family atmosphere, to compromise with the truth.

'Gilbert, I regret, was an abominable child, which wasn't to be wondered at. They ruined him, his parents, his grandparents. Because he was an only child, and born late in life to Mildred.'

'I was late. You were expecting the menopause,' Emmeline murmured. She had once overheard her mother talking about family planning: *I left that sort of thing to Daddy*, and ever afterwards regarded herself as a fit of absent-mindedness on her father's part.

'I don't think we need discuss the timing of your conception. Go and comb your hair, my dear. And might you do something about your clothes?' Mrs Dash spoke with affection and some despair. Emmeline's pullover was on inside out and she had lost the buttons of her shirt sleeves. Or someone's shirt, it was far too big for her and could have been an old one of her father's. She stared guiltily down at herself, scooped off the dogs and went out.

Mrs Dash said, 'She does make an effort when one reminds her. It simply doesn't occur to her she might look as if she's just cleaned out the cellar. Now, what were we saying? Ah, yes. Grief alone is hard enough to bear, but for Gilbert there are the extraordinary circumstances, the unanswered questions.'

'How is he coping, then?' Henry asked. 'Doesn't he have to run the firm?'

'He never did, you know, Mildred was always at the helm. There is a cousin, or something very distant. Wilfred, his name is. Let me see, would you have known him?'

They sipped their sherry, searching their thoughts, attempting to place Wilfred in a shared time.

'I don't think so,' Henry said at last; a crowd of faces and names had occurred to him, he could not isolate a Wilfred. Since the previous day, stray memories of Gilbert had returned, unwillingly: none of them was pleasant.

'No. His family lived over the other side of town, Mildred never had much to do with them. And he's quite a bit older than Gilbert. He married a local girl and they moved away, Birmingham, I think, somewhere like that. Mildred's always regarded them more as a cross she had to bear . . . She might have been a blindly doting mother but she was shrewd in other respects. When Gilbert's father died she took Wilfred into the business. He's a terrible busybody, I believe, but he must be efficient, or she'd never have kept him on. I daresay it was always at the back of her mind that Gilbert would need someone to lean on one day. It's the sort of thing a mother does think about.'

A suggestion of something less than her usual vigour made Henry look at her curiously. 'You don't worry about the girls, do you? They're both independent.'

'Financially, yes, they're singularly fortunate. Emotionally independent? Olivia is, but Emmeline . . . She's a dear, but you must agree there's something of the waif about her. She could have gone to drama school, you know, she has just as much talent as Olivia, but the idea of making a career away from home horrifies her. She can't bear the thought of living anywhere except in Avenridge.'

'She loves it. It's where she has her being.'

'What an apposite phrase, Henry.'

'And you're not holding her back, if that's what's worrying you.'

'It does occur to me occasionally. And thinking of Gilbert — '

Henry could see Gilbert descending on her like a black cloud. Did he have this effect on everyone?

'It's the comparison, if there is one. Mildred and Gilbert.

She took away his will to be independent, to be free of her. And in its place she gave him an image of himself. But, Henry, it's nothing to do with reality.'

The earnestness of her tone made him laugh. 'You're not suggesting there *is* a comparison — '

'Oh, I do hope not.'

'Emmeline doesn't need you to provide her with an image of herself. She has her own. Several, in fact.'

'Quite. That's the actress in her. She lives so much in her own head.'

Henry thought it wasn't a bad place to be: in Emmeline's head anything could happen. Once . . . once she had formed Avenridge's only flying saucer society, it had been her dearest wish to be taken aboard one on a visit. As far as he knew she still considered it a possibility. And who was to say she was wrong?

'You see, I have very little imagination,' Mrs Dash said. She had none at all. 'I've never tried to stand between her and reality, which is what Mildred did with Gilbert. And now he has to adjust to what he really is, not what she pretended he was. And he's not very nice.'

'We're in for a crashing time.'

'I'm afraid so.' Mrs Dash took a steadying sip of sherry. 'But we must do our best, mustn't we?'

She gave him the look that had once sent his conscience on a panic-stricken search for unconfessed sins. Now he could smile, he had long since passed through the untraceable processes that made her goodness accessible to him. But it was the small boy who had not done his homework, who had extorted Olivia's sweet ration out of her by teaching her new swear words, who answered meekly 'Yes, Mrs Dash'.

Gilbert arrived, white-faced, out of the weeping day,

tremulous in his need for sympathy. He had not expected to share the attention of the ladies and had no more than a glance for Henry, receiving the impression of powerful, masculine ease and a style he could not hope to measure up to; so he ignored it and murmured something about not remembering. 'You must,' Emmeline said, aghast that anyone should regard Henry as a passing stranger. 'He's more or less family.'

They all explored past occasions when Henry and Gilbert were sure to have met, until Gilbert apologized, piteously, 'I'm sorry, I'm a little confused.' But he grasped at the memories offered to him — his mother being embalmed in them, in all her perfection — and converted them to his own comfort, talking relentlessly through the soup, roast beef and Yorkshire pudding. With the dessert he began on Wilfred and Linda, exercising his spite and sense of betrayal, resisting every effort to change the subject. Conversations occurred surreptitiously around him but he appeared not to notice beyond an occasional, 'What? Oh . . .' in case it was anything that concerned him, losing interest immediately when it did not.

A fractional desperation appeared on Mrs Dash's face. Henry said, 'Coffee, I think,' and went into the kitchen.

Emmeline followed him after a while, carrying plates. He looked at her sideways. 'This is a fine mess you've gotten me into, Stanley.'

'I know. He's started to cry. Mummy's taken him into the sitting room.'

They sat at the kitchen table and smoked cigarettes, waiting for the coffee, talking quietly. Emmeline said, 'Perhaps it's a sort of madness people go through. Then they get over it, and forget. We weren't like that after Daddy died, were we?'

Henry remembered the helpless quiet of their grief and how, sharing it, there had come to him for the first time the true meaning of the words 'cherished memory'. So they had cherished in one another the love that the dead man had given them. 'You had each other,' he said.

She sat thoughtfully, chin in hands. 'Yes. And you.'

'To say nothing of the three million Dash relatives,' he added.

'Yes. One doesn't realize, till they're all together, how many there are. You know what Olivia said afterwards.'

'Yes.'

'That Mummy was like Aunt Ada Doom holding a counting: 'there's always been Starkadders at Cold Comfort Farm' . . . There's no one at The Laurels for Gilbert. Poor sod.' Emmeline got up and went to the dining room to collect more plates. On the way back she listened at the sitting room door. 'Trumpeting sounds,' she reported to Henry. 'Gilbert blowing his nose. Pulling himself together. Mummy's giving him advice about Mrs Blunt.'

'That lady of terrifying rectitude who does for you? Speaks as she finds.'

'Is beholden to no one.'

'Keeps herself to herself . . .' Having exhausted the few words Mrs Blunt was disposed to speak, Henry said, 'But what has she got to do with Gilbert?'

Emmeline shrugged. 'I don't know. But she does for the Hewitts as well.'

They took the coffee into the sitting room. Gilbert was tucking away his handkerchief , saying, 'Mother was very generous to her in her will.'

'It would be most unfair of you to take advantage of that,' Mrs Dash said firmly. She explained to Henry and Emmeline that Gilbert was having trouble with his domestic arrangements as Mrs Blunt could not spare him any extra time.

'Of course not,' Emmeline said. In spite of her vagueness she had the same thought for others that her mother had. 'And she must be getting near retirement, anyway, time she took on less, not more.'

Henry suggested, tentatively, that Gilbert ask Mrs Blunt if she could herself recommend someone to help out.

Gilbert reacted as if struck, his porcelain skin flaring pink. 'Impossible, too embarrassing for words. Mother did that once years ago, when Mrs Blunt was ill, and Mrs Blunt's ghastly niece came. It was a disaster, not only was she inefficient, she stole. Money.'

Too preoccupied to notice the glance exchanged between Emmeline and Mrs Dash, Gilbert went on, 'Whatever Mrs Blunt's faults, she's honest as the day is long, Mother couldn't humiliate her by bringing in the police. She had a quiet word with her, smoothed the matter over, and it was never referred to again. But so hideously embarrassing. We never dared raise the subject of a stand-in again.'

'And, under the circumstances, Mrs Blunt would not be likely to recommend her niece a second time,' Mrs Dash said, with the finality of a subject closed.

Gilbert, not listening, smugly reviewed with dignity the years of Mrs Blunt's employment, their generosity to her in the matter of holidays, Christmasses, unwanted personal and household effects. 'So I don't know what I'm going to do. It's not just the housework, it's clean shirts and ironing and ordering the groceries and — everything.' His voice trailed off, he stared into his coffee cup, defeated by the minutiae of everyday life.

Emmeline said what about advertising for someone and for a while they discussed the wording and placing of advertisements; it was plain Gilbert had no idea how to go about such practical matters and resented having to concern himself with them. Mrs Dash's face had taken on the stoicism of a woman fighting off a headache. Henry said, 'It's time we gave you a rest. Put your feet up and read the paper, we'll do the washing up, Gilbert won't mind helping.'

Gilbert's idea of helping was to keep up a monologue about Mrs Blunt and get in the way while Henry and Emmeline worked round him. Henry said, 'I never knew she had anything as humanising as an errant niece.'

'Surely you did,' Emmeline said. 'She was often around. I used to give her casual jobs in the workshop sometimes. She's clever with her hands.'

'Yes. Thieving.' Gilbert gave a snicker, his face venomous. 'And an appalling slut, she's anybody's who'll have her.'

'That's a disgraceful thing to say.' There was an edge to Emmeline's voice that made her sound suddenly like her mother. Henry looked at her in surprise, he had never thought it possible she could run out of patience, but Gilbert seemed determined to try everyone beyond endurance.

Gilbert retreated, gaping, fish-like. 'Well, it was just what I heard.'

'That's even more disgraceful. You can say what you want about someone if you know at first hand it's true. Do you?'

Henry disappeared inside a cupboard, putting plates away, hiding his smile. If he had been asked to describe a mouse in a rage, it would have been Emmeline.

'Do you?'

'No, Emmeline,' Gilbert stammered, aghast at the thought of anything first hand with the cleaning woman's niece.

'Of course not. How do you know anything about Rosa? You haven't set eyes on her for years, you wouldn't know her if you fell over her.'

'No, but — It was Wilfred, he told me. He's always saying things like that.'

'Then you should know better than to repeat them. Right. Change of subject.'

After the pressure of a hurt silence, Gilbert excused himself in a choked voice and went out to the downstairs cloakroom. Giving up the attempt to keep his face straight, Henry emerged from the cupboard.

'What are you laughing at?' Emmeline said.

Henry watched her vague charm re-appearing, settling into her expression; without it, she had looked momentarily lost. 'You. Sitting on Gilbert.'

'Was I?' she said, contrite. 'He's probably having a blub in the lav. Was I a beast?'

'Come on, Emmeline, he asked for it.'

'He did rather. Still . . . We'll have to be nice to him when he comes back. I know, tell him about Marchstearn.'

'Do you really think he's interested in anything except himself?'

'No, but we can try. Anything to shut him up about his mother and saying awful things about people.'

When Gilbert returned, she began hopefully, 'Henry inherited a house from his aunt last year, in Marchstearn.'

'I wonder if I should take one of my tranquillizers?' Gilbert said.

'It's a super place, one of those magic villages on the edge of the Cotswolds,' Emmeline persevered.

Gilbert showed interest: Mother had been very found of the Cotswolds, they'd spent quite a lot of time there together . . . Sinking beneath the flood of reminiscence, Emmeline looked wildly at Henry, then the phone rang and she went off to have a long talk about hang gliding. Henry continued to tidy up, to put things in Gilbert's long, inept hands and watch him wave them about and put them down again. He listened, made automatic responses, fully aware that nothing he said would make any impression. Mrs Dash had been right. Gilbert was collapsing inwardly, in pain and confusion, towards the image his mother had given him of himself. When he finally encountered reality the shock would free him to create his own image of himself. He'd do it, Henry thought, considering him, he had enough arrogance.

When Emmeline finished her phone conversation she took Gilbert to show him the conservatory, because she could think of nothing else to do with him. Henry saw to his overnight bag and put it in his car. Then it was time for tea. Afterwards, Henry offered Gilbert a lift, to Mrs Dash's silently signalled relief.

'Oh, now?' Gilbert muttered, a child dragged away from a party.

Emmeline said, 'I'll walk with you, Gilbert. It's stopped raining and we can take the dogs.'

Gilbert agreed, consoled. Henry would leave him at his door: Emmeline could be persuaded in, to soothe his loneliness with sympathy. Henry read his intentions and so, with a flickering sideways glance, did Emmeline. Henry smiled at her. Her good intentions were self-limiting, beyond them, she was herself and Gilbert, his eyes fixed hopefully on her, would have to look elsewhere for company. Like so many other people, he was misled by her vagueness, he could have no idea how much determination there was in such a wisp of a woman.

The misty radiance of lights from the long windows was swallowed in the blackness of the garden. In the porch, Emmeline said goodbye to Henry, 'Will you come next weekend?'

'Yes, if I don't go to Marchstearn.'

Gilbert had gone on down the drive. 'Emmeline,' he called, proprietorially.

Henry couldn't resist teasing her, whispering, 'He thinks he's got you for the night.'

'Oh, be still my heart,' Emmeline moaned.

Henry watched them walk away between the dripping shrubs. Emmeline shrouded in her groundsheet; Gilbert, beside her, his head tilted, talking, talking . . . He turned back to the door, to Mrs Dash, and kissed her cheek.

'Sorry it's been such a bore,' she, too, was watching the figures on the drive. 'I didn't know Gilbert was in quite such a state. I do hope he doesn't do anything foolish.'

SEVEN

Seven people in the medium's back room crowded the dim-lit obstacle course of its unwieldy furniture. Gilbert, the last to arrive, caused the settled company to shuffle, redistribute itself, while he stood about, conspicuous and immaculate, waiting for a seat to be offered. It was a vast armchair, he perched on the edge of it, his buttocks cringing from its sinister depths.

The medium wheezed, began to speak. 'There's a dear one here. Her name begins with M. She's very distressed. She can't get through. This is ever so strange. There's something wrong.' She looked around the room with an air of agitation. Her gaze rested on Gilbert. 'There's something ever so wrong, dear. I can't understand it.'

He stared, mesmerized, at her fat, shapeless face. His mouth opened and shut. A small, indefinite sound issued.

'M. It's M. Did she pass over to the other side recently? Mother? I can't tell, there's too much distress. I can't get anything. I don't like this at all, it'll upset the others. I'll have to let her go. She's exhausting me.'

She sank back in her chair. Embarrassment and concern spread furtively amongst the visitors. 'Shall we get her a glass of water?' someone whispered. 'No, she's best left. She'll come round,' an elderly woman whispered back, with the authority of the regular.

The medium heaved herself into an attentive posture and, as if nothing had happened, began to address each person in turn, conveying messages, offering reassurance. She had no further word for Gilbert until the session ended. In the jostle of leave-taking, from which he flinched, she edged beside him. 'Come again, dear, if you want, she might be able to come through next time. I know she's got a message for you. I can't think what went wrong.'

Gilbert muttered a choked thank-you-good-evening. The failure, she had managed to convey, was somehow his. He was the first to leave, letting himself out by the front door and hurrying along the street. Round the corner, out of sight of the house and whoever might be issuing from it, his impetus deserted him and he came to a halt. He was confused, humiliated, and close to tears.

And, momentarily, lost. This was north Avenridge, a district he never visited and only occasionally passed through. There were no grass verges, no trees: in steep, shabby streets the high terraces squeezed together, row upon row of bay windows and steps going up from the pavement. On the corner opposite him stood a pub from which issued raucous sounds.

He stared about with disproportionate wretchedness, the effort of choosing a direction too much for him.

A step sounded on the pavement. A young woman, quickly rounding the corner, halted beneath the street light. She said, 'Mr Hewitt? I'm glad I caught you up, there's something . . . I'd rather like to speak to you.'

He peered at her. Disorientation robbed him of words.

She went on in a pleasant, diffident voice, 'I hope you don't mind. I recognized you in there — the — er — seance.'

'Oh, were you . . .? The lighting was so bad . . .' He had taken no notice of the other people in the room, being interested only in himself.

'It was rather. My name's Veronica West, we haven't met, although I know you by sight. And I did meet your mother once or twice, we helped out at the same bazaars. I'm very sorry about her death, such a dreadful shock for you . . .'

She murmured condolences: regret, admiration, respect. He stood listening, soothed; he knew where he was with sympathy. 'Thank you,' he said, when she had finished.

She shrugged deeper into her coat. It was icily cold. As they talked their breath hung vaporous in the air. 'Look, there's something I need to tell you. It won't take long. But not here.'

'I've got to get a taxi.'

'You don't have a car? I have, it's just down here, come along.'

They began to walk. He said, 'I've rather lost my bearings.' He might have been referring to the unfamiliar streets or to his loss, his continuing grief. Then, 'That woman . . . a charlatan.' That, at least, was unequivocal.

'No. Well, not really. It's about that, actually.'

'I don't want . . . I'd rather forget the whole thing. I wish I'd never gone. I heard talk, I shouldn't have paid attention. She has a reputation . . . I can't imagine why.' There was contempt in his voice, for the medium, for all who resorted to her — with the exception of himself. He was a special case, the arrogant tilt of his head asserted this; but there was something overwrought about him, a small boy crying in the dark. 'I wish I'd never gone,' he repeated.

'Don't say that. Everything we do is significant in some way, even if it seems like a mistake at the time.'

The gentle urgency in her voice made him turn to look at her. She shrugged again, her smile rueful. Her face was open, attractively composed; she was tall, slender, dressed in neat, unremarkable clothes. In spite of her diffidence she had warmth, and it was to this he responded, or, rather, speaking from his own need, he said, 'You don't know what it's like.' He was too taken up with himself to consider that she might be bereaved, or might be in that state of dismay where reassurance is sought in unlikely places.

They reached her car, parked on a small open space beside a fish and chip shop. Litter surrounded it, a group of youths scuffled, obscenities resounded.

'I must get away from this dreadful place,' Gilbert said. He folded his length, all untidy angles, into her small car.

'It's a bit cramped,' she apologized. 'Not built for big guys. Now, you live south, don't you?'

He gave the briefest directions. She did not question them, play on his ragged nerves with quibbles about turning left here or going straight on there, she merely murmured, 'Ah, yes,' and set off decisively.

Responses long congealed began to loosen and stir in Gilbert. Something exceptional in his character had drawn this young woman out of the night, turning his defeated enterprise, imperceptibly, to adventure. 'You wanted to speak to me.'

'Yes. But can we wait till I get you home? You've been very much out of your element. Unsettling. Meanwhile, I'd better explain myself . . .' She worked for a firm of office suppliers that had been based in Avenridge for some years, her job took her about a lot; she had a flat in one of the solidly respectable old houses behind the Winter Gardens. Gilbert automatically registered familiar names and places, discarded them as lacking in interest. Where had she met his mother, he wanted to know.

'I do voluntary work for one or two charities. I can't claim to have known her, but she was always on the organizing side. I don't remember meeting your father.'

'He died, twelve years ago.'

'Ah. But you have family? Cousins, aunts, uncles?' she

glanced at him quickly, questioningly.

He shook his head. 'No,' not mentioning Wilfred. He never mentioned Wilfred.

They drew up before the porch of The Laurels. In the faint glow of the dashlight her smile was again rueful. 'Well, I thought it best to account for myself, so you know I'm not likely to pinch the silver.'

'I'm sure not,' he said inattentively, concerned only that this should not be yet another evening he would sit alone in the house so appallingly empty of his mother's presence.

In the drawing room, after he had taken her coat and poured drinks, she said, 'How on earth do you manage all on your own in this huge place?'

'I have a daily woman, devoted to me, but not really up to it,' Gilbert said, bitterly unjust to Mrs Blunt who, plain woman, was incapable of those touches that had been entirely his mother's inspiration and given the house its high, glossy grace.

'I suppose you go out a lot, though,' she said, and her assumption that he was a busy man, much in demand, made him look at her with renewed interest.

What had drawn this attractive woman to him from the night, from the mist? He tried to find some gallant way of phrasing this but, failing, settled for a polite query.

'I'd like you to understand,' she said, 'I'm a perfectly ordinary person. I don't have any — what? Psychic abilities. I'm not sure I even understand the term. I went to that place tonight because — I had a friend. He died some while ago. It's so hard to make sense of things, one looks for — I don't know, difficult to put into words, isn't it? I don't know what I expected. Certainly not what happened.'

'Nothing happened,' Gilbert said peevishly. 'That woman ought to be sued for false pretences.'

'No, you're wrong,' she was uneasy, urgent. 'Something very strange happened in that room tonight, so strange I just obeyed an impulse and came after you. I felt I had to. Now . . . now, I'm not so sure.'

'Something to do with me?'

'Very much so. That's what is so extraordinary. She scarcely spoke to me — did you notice?'

'I noticed very little. She was so ridiculous, and the room crammed with quite awful people, and those ghastly lights, one could see scarcely anything. I just sat wishing I hadn't gone and not paying attention to anybody.'

'I can't say I blame you. I changed my mind as soon as I sat down, but it was too late then. I just had to stick it out.'

'I didn't mean,' Gilbert said belatedly, 'that you were one of the awful people. I hope you didn't think — '

'Oh no, no. They were pathetic, weren't they? Hanging on to every word. You have to be pretty hard pushed to be grateful to someone like that. The minute you walked in I could see you were as out of place as I was. I knew your face, but it didn't register straight away who you were, then I realized I'd seen your picture in the local paper, presenting prizes at various functions and things. But, of course, we don't know each other, that's why it's all so odd . . . You remember, first of all, she asked for silence. Well, that was when it began to happen.' She hesitated, took a sip of brandy.

'What?'

'Something made me look towards you. There was a kind of — a pale glow about you. Like, like an aura. I've heard of such things but never seen one. It made everything immediately surrounding you sort of blurred, out of focus. Then I heard a voice, terribly faint, I think a woman's voice. It said, "Gilbert, I must tell . . ." then it faded. Then came back again. Just those few words. I was riveted, I didn't know what was happening. I couldn't move or speak. Part of me was aware that the medium was talking to you — about distress, something wrong, or in the way. I can't remember her exact words, can you?'

He shook his head, staring at her. His mouth had fallen open.

'Oh, I can see you think this is all mad. I shouldn't have followed you out of there. But I didn't seem to be able to help myself.'

He found his voice, it was eager. 'Go on.'

'You mean, you do believe me? This isn't upsetting you?'

Gilbert blinked, collected himself. 'I was more upset by that frightful woman and her pretensions. I couldn't make out what she was talking about.'

'I grasped some of it. There *was* a tremendous force in the room. She said it was exhausting her, and the awful thing was, it came from me — quite unintentionally. I didn't even know what was happening. I seemed to be at the centre of some turmoil, this voice calling, fading, images filling my head, this light shining round you.'

Gilbert looked cautiously down at himself. 'Is it still there?'

She smiled, shook her head. 'No, it went as suddenly as it appeared. Everything just — stopped. But some of the scenes were so clear, so detailed, they stayed here — ' she put her hand to her brow, then, at a loss, shrugged.

'What sort of scenes?'

'Well. I saw a child, sitting up in bed. All the furniture, the bed, the cupboards, the chairs, were a lovely blue. Beautiful toys: a dappled rocking horse with a red saddle, dolls, a miniature farm — that was set out on a table by the window. And on the bedside table some figures from the farm — a horse in the shafts of a haywain, a farmer — brown breeches and gaiters standing next to it — a sheepdog — '

Gilbert made a sound, interrupting her, then words gobbled out, 'How could you know? How? My room, my old room, my rocking horse, my farm . . .'

She considered him warily, puzzled. 'Don't ask me. I can't

tell you. I *felt* the child was you, I didn't *know*. You must have been very young, there was nothing the least like you as you are now and people change out of all recognition as they grow up, don't they? And I've never met you in my life, there was just this immense conviction that I was seeing you as you were — '

'The bedroom's still there, the nursery, just as it was. I could show you — ' But he made no move to get up, he was too intent on hearing more. 'What else? What else?'

'There was another picture. I couldn't see the surroundings clearly. A corridor? Hallway? Green velvet curtains at a window. In a corner an archway, a huge fern in a brass pot. A woman, I couldn't see her face, but she was wearing a lovely kimono, rich, shining gold, with peacocks embroidered on it — '

Gilbert gave a small cry — 'Mother. She used to wear that when I was a child, I remember it. And the landing, we had green velvet curtains there, years and years ago, and a fern — it's gone now — '

'How extraordinary.'

'But — what does she do? What can you see?'

'Do? Nothing, really. She was just walking along, then she put out her hand, to open a door, perhaps, reach out to someone. I don't know. Then the picture faded. How strange, though, two pictures from your childhood, all that time ago.'

'What can it mean?'

She shook her head, retreating before his fevered, emotional pressure. 'I don't suppose it means anything. Nothing like this has ever happened to me before. I've occasionally had dreams about things that have come true, trivial incidents, nothing I've paid any attention to.'

'But why me?' Gilbert cried, placing himself, as always, at the centre of events. 'Why me?'

'Well . . .' She was thoughtful for a while. 'I daresay if you hadn't been there tonight I wouldn't have had any of of those weird . . . symptoms. You were the one person in that room who was experiencing really extreme emotions, grief, confusion. I sort of — picked them up, monitored them, you could say.'

He gave a short, crowing laugh. 'And that dreadful woman, who was supposed to be so sensitive, had no idea — '

'Not quite. She knew there was something. But whatever was happening wasn't on her wavelength. The atmosphere, you being there, combined to touch off this response in me. I have heard about this sort of thing happening to people, just once, out of the blue, because the circumstances were right — '

In the hall, the telephone shrilled. Gilbert jumped, turned his face stupidly towards the door.

'Shouldn't you answer it,' she said, when he made no move.

He looked resentful, went out quickly. When he picked up the receiver, Wilfred's voice issued loudly, 'Hello, Gilbert.'

'What do you want, Wilfred?'

'I forgot to mention, at the works today. Friendly snooker match at the Conservative Club tonight with the chaps from — '

'Really, Wilfred, I'm not in the least — '

'I'm just on my way, should be a good night. Lin said why not give you a ring and see if you'd like to — '

'You've called at an extremely inconvenient moment. I'm occupied. I have a guest.'

'Oh,' Wilfred said, interested. 'Who?'

'No one you know. A lady. Goodnight.' Gilbert put the phone down.

When he returned to the drawing room she was sitting back against the cushions of the sofa, neatly disposed, but with an air of weariness. She turned her face to him with her smile, her gentle attention. 'I'm sure I'm keeping you from something important.'

'No, no,' Gilbert said, dismissing the interruption. 'Ghastly people, pressing themselves on one.'

'Oh dear,' she reached out for her handbag on the sofa beside her. 'I'd better be — '

'No,' Gilbert said urgently. 'Don't go. I didn't mean — You must stay, please. We have to talk. And I must show you — the nursery — '

'I'd rather not, if you don't mind. I've had a long day, and I'm tired. Probably because I'm hungry, I didn't have time for anything earlier. I must get home and get some supper — '

'No, we have to talk. Let me take you out to dinner, I haven't eaten yet.'

'Were you going out?'

'Well, I was . . . Well, I hadn't . . .' In his agitation he stood over her, making flapping gestures with his long, pale hands. If he had made any plans beyond the visit to the medium, the evening had turned out so unexpectedly he had forgotten what they were.

'I think I've had enough going out for one evening. Look, if you've got something in the kitchen, I'll share it with you.'

'Yes, yes.' He circled her excitedly, ushering her to the kitchen where she looked round in a practical way and said that with a fridge full like that they should have no trouble putting a meal together.

She set about this, hindered by his helpfulness. He opened a bottle of wine and, as they ate, drank several glasses, pressing her all the while to repeat what she had told him. She was patient, going over the details again and again, and when they had eaten and finished their coffee, she washed up carefully and put everything back as she had found it.

Gilbert urged her to stay, but it was late, she said, she was tired and had a busy day ahead. 'And you need to rest, this has been a bit much for you, you're rather overstrung. Do you have any sleeping pills? Or tranquillizers? I think you should take something — not too much.' She organized him, and he scarcely noticed. The evening had gathered momentum, carrying him from his defeated enterprise to a hectic, garrulous state; when she left, suddenly, the echoes of his voice shrilled on, questions, speculations, as he stumbled up to bed.

He woke early, filled with dread, because something essential to his well-being had slipped away in the night. Her name. Had she told him her name? Where did she live? Had she told him that? How could he find her again?

Downstairs, in his pyjamas, the clocks ticking loudly through the silence, he searched for traces of her. There were none. His brandy glass stood on the rosewood table in the drawing room. His. Not hers. The cushions were smoothed in the corner of the sofa where she had sat. In the kitchen everything was in place, the china and cutlery of the night before might not have been used. It was as if she had never been there.

Distracted, he wandered to and fro, then crept up to his mother's room, opened the wardrobe, stroked her dresses, took out her mink coat and caressed it. After a while he grew cold, the radiators had long been turned off in this unused room. He slipped the coat on. It was tight across the shoulders, short in the sleeves, but he was the same skinny build as his mother and was able to wrap it round, hug himself into it.

He went to the window. Between the lines of naked trees, along the curving avenue, a milk float jolted, stopping and starting. It was too early for anyone else to be about. He gazed into the blurred grey of the morning until desolation crept over him.

How could he find her again?

He was half dozing, crumpled on his mother's bed, when the telephone rang. He stumbled down the stairs, snatched up the receiver. Her voice came to him calmly, sweetly, 'Gilbert? It's Veronica.'

Veronica, he said to himself, and hung upon her name, speechless.

'How are you this morning? I was worried about you.'

Suddenly he began to gabble. 'Where are you? I forgot your — you didn't tell me — I couldn't think how to get in touch with — '

'Oh dear, you still sound rather overwrought. It was quite a strain for us both last night.'

'You left so suddenly. And this morning — I began to think you weren't real.'

She gave a soft laugh. 'Oh, I'm real all right.'

'I must see you again, we must talk.' He fumbled with the pen and pad beside the telephone. 'Listen, I've been thinking. Should we go back to that medium?'

She was silent. He strained for background noises, a whisper of her breathing. Alarmingly, there was nothing. He began to shout, 'Hello — hello — are you there?'

'Yes, I'm here. Well, you can go if you want to. I'm not sure it would be the right thing, though. We'll talk about it, shall we? I had the strangest dream last night.'

'What? What about? Me? Mother?'

'I'll tell you when I see you. I must go now, I'm late. I have to be out of town today. I'll phone you when I get back.'

'No, wait,' he cried. 'Wait — ' But the line had gone dead and he stood in the hall, in his pyjamas and his mother's mink coat, clutching the receiver, shouting, 'Don't go, don't go—'

Later that morning he walked into town, got in Wilfred's way at the office and hurried home. There was no message on the pad. Mrs Blunt detested the telephone and pretended not to hear it. He stayed in that evening, waiting, missing a meeting of the Historical Society.

Next day he could not bear to leave the house at all. He occupied himself somehow while Mrs Blunt stomped about her work. When the telephone rang he rushed to answer it and at the sound of the sweet, gentle voice: 'Hello, Gilbert?' He cried, 'Veronica — '

There was a pause. 'Er — It's Emmeline Dash.'

'Oh.' Gilbert subsided. 'Hello, Emmeline.'

'I hope I'm not disturbing you.'

'Well, I'm rather busy.'

'Sorry. I'm having a party at the hotel a week on Saturday. Fancy dress. Anything you like. Do come.'

'A week on Saturday?' Gilbert sounded doubtful, booked up.

'If you're not doing anything. Eight-thirtyish. Please bring a friend.'

'Yes. I probably will. Thank you, Emmeline.'

The prospect of taking Veronica to Emmeline's party was so pleasant he dwelt on it, not noticing time passing, until the telephone rang again.

It was Wilfred, reminding him he had a business lunch. 'Oh, you go, Wilfred, I've got a dreadful migraine.'

'Sorry about that,' Wilfred bellowed. 'I wish you'd let me know, though. Haven't you been to Harper's, then? You were going for a fitting for your new whistle and flute.'

Why couldn't Wilfred say suit, like any civilized person? 'I've cancelled it,' Gilbert lied.

The third call was unnerving. The receiver was mute. Gilbert kept saying hello, repeating the number, his voice squeaking into a dense, immeasurable silence. Was she trying to contact him — defeated by the vagaries of the G.P.O? 'Veronica,' he shouted. 'I can't hear you. Can you hear me?'

'Time I was off,' Mrs Blunt said flatly, making Gilbert give a small shriek and whirl round.

She was standing behind him, square as a tombstone in her grey coat. Gilbert fumbled the receiver back into place. 'Er, thank you, Mrs Blunt.'

'Silver needs doing.'

'Yes. Does it? Yes, I suppose so.'

'Cloakroom tap not been seen to. Dripping.'

'What? Yes. I'll — I'll get someone.'

Mrs Blunt hoisted her shopping bag and launched into a paragraph. 'It took your mother *and* me to keep this place right, Mr Hewitt. I shan't be able to carry on like this. You'll have to make other arrangements.'

Gilbert stared into her impassive face. The nature of her other arrangements stupefied him. He could not admit as much. 'I have matters in hand, Mrs Blunt.'

She gave a nod and without another word surged across the hall and let herself out.

Veronica telephoned in the afternoon. 'That awful line yesterday. We were cut off, I haven't had a minute to call back. I was going to at lunch time, but — '

'Oh, it *was* you. There was something wrong with the line again.'

'No,' she said patiently. 'Not me. I was just about to dial the number when someone interrupted. Anyway. Can I take you up on that invitation for dinner?'

'Of course.'

'Tonight? Shall we try Ferdinand's Bistro? I haven't been there yet.'

'Yes, yes.'

'Good. I'll pick you up. Seven thirty.'

EIGHT

Ferdinand's Bistro was fashionably subterranean with rush matting and wall lights feeble enough to cause eyestrain. They sat at a table set in a high wooden booth in a secretive, enclosed atmosphere. Gilbert kept knocking things over until Veronica efficiently produced matches and lit the candle on the table. The flame cast its glow over her face, the tiny smile at the corners of her mouth as she righted the salt and pepper pots, put the bread sticks back in their bowl. She made no reference to his clumsiness and Gilbert pretended not to notice. Politely conversational, she asked if he had found out who his mysterious caller had been.

Gilbert, pouring wine, became serious. 'No. But I've been thinking. What time were you going to phone?'

She considered. 'One. Near enough. Why?'

'Mrs Blunt leaves at one. On the dot. That's when the call came.'

'But, Gilbert, I told you, I didn't even dial your number.'

'Perhaps you didn't need to.'

'What?' She gave a disbelieving half-laugh.

'There's been some kind of contact between us since that first night. You have to admit it.'

'Oh, well . . . yes. And these peculiar dreams I've been

having. So insistent, not like any dreams I've ever had before.'

'About me?'

'Who else? In and out of my sleep I don't seem to be able to shake you off,' she said ruefully. 'Part of this is odd, so don't laugh. Well, there you are, a child again, in your room, the way you were before, or on that landing. There's a bit more detail — a large carved chest, and a pretty velvet chair.'

Gilbert put a hand to his mouth, an involuntary gesture. 'They're still there.'

She shrugged, resigned to the exceptional. 'It's mixed up, the scene changing, the way dreams do. Don't laugh — you're wearing girl's clothes.'

The unexpectedness of this made him draw back, his vanity assailed by the ridiculous. But there was something more: a concealed hazard, this blurring of his gender, his identity.

'I know. Nonsensical. Then, I thought — children are always dressing up, pretending to be someone else. It's part of the growing up process. I'm sure I did it, although I must admit I can't remember.'

'Neither can I,' he said.

'Can't you? Are you sure? I was right about everything before, wasn't I? Anyway, there you were, running about, playing, all the innocence and daring of a child getting up to mischief.'

It was his turn to shrug, to say indifferently he couldn't see it meant anything.

She agreed that on its own it didn't. 'But there was something else.'

'What?'

'Someone falling.'

Emotions sped across his face, broke into a single word, pleading, dismayed, 'Mother?'

'No, no,' she said reassuringly. 'This was a flight of stairs.'

He drew back slowly from the pain of the immediate past: the years accelerated, like a film run in reverse.

'What is it?' she asked.

'When I was very young. There was an accident. My grandmother fell down the stairs, she was killed.'

They sat for a while not speaking, studying each other. Eventually, Veronica said, 'Do you think that's it?'

'It must be. But why . . .'

She shrugged. 'Don't ask me. I recognized the stairs at The Laurels from that — vision — or whatever I had at the medium's, when I saw your mother in the dressing gown. And I *have* seen the stairs . . . from the hall, though, not the landing . . .'

'But it was so long ago. It seems,' Gilbert sought for a word, 'inconsequential.' What he meant was that anything not connected to his present condition was irrelevant.

'Mmmm.' She thought this over. 'I suppose it was the association. My being in the house. I picked up this event — from the atmosphere. It seems when I'm anywhere near you I turn into a walking transformer. Or do I mean receiver? Disturbing.'

The waitress came to the table, bringing their food — lasagne and salad. Veronica began to eat, commenting on how good the food was. Then she asked, 'Did your grandmother live with you?'

'And grandfather. It was his house before it was my father's. My great-grandfather had it built in 1840 . . .' Gilbert talked on, managing — immodestly — more than a hint that such continuity of family and ownership contributed to what was exceptional in himself.

But the tide of his heritage had long since turned, bearing away the robust families with their businesses, property, alliances. The Hewitt men had got into the habit of marrying genteel, wilting women who bred too late in life, beyond their strength. Gilbert's sense of himself as representative of a tradition did not permit the reality of himself as its stranded survivor: epicene, myopic and incompetent.

He paused on some impressive detail to take a sip of wine, and Veronica returned at once to the accident. It was almost, unbelievably, as if she had not been listening. But his doubts fled, her concern was for him.

'It must have been pretty traumatic for you.'

'I don't remember, I slept through the whole commotion. Mother told me about it afterwards. To be honest, I don't really remember my grandmother.' In a dark place in his memory something urgent moved, and was still. 'You see, just after she died, I had meningitis.'

'Oh, how awful. That's terribly serious, isn't it?'

'Terribly. I was fortunate to come out of it so well. It affected my eyesight and my memory. I do just remember grandfather, because he lived a little while longer. Not much, he was terribly doddery, and I suppose the shock of Grandma's death . . . After that, though, things are absolutely clear. I got stronger — ' Discarding uncertainty, Gilbert moved on in time. He was prepared to talk endlessly, the excitable, pampered child, of escapades, treats, parties; how clever he was, how admired.

Veronica finished her meal, lined up her knife and fork exactly in the centre of her plate.

A figure loomed beside the table. 'Good evening,' Wilfred said, stereophonically.

Gilbert stopped speaking. His face took on a frost-bitten look.

'I was just sampling the vino in the bar. Thought I saw you on my way to the gents.' Wilfred told everyone in the restaurant.

'Good evening,' Gilbert said, staring straight ahead.

'Nice to see you up and about. Bound to do you good. And in charming company.' Wilfred inclined his bulk forward confidentially. 'Wilfred Hewitt.'

Veronica had drawn back beyond the nimbus of the candelight, her face a smudged oval in the shadow of the high, dark booth. 'Veronica,' she said quietly.

Wilfred repeated her name with approval. Straightening up and looking about, he said generally, 'Nice place.' Then, to Gilbert, 'Lin's always on at me to bring her here. You know how she is for anywhere new. Put her nose out of joint to know you've beaten her to it.'

Gilbert did not reply. In the momentary silence Wilfred's gaze ranged over the two of them. Dipping his large head and speaking with grotesque intimacy, he said, 'I think I'm intruding.'

'Wilfred, you are intruding,' Gilbert said.

'Glad to hear it. Good for you.' Wilfred gave Gilbert's shoulder a manly thump and went away, smiling enormously.

Veronica spoke from the shadows. 'I thought you said you didn't have any relatives. His name's Hewitt.'

Gilbert was disparaging, his voice ragged with embarrassment. 'A very, very distant connection. So distant it simply doesn't count. Mother and I always — '

'And who is Lin?'

'Wilfred's wife. Frankly, she's dreadful. Common. And she leads him a terrible dance. But it's his own fault for marrying her. *Had* to, you know. Shotgun wedding. Although whether the child was *actually* his . . .' He shrugged elaborately, inviting comprehension. Disconcertingly, Veronica still sat back from the table, he could not read her expression although he craned forward, intent on picking up some responsive signal. Assuming her interest, although she said nothing, he continued.

'And their second child. Well, Wilfred would be very rash to claim *exclusive* paternity. Everyone knows, except Wilfred, of course. Someone should tell him. And her extravagance, they must be knee-deep in debt . . .'

Veronica spoke at last, mildly. 'It worried me to think you were alone, Gilbert, but here I find you have a clutch of nearest and dearest.'

'They're not,' Gilbert said, alarmed. Inviting her to despise them, he had misled her into thinking he claimed them.

The waitress came to the table. Gilbert ordered fruit salad for Veronica, cheese for himself and, distractedly, another bottle of wine. Veronica excused herself, picked up her handbag and went to the ladies. She was gone for a long time. Gilbert fretted, drank to calm himself and peered out of the booth, this way and that.

When she came back she slipped into her seat without a word and began to eat her fruit salad.

Gilbert strained towards her silence, the barrier that, temporarily, excluded him. It was all Wilfred's fault; Wilfred, with his jokes, his curiosity, his blundering presence. Helplessly, he dwelt on revenge.

Veronica said, 'I have a decision to make, and in a way it's helped — knowing you've got someone close to you.'

'But — I haven't — '

'You were right, what you said earlier. It's as if there's something of extraordinary significance lying between us, waiting for us to discover. But *what* it is, *why* it is — that's beyond me. And I've begun to understand what a terrible burden you carry — more than grief, the uncertainty, the question that must always haunt you. Why did your mother go to the Ridge that night?'

His lips quivered uncontrollably. He pressed his handkerchief to them, said something muffled behind it.

She nodded. 'Yes, you're very brave. And at least now I know you're not alone. That's important because I want you to look at things from my side. I'm a stranger, an outsider, and I'm intruding — that makes me very uneasy. Do you understand?'

He stared at her blankly. He understood nothing except his own needs.

'Good. So the time for me to pull out is now, before I get in any deeper — '

'No,' Gilbert said faintly.

'And what's happened, my firm's being taken over. They're reshuffling the branches, closing some down. My branch here. But I've been offered promotion, in Newcastle.'

Gilbert was having trouble with his voice. It was saying something urgent but she did not seem to hear.

'. . . so I'll have to make up my mind soon. Move, or start looking for another job. I like it here. On the other hand, I have my future to think of. . .'

Gilbert found fragments of speech: *can't go — need — alone.*

'And what I've been thinking about particularly is this. If I go away, I'll remove myself from this influence. You see? It's only happened because I'm here, here in Avenridge, in touch with you. If I break that contact, cut myself free, I'll return to normal, I'm sure I will —'

Her voice continued. Gilbert peered at her, his thoughts had broken loose and were sliding about wildly in his head. Someone knocked over a wine bottle and sent it crashing on the stone flagged floor; someone was shouting. The voice sounded rather like his but it could not be him because a Hewitt did not make scenes in public.

'It's time we left,' Veronica said.

Rain, and lamplights giddy in the dark. The car stopped. Veronica said something and got out. Then she opened the door from his side.

'Puncture. Come on.'

'What?' he said foggily. He clambered out, clutching his overcoat about his shoulders. The car was in the gateway of The Laurels, bushes dripped around them. 'But we're home.'

'Just. That's something. I can leave the car here, at least it's not in anyone's way. Come along, where's your door key?'

He fumbled for it, trotting beside her up the driveway

through the pelting rain. When they had let themselves in and were in the hall, he stood as if clamped to the floor, his long body weaving, his eyes two mad points of light staring at her. 'Don't go away, Veronica. Don't leave me.'

'You're in a terrible state,' she said gently. But she was practical. 'I'm damned if I'm going to start changing the wheel in this weather. I'll sleep here, in one of your spare rooms.'

'Don't go away. Ever. Please.' He began to cry.

'Gilbert, go up and put yourself to bed. I'll bring you a hot drink, you need one.'

'No. Not till you promise. No one can help me except you. No one likes me. Mrs Blunt is going to leave. She's an old cow, I hate her. I can't look after the house. I can't do anything on my own.'

'I'm not going to promise you anything. If you don't do as I say, right now, I'll walk out of that door and never come back.'

He glared at her through his rain-smeared spectacles, caught his breath on a sob of outrage as she made to move towards the door. Flinging his coat on the floor, he stumbled towards the stairs. 'I'm going, I'm going, I'm going — ' His voice was high, like a child's, ringing with echoes of old tantrums, of long ago threats and appeasements.

She waited in the hall, watching him blunder up the stairs. 'My, master Gilbert's in a fine old rage,' she said. As he knew she would, because they always said it: Mummy, or Daddy or Grandpa, or the other grownups. All those people, remembered or half remembered, who waited in the corners and crevices, the years and memories of the house.

She came to his room very early in the morning with tea and biscuits. He had been lying half awake, not moving or thinking; it was impossible to tell if the day had begun beyond the heavy, lined curtains at the windows.

She switched on the bedside lamp and he sat up, blinking, not reaching for his spectacles. Without them everything lacked definition and her figure was no more than a comforting shape, which was all he required. But she passed him his spectacles and for the sake of his dignity he put them on. She came into focus: a neat and efficient woman, equipped for demands beyond his range, appointments to keep, places to go. He looked away from her. His clothes were scattered about the room, he did not remember taking them off; on the bedside table stood a mug of milk from the night before, cold skin on its surface. He did not remember her bringing it in.

She said, 'I've changed the tyre and had my breakfast. Shall I make some for you?'

'No thank you, this is all I can manage. I'm sure I haven't got a bad bout of flu but I'm not up to a hearty breakfast.'

'Flu?'

'I had been feeling off colour all day, but one tries not to give in. The way it struck me last night, though, quite devastating.'

She sat on the end of his bed, regarding him thoughtfully. 'Ah. I see.'

He was busy pouring his tea. Even in such small matters he had known she would be aware of his preferences. The tray was set with a lace-edged cloth, the breakfast china and small teapot. When Wilfred and Linda had stayed, Wilfred had brought his tea in a thick pottery mug: Gilbert, not knowing where it came from, suspected it was the one Mrs Blunt kept for her own use and refused to drink from it. 'I must have behaved quite strangely. I suppose you wondered what on earth was the matter.'

His silver teaspoon tinkled busily. When at last it stopped, she said, speaking carefully, 'Well, we both know now, don't we?'

He gave her a pleased smile. He had not invented his indisposition, it was simply that the events of the previous evening, having rearranged themselves inside his head, had presented it as the most acceptable explanation. And Veronica, by her agreement, confirmed what he had expected: that he need trouble himself no further with what had happened.

She saw that he was comfortable, had books, his radio. Then she prepared to leave. 'I wouldn't like to run into your daily woman, she might get the wrong idea and start spreading gossip.'

'Mrs Blunt has always been discreet,' Gilbert said gravely, as if reviewing a rakish past. 'But you're quite right, one can never tell.'

At the door she paused and looked back at him. 'Gilbert, you don't walk in your sleep, do you?'

'Not as far as I know. Why?'

'Oh, nothing.'

'You will come back, won't you?' he said, confident of her reply.

'Of course. This evening. I'll make supper for us. That is, if you feel up to anything.'

'Oh, I expect I shall.'

He heard her walk down the landing to the stairs, then the space and solid walls of the house muffled the sound of her leaving.

There were flowers in The Laurels again. Veronica brought them, an armful of colour, swooningly scented. Gilbert trembled with delight. 'We always have flowers on a Friday. Always. How did you know?'

'I didn't. I just thought I'd cheer up the invalid.'

With un-invalid vigour he collected vases and jugs, rushed out into the garden in the falling light to cut evergreens. He let her help with the arrangements, he was very precise, showing her how to get the best effects. She admired his artistry, complimented him on his taste. When they had finished they placed the flowers round the house and went back to the kitchen.

'This is a huge place, isn't it?' Veronica said. 'I was looking round while you were in the garden. Through here . . .' She opened a door off the kitchen. There was a passageway, a small living room, a bedroom cramped with two beds, a bathroom. The furnishings had always been cheap, time reduced them to squalor. Paper peeled from the walls, the air was musty and clingingly cold.

Gilbert accompanied her reluctantly. The passageway ended in a small lobby, a narrow flight of stairs. He said, 'We don't bother with this bit. Mother never liked me to come here.'

'No, well, of course, she'd hate it. Not her sort of place at all, a woman of her refinement, much too sordid. Servants' quarters, I suppose.'

'They used to be. We had live-in maids, or something, till the war. Then it became more and more difficult to get people. So we just shut all this up.'

She looked at the staircase. 'Where does this come out?'

'At the end of the landing. There's a door.'

She murmured she hadn't noticed it and drew aside a curtain, stirring dust. 'Another door. How confusing this all is. Where does it go?'

He fidgeted. It was depressing standing there, and cold; he remembered his flu. 'Through the kitchen garden, only we haven't grown vegetables for years. It goes to the side entrance, there's a door in the wall, it lets on to the alleyway between the houses.'

'For the domestics to use, make sure they knew their place. You couldn't have them walking up the drive.'

'Well, it was like that when these houses were built. I'm cold, Veronica, it's very grubby here.'

'Yes.' But she lingered, looking round, crossed her arms in a shudder. 'There's something — I don't know — very peculiar here . . . Come on, I'll make us supper.'

They ate in the small morning room, Gilbert detested eating in the kitchen, even when he was alone. Afterwards, they took their coffee into the drawing room. Veronica had brought him a present, a jigsaw puzzle. 'Silly, I know, but you said you liked them.'

He did not remember telling her that; but then, his preferences seemed to be implanted in her consciousness. Even the design — a castle — was one of his favourites.

'Actually, I believe they're quite good therapy,' Veronica said. 'They induce serenity.'

Tranquillizers and wine added their soothing effect. Gilbert fumbled the jigsaw pieces, touched the tremulous edge of all that was lost and cherished: Mummy home from business on a winter's evening, the fire bright, the curtains drawn. 'Now, what has my little man been doing today?' Mr Hewitt, that eclipsed individual, seldom figured in Gilbert's memories. And childhood had its own imperatives: the adult world, boring and harsh with complicated requirements, existed only where it touched his world. He never asked Mummy what she had been doing. He did not ask Veronica.

'Gilbert. Where did you hear about the medium?'

'The . . .' He struggled; the past released him reluctantly. 'Oh, I don't know . . . It was when Wilfred and Linda were staying here. Linda had a crowd of her friends round one day. A very showy, overdressed lot they were, empty-headed enough to be impressed by that kind of nonsense. They were talking about her and someone wrote down her address, I found it on a piece of paper afterwards. It might have been Linda, only I doubt very much if she can write.' He smiled spitefully. 'Do you think — should we go back there?'

'You can if you want. I'm not.'

'Oh, I wouldn't go without you.'

'I was wondering. If your cousin — Wilfred— asks where we met. That is, if he wants to know.'

'Wilfred wants to know everything. I shan't tell him. He's paid to run our business and mind his own. Not that he ever does.'

'We'll keep it secret from him.'

He gave a gobble of laughter, delighting in their triumph over Wilfred. 'Yes, yes.' Then, because there was room in his arrogance for the illogical, 'Besides, I wouldn't like anyone to think I'd had anything to do with that frightful woman.'

'I don't think I would, either,' she agreed.

He finished off his wine. An inner spurt of excitement from a source too obscure — and he was too fuddled — to trace, prompted him to say something daring. He glanced at her slyly. 'You're a secret person, aren't you, Veronica?'

'I'm a private person,' she answered composedly.

'I don't know anything about you.'

'You know what you need to know.'

He smiled wickedly, challenging her to a game of question and answer. Confident, too; here, on his own territory, he always won, everything had been arranged for him to win, long ago. 'Suppose I asked you — '

'Let's get this straight, now,' she interrupted pleasantly. 'I *mean private*. I don't care to involve anyone in my life. I involve myself in yours because something exceptional holds us together, and I mean to discover what it is, as much for my own peace of mind as yours. But I do it on my terms. If you question me, or try to find out anything about me — I shall know. I shall know, Gilbert, and you'll never see me again.'

Her strength filled the room, the pressure of it was so intense he was unable to speak and could only nod. It was the strength on which he leaned, in which he found affirmation of himself; but he comprehended it, momentarily, as a great darkness, blotting him out. And that, too, terrifyingly, he craved: an ineffable ravishment.

'I make no demands on you, do I?' she said, still pleasant.

'No . . .' his voice was faint.

'So this relationship is very much in your favour. I meet the demands you make on me, but I need my own private area. You see?'

He sat with his hands pressed between his knees, his shoulders hunched, his fine skin flaring pink at the cheekbones. 'Yes, Veronica.'

'Good. Now I think you should go to bed. You're over-tired.'

'Can I stay up just a few more minutes, I want to tell you something. Something nice.'

'What is it?'

'Well, I forgot . . .' He told her about the telephone call from Emmeline, the invitation to the party.

'Who?' Veronica frowned.

He explained the Dash's, the old hotel. She said thoughtfully, 'A week on Saturday. Fancy dress.'

'Yes. Do let's go, Veronica.'

'Oh, am I invited, too?'

'Of course. I love dressing up.'

She shook her head. 'I don't know. I don't think you're up to it.'

'Oh, please — '

'Your nerves aren't strong. People, excitement — '

Mummy had always said that to him when he was set on something. But he'd known how to wheedle his way round her, knowing she could not endure to deprive him of something he desired. '*Please*, Veronica . . .'

Cold woke Gilbert.

He sat up. He was uncovered, the sheet and duvet at the foot of the bed. A draught of air blew over him; the darkness formed dissolving shapes. His door was standing wide open.

He fumbled for his spectacles, clattering the cup and saucer on his bedside table. The noise was raucous in the heavy silence and when its last echoes died away another sound occurred, unidentifiable, unlocated, making him freeze.

He tried to say 'Veronica . . .' in case he had made a mistake and she had not left after all, but put herself quietly to bed in the spare room after he had gone to sleep. But his voice was no more than a quavering whisper and he waited a long time before his withering will set his body in motion. He dragged on his dressing gown, went out on the landing and there, staring, saw a faint illumination at the end of the landing, beyond the stairhead. He crept towards it, finding courage only in the thought that Veronica *had* stayed and was in the bathroom and it was the sound of her going along the landing that had woken him.

Door ajar, the bathroom was in darkness. The light was seeping from the turn in the corridor beyond and he was drawn helplessly on, baffled and trembling, until he reached the corner and, standing in the engulfing cold, saw that the door to the back staircase was open.

The thought of burglars so terrified him he became paralyzed and stood gazing down the narrow staircase. The weak bulb was unshaded, dangling on a long flex that stirred to and fro on a current of air; the light shifted over the dingy wallpaper; the stairs were sharply angled, the lobby below in darkness.

Then, from far away, came the thin, piping chant of a child's voice: 'Gilbert . . . Gilbert, 'fraidy cat, 'fraidy cat . . .'

The senselessness of the situation touched a brief fury in him: children, how dare they? Play pranks, violate his privacy.

'Gilbert . . . 'fraidy cat . . .' The voice called again from the darkness, an eerie thread of sound, and bewilderment surged, extinguishing his rage.

In a sickening reversal of time he was a small boy again,

taunted by those cruel, strong children who prowled his cossetted boundaries, children who had the glamour of their own wildness, the daring of knowledge and acts that tempted and terrified him. He had always needed protection; there was humiliation for him in their busy, snatching hands, their bold eyes . . . But who was to protect him now?

He jerked into a frenzy of movement, slammed the door, thrust back the bolt and fled, limbs threshing, back along the landing.

He shut himself into his room, but there was no lock on the door. He grabbed the armchair from the window bay, dragged it to barricade the door, then collapsed on to the floor and huddled there, whimpering, his hands pressed over his ears.

Perhaps there was scampering, whispers; perhaps there was the sound of someone falling. In the tumult of his mind these things occurred, again and again, while he crouched there, and the night passed.

NINE

The ringing of the door bell brought Gilbert to life. He pulled the armchair out of the way, ran down the stairs to the half landing window and yanked back the curtains. It was daylight, crusted with hoar frost, and Veronica's car stood in the drive.

He began to gabble at her before he had opened the door. She stepped in. 'Gilbert, what on earth . . .' But his teeth were chattering violently, he made no sense, trying to clutch at her, then flinging his arms about in distracted gestures.

'You're freezing — ' She led him through to the kitchen, to sit him in front of the Rayburn and make him a hot drink. She kept her coat on because the house was unnaturally cold. 'You haven't had any windows open, have you? Not in this bitter weather?'

He said, 'Last night. Terrible things. Noises. The door.'

'What door?'

He pointed, waveringly.

'Through there? Where we were yesterday?' she said, puzzled.

His despairing yelp followed her as she crossed the kitchen. He would not go with her but sat hugging himself in a distress close to physical agony, mouthing her name, until she returned.

'Gilbert, that back door's wide open, no wonder every-where's so cold. What have you been doing?'

'Not me,' he wailed. 'Not me,' and began to sob.

She made tea and, sitting beside him, coaxed and encouraged him until he had calmed down enough to give an account of what had happened.

She said, 'Oh, dear . . .' thoughtfully.

His voice was shrill. 'That landing door's always kept bolted. Mummy said we can't have the servants coming up the back stairs into our part of the house. They can't be trusted, Mummy said, they pry into things. They must keep to their *place*.'

'Yes,' she agreed carefully. 'They must.'

'Well, who unbolted it last night? Who did?'

She studied him without speaking for a moment. 'Perhaps it was you, Gilbert.'

'It wasn't, wasn't, wasn't.'

His cries buffetted against her calm. She was very serious, asking him if he remembered — when she had stayed overnight — she afterwards asked him if he walked in his sleep. 'You see, I heard something in the night.'

He gaped at her.

'I got up, I was half asleep. I didn't know if I'd been dreaming, dreaming of a child's voice calling — '

Tea slopped from his cup, the stain spreading, disregarded, on his dressing gown. 'You . . . You heard it.'

'I wouldn't say that. I wasn't sure. *Something* woke me. I went out to the landing — of course, there was nothing to see. Your door was open, you were asleep, very restless, muttering to yourself. That was why I wondered . . . if you'd been sleep walking, that night, last night — '

He shook his head violently.

'No. No, I don't think so, either.'

'I was *afraid*,' he whispered.

'I'm sure you were, it's very disturbing. But I can't help

thinking . . . The odd things that have happened. The peculiar effect this house has on me — or I have on it. Did I spark it off?'

He was beyond understanding anything, sat glazed and wretched, his body shaken by long shudders.

'Well, never mind that now. You're cold, you'll get pneumonia, and you must be exhausted. Go and get some sleep.'

He tried to protest, he could not bear to be left alone. She assured him she would stay, took him upstairs and, while he was in the bathroom, made his bed, tidied his room.

'It's funny, as soon as I woke up this morning, I *knew* I had to come round here. Good thing it's Saturday, and I don't have to go to the office.'

Saturday? Was it? He swallowed his tranquillizers, climbed wearily into bed.

'We can have the weekend — ' she began. Then the doorbell rang.

It was an ear-splitting sound, they both started, then fell still, gazing at each other.

'Are you expecting anyone?' she asked.

'No. I don't want to see anyone.'

'Of course not. Hang on, I'll see if I can see anything.'

She went out, returned quickly. 'There's a yellow Cortina in the drive.'

'Wilfred,' Gilbert said meanly. 'I don't want him.'

The bell kept ringing.

'Neither do I. Honestly, I don't want to start explaining you, the state you're in, what's happened.' She gave an unexpected gulp of laughter. 'Let's ignore him.'

'Yes, yes.' They began to speak in lowered voices for no other reason than the pleasure of conspiracy, Wilfred could not possibly hear.

The bell stopped ringing. 'Perhaps he's gone away,' Gilbert whispered. Then, 'Your car's outside.'

'Doesn't matter, he doesn't know it's mine. He'll think — that you've gone out for a walk with a friend . . .'

They muffled their giggles, listening. There was a pounding on the kitchen door. 'Everywhere's locked up, isn't it?' Veronica said.

Gilbert nodded.

'What does he want?'

What did Wilfred ever want? The satisfaction of his perpetual, vulgar curiosity. The triumph of not merely frustrating it, but tantalizing it as well, made Gilbert almost suffocate with glee.

The sound of Wilfred's tramping footsteps broke into their attentive silence. 'He's walking all round the house.' Veronica said, and they almost exploded, holding back their laughter. She crept to the window and knelt by the sill, moving the curtain an inch. 'I say, Gilbert, that door in the garden wall is open . . . He's going along the path to it . . . He does look ridiculous. He can't make it out, standing there, scratching his head. He's closed it now. Where *does* he get his clothes? That shiny black overcoat, he looks like an earwig . . .'

Gilbert smiled blissfully, eyelids drooping. The tranquillizers were very strong, already easing him down through the layers of stress to his loosened, lulled self.

'. . . He's going back now, round the other side of the house. He's made the complete circuit. Could he get in if he wanted to? Has he got a key?'

'Key,' Gilbert murmured.

'Well . . . when he and his wife stayed here, they must have had keys.'

'Gave them back.'

'Mmmm. They could have had one copied. You wouldn't have been in any state then to know what was going on. And your daily woman? Does she have a key?'

'Mmmmm?'

'You see, you're vulnerable here, all alone. How do we know it wasn't one of them who came in the night. Only don't ask me why . . .'

Gilbert began to wake. Calamities crowded the border beyond sleep and he shrank back from the process of consciousness that contained the undefended instant of truth: he had no resources to order his own life.

Veronica was drawing back the curtains, letting in the hard grey light of the afternoon. When he was a child his indispositions were decently shrouded, to protect his eyesight, his headache, his fever. No one expected anything of a sick child except that he should recover, slip back into place in the uninterrupted rhythm of the house.

He whimpered, 'You can't go away, Veronica.'

She gave a small sigh. 'I've got tea ready downstairs, I'll bring it up. You go and wash your face and brush your teeth.'

'I can't.'

'Yes you can. Listen, I shall be here all weekend. If anything happens in the night you won't be alone. I can come in the week, as well. I can take some time off from the office, they owe it to me . . .'

She talked on, her soft voice drawing him to sit up, to fuss with his disordered state. As scrupulous about his appearance as he was himself, she had found his second dressing gown and removed the one with the tea stain. He padded off to the bathroom to make himself presentable. His difficulties, passed into Veronica's keeping, had shrivelled to minor inconveniences.

She brought tea up on a tray: the china tea service, scones and cake, his favourite raspberry jam. 'But I don't want to run into your daily woman. I'm damned if I can take her on as well, that's too much to ask,' Veronica said. 'And isn't she leaving, anyway?'

He had forgotten he had told her that. Unwelcome, the figure of Mrs Blunt barged through his consciousness, manhandling furniture, banging about with the vacuum cleaner, slapping in front of him any odd bits of crockery she could lay her hands on. *Excellent woman*, his mother always insisted. But without his mother's direction, Mrs Blunt ran amok arranging the house, and Gilbert, around her own spartan notions. The effort of replacing her, even if he had the least idea how to go about it, was no longer his concern. His gaze dwelt on Veronica. Inside his head, all kinds of things were accomplished — or accomplished for him, by her.

Then she said, casually, 'Get in first. Sack her.' And his expression reeled.

'I — couldn't,' he squeaked. 'You . . .'

'No fear. I have the distinct impression if I ever set eyes on that woman she'll turn me to stone.'

'That's what she does,' he said faintly.

'Yes, well . . .' Veronica ate some cake, thinking. 'Well then. You write her a letter. Tell her you're going away soon, on holiday — '

'Holiday.' This new element confused him. He had never taken a holiday without his mother.

'It's a good excuse, you don't need her when you're away. And why not? You could do with a break, we could go somewhere for a week. I told you the office owes me some time. Anyway, we'll think about that, I can get some brochures from the travel agents.'

'I suppose . . .' He looked at the bleak day beyond the window, thought of warmth, colour, spice-laden air.

'You can say that you find you're in a position to dispense with her services. You can enclose a fortnight's pay in lieu of notice. Or a month, whatever you think. And ask her for the house key back, she can put it through the letter box.'

'She might . . . She might knock on the door.'

'Don't answer it. The phone either,' Veronica said, simplifying everything.

'You are clever,' Gilbert said, admiring, not her, but himself. If the idea for disposing of Mrs Blunt was entirely Veronica's, then the responsibility, should there be any unpleasantness, would be entirely hers, too.

Later on, Gilbert got up and spent some time grooming himself to produce an elegantly convalescent look.

Downstairs there was a gleaming air, the rich comfort of a house cared for with subtle touches: the scent of flowers, the velvet curtains drawn across the long windows, the fire burning brightly in the drawing room. Veronica had the dinner in preparation. Gilbert helped her to set the table in the dining room, then they drank sherry and he sat down and wrote the letter, at Veronica's dictation, to Mrs Blunt. He read it through when it was finished, it had just the right note of firmness and condescension, he congratulated himself on it. 'I'll put it through her door tomorrow,' Veronica said.

After dinner Veronica produced an assortment of Gilbert's old picture books, relics of his childhood. She thought it would be fun to see if they could find ideas for Emmeline's fancy dress party. They looked through them together, exclaiming, pondering. Gilbert loved dressing up, he wanted to be everything. Veronica suggested making a short list, they could take it round to the theatrical costumiers in the week.

'Will Wilfred be going?'

'Good heavens, no.' He was surprised she should ask. 'He has his own social level.'

'Yes, I suppose he would have. But . . .' her voice became gentle, 'Wasn't he with your mother at the Pavilion that night when . . .'

'Only because I was away.' Gilbert's expression twisted with recollection. 'He forced himself on her, it's the sort of thing he does.'

'How awful, that he should that particular night. But wasn't Linda there, too?'

'*Linda*. Mother couldn't stand her company in private, in public it was out of the question. So overdressed and vulgar, flaunting herself. No, Linda was allegedly at a dramatic society meeting. I'm pretty sure she was off on one of her squalid assignations.'

'Really? Who with?'

'Goodness knows. Probably her best friend's husband. She loves doing that sort of thing.'

'Does it work in reverse?'

He looked at her blankly, then, comprehending, gave a shrill, scornful laugh. 'Wilfred? Serve her right, wouldn't it? Pay her back in her own coin. No. I daresay he'd like to, he's very coarse in his tastes, but who'd have him?'

'So nobody knows where she was that night. Didn't the police ask?'

'I suppose they did, they made all sorts of enquiries.' Gilbert had drunk a great deal of wine with dinner, he was on to the brandy: alcohol took him back to the desperate depth of his grief, he talked about how confused he had been, how things had gone on around him he could not grasp, could no longer even recall. His voice began to tremble.

Veronica interrupted briskly. 'Well, they sound a thoroughly slippery pair, you're quite right not to trust them.'

As Gilbert had never trusted them with anything, it had never occurred to him to add untrustworthiness to their many failings. However, he nodded gravely at Veronica, she must be right.

'I certainly don't want anything to do with them.'

'Oh, they never come here,' Gilbert said hurriedly.

'Wilfred did today. You said he's always forcing himself on you. I wonder why he never came back?'

Gilbert said they'd probably gone to Birmingham for the weekend where Linda's immense family was constantly engaged in weddings, christenings, twenty first birthday parties —

'Phoning you. Coming here. Lying in wait for you at the end of the drive next.'

Gilbert gave a weak laugh, fumbling for reassurance, not daring to commit to words the possibility that Wilfred and Linda might drive Veronica away from him.

'I've been thinking,' Veronica said. She was very serious.

'About me?' Gilbert leaned towards her.

'Well. The voices last night, things happening — *because* I'm here. I feel — no, I *know*, Gilbert, that your mother is trying to get in touch with you. *Through me.*'

He felt a great yearning, and in the anguish of it closed his eyes. Her voice continued gently.

'I can't think why she should have chosen me, or what it is she wants to tell you. She's coming closer. I think she'll be here soon. You want to hear what Mummy has to say to you, don't you?'

He opened his eyes. Her face blurred beyond his unshed tears. 'Yes, yes.'

'But . . . we have to be careful. Other people wouldn't understand.'

'I wouldn't tell anyone.'

'Of course you wouldn't. But they might try to find out — spite, envy.'

He nodded vigorously. It was not necessary to say that such things were associated, principally, with Wilfred and Linda, which was why he had always been on guard against them. But it was Mummy who had watched, shielded: now it was Veronica who had taken over that role, and she would be doubly vigilant, because there was so much at stake. It was not very clear to him, but the importance of it all was borne in on him as they talked. Veronica would see to everything. But she must protect herself, too, and he must help her do that. Yes, yes. And they would wait, and be ready, for when Mummy came.

On the Sunday evening Wilfred and Linda drove back late from Birmingham. Amabel slept on the back seat, worn out by a raucous weekend of cousins, aunts and uncles.

'Well, where was he, then? Don't tell me he was out first thing in the morning. Where'd he go? He was just ignoring you. He always has,' Linda said, shrewish. Wilfred had enjoyed his weekend, he was popular with her family. It annoyed her, on the journey home she always had to find some way to reduce him to his secondary status. And she had a genuine grievance: her foundered expectations of the Hewitt money. Her family had been vocal on the subject, her humiliation was still burning. It had to be Wilfred's fault, not that he would admit it; so they argued, low-voiced, for miles.

'He's always treated you like dirt. So did she. And where's it got you? Not a penny in the will. No rise. No partnership. Your trouble is, you've got no guts.'

'True,' Wilfred agreed ruefully. 'But I've got staying power.' He reverted to his unsuccessful call at The Laurels. 'Perhaps he'd been out all night.'

'Don't talk stupid. What woman would put up with him for an hour, never mind all night.' Linda took it for granted no one had an innocent purpose for sleeping away from home. 'You're obsessed with sex.'

'I never mentioned it,' Wilfred said mildly.

'There's his girl friend,' Amabel said from the back, startling them; they had not realized she had woken up and was listening.

'What are you talking about?' Linda twisted round in her

seat, her beautiful face petulant but attentive. Amabel was a gatherer of gossip, all she had to do was listen, which required no exertion. Conscientiously, in her monotonous voice, she repeated everything she heard to Linda. The more outrageous or scandalous the information, the more gleefully Linda passed it on; her favourite position as centre of attention at her endless coffee mornings owed a great deal to Amabel.

Encouraged, Amabel told a convoluted story about her friends' older sisters, and their friends, who had seen, heard . . . The network spread; somewhere, Rosa came into it.

'Mrs Blunt's niece. She'd say anything,' Linda said. 'And you know I don't like you to have anything to do with relatives of domestic servants, not in our social position.'

'I didn't. Someone who knows her told Daphne's cousin's boyfriend, who said . . .'

'It's like the bloody Mafia,' Wilfred muttered; but he always listened to Amabel, too.

Amabel moved on stolidly to a further episode: someone else, who had an evening job as a waitress at Ferdinand's. — 'They were there that night you were, Dad.'

'You've been to Ferdinand's? *I've* never been to Ferdinand's,' Linda snapped.

'I just popped in for a jar on my way to the Con Club. I'd forgotten about it.'

'You mean you didn't want Mum to know. Honestly, Dad, what makes you think you can get away with anything?' Amabel said. Lack of animation prevented her from treating him with contempt, but in her general attitude she took her cue from her mother and managed a weary scorn.

'You're tired, you need your rest. It's easy to overdo things when you're a growing girl,' Linda fussed. This was one of her tactics. Amabel, slow but not stupid, knew she could rely on it: when she successfully divided her parents her reward was her mother's engulfing solicitude. She settled back in her seat to enjoy it.

Wilfred was ostentatiously ignored — not dismissed, held in reserve. Beneath her maternal sweetness, Linda was seething.

In the privacy of their bedroom they said the things they had not wished Amabel to hear, although the inadequate sound-proofing allowed her to eavesdrop without difficulty, until she fell asleep, which was quite soon.

Wilfred placated, 'I knew it would upset you, Lin. Not just me going to Ferdinand's without you — '

'Am's right, she's got more sense in her little finger than you have in all your great fat body. I was bound to find out — '

'Not just that, but thinking Gilbert had got himself a girl-friend.'

'Thinking. He has, hasn't he? Everyone knows it — except me. I had to be the last, all because my husband's too spineless to tell me.'

'I knew it would upset you — '

'Spineless. You make me sick. Look at you. Spineless.'

He was doubly helpless, deprived of the decent protection of his clothes. His shoulders were narrow and sloping, his chest hairless, overdeveloped. From this soft womanliness he spread out, white rolls of flesh settling round him as he sat on the edge of the bed to take off his socks. In all the bulk of his body his genitals were disproportionately small; Linda had always had a great deal to say about that. 'Listen, Lin, what harm is there if — '

She sat at the dressing table, furiously engaged in what she called her beauty routine: lotions, creams, curlers. 'Harm. You know what bloody harm. Supposing he marries, has children?'

'We always said he wouldn't — '

She gave a strangled shriek of scorn. 'And who are we to stop him if some gold digger gets her claws in him. You can't even provide for your own wife and family as it is. Now we're going to be done out of our prospects.'

'I've done my best.' His voice hardened. 'You could get a job —'

There was a great deal of her inside her nylon nightdress. Incensed, voluptuous, it wobbled. 'My place is in the home,' she yelled.

The old arguments began, spiralling, fragmenting, subsiding. Matters were never settled: their debts, her extravagance. Matters were never faced; her infidelities. Gilbert became the rag they tore between them. Whatever divided them through all the years of their marriage, this at least held them together. Linda had had enough of being pushed around by the Hewitts (on these occasions she did not count herself one), she would have it out with Gilbert, find out who this woman was, what was going on.

'You can't,' Wilfred pleaded, although the whole course of their quarrel had led to this. 'He's in a funny state. You could, I dunno, make things worse.'

'It's time he faced up to his obligations. You've only yourself to blame, letting things get this far with him and this. whoever it is. But you daren't do anything about it, oh, no.'

'I'm sorry, Lin —'

She had taken on a sleek look. A really blazing row was the only sexual stimulant she knew: the longer it went on, the more abject his apology, the more she was likely to allow him to make love to her. Although love had ceased to have anything to do with it and, latterly, Wilfred's simple lust could not stay the course. By the time he was on his knees, begging her forgiveness, forgiveness was all she needed to dispense. Which completed her conquest and was far more satisfying than an orgasm.

Devastatingly overdressed, she was at The Laurels at eleven

o'clock the next morning. She knew Gilbert was not at the office, she had telephoned Wilfred to make sure. He had pleaded with her again, unavailingly, a long conversation, embarrassing for him with people about, but she kept it going, stoking her self-righteousness.

There was no answer when she rang the doorbell. She opened the letter box and peered in. The distant sound of a radio was cut off; somewhere a door closed. She rang again, shouted Gilbert's name, went round to the kitchen door, which was locked, and banged on that. Teetering to the front again on her platform-soled boots, she thumped on the door, opened the letter box and shouted, 'I know you're there. Gilbert, stop behaving like this. Open the door.' The lack of response touched off her temper, she made no attempt to control it. 'I know what's going on. I'll put a stop to it, you'll see.' She straightened up, stood thinking for a moment, then bent to the letter box again. 'Where's Mrs Blunt? She should be here. What have you done with Mrs Blunt? I'm going to fetch her.'

She flared off, making screaming noises with her car down the drive, narrowly missing the gateposts.

Mrs Blunt did not ask her in. She stood in the shelter of the doorway of her small house, unyielding. If Mrs Linda Hewitt, done up like a tart and putting on airs, wanted to make a show of herself, Mrs Blunt did not care if the whole of Kitchener Terrace listened. It did.

'You mean he's sacked you? Sacked you? Just like that?' Linda kept repeating, her voice rising. Mrs Blunt had delivered the information flatly, unadorned by detail, she had nothing to add.

'How dare he? After all these years. Just like that. What's he up to? What's going on in that house? What?'

'What?' Mrs Blunt repeated impassively.

'You must know. You're there every day.'

'Not now.'

'What are you hiding? Who's that woman he's got there?'

'What woman?' Mrs Blunt said, demonstrating her ability to be gloriously and adamantly bloody-minded.

Linda shrieked, 'Haven't you got any loyalty? You did well enough out of Mildred when she was alive, then her legacy. Don't you care what happens to Gilbert? You should be helping me to find out, not just standing there pretending you don't know anything.'

'Keep myself to myself.'

'You stupid old bag —'

Mrs Blunt shut the door.

TEN

Henry was spending the weekend at Marchstearn. Sunday morning, with the landscape locked into frost, Emmeline arrived unexpectedly, on her way home from a three day craft fair. She parked her camper, in which she slept and transported her exhibits, under the great hoar-spangled chestnut trees that bordered the common opposite his house. He was relieved to see she did not have her hang glider strapped to the roof: she might have had some notion of giving him a practice flight off Marchstearn Hill.

'No wind today,' she said.

'Emmeline, I jest.' He untangled her from a scarf of heroic length; she appeared to be wearing it instead of a coat. Underneath, she had on several jerseys and a long skirt of soft blue wool. 'Keep going. A few more turns and I'll have you free.'

She revolved slowly. 'I hadn't thought of any sites round here,' she said seriously. 'I must view the possibilities.' She stopped and said softly, 'Aah, Wanda . . .' to the Italian greyhound that had woken from its doze by the sitting room fire and come to pose exquisitely in the hall. Lydia Marshall, Henry's next door neighbour, had gone to church and left the little dog in his keeping. Emmeline picked her up and hugged her. 'Come upstairs with me, we'll view the possibilities together.'

'Emmeline, put her down, you'll trip on your skirt,' Henry said. He was expecting guests, he didn't need Emmeline flat on the stairs with a bleeding nose and the dog squashed beneath her. It was not unusual for such catastrophes to attend Emmeline.

Emmeline put Wanda down and they went off together to the top of the house, the long attic room where windows at either end gave a view of the two hills that, tapering down, held the village in their arms.

Henry went into the kitchen, leaving Emmeline to herself. She knew her way about. She had a curious passion for inspecting other people's domestic arrangements — curious because he had to assume it extended beyond himself and the various flats he had occupied over the years, although he had never heard her talk about anyone else. She had begun at ten years old, insisting that Mr Dash take her to visit Henry and his father in Manchester, it was just after Henry had finished his National Service. A strange, small, scarecrow figure inside her expensive clothes, she had inspected the two–up–and–two–down terraced house with extreme politeness, solemnly amazed by the lavatory in the back yard, the absence of a bathroom, the tin bath hanging in the wash house. Later, she explained these interesting arrangements to Olivia, and Mrs Dash had been very angry when Olivia said scathingly, 'Emmeline, that's a slum.'

Not that Emmeline or Mrs Dash told him that. Olivia did, the splendid bitch, when she had turned up at Marchstearn, stunning the village with her presence and, later, Henry, upstairs in the feather bed. 'Well, you've been looking at me with lust written all over you since I was sixteen.' 'Fifteen,' Henry said. 'And I can only thank God you waited till I'd got the experience to cope with you.' They would not have dreamt of telling Emmeline, it was their business, too briefly for Henry. Although, afterwards, Olivia amused herself by reminding him, speaking under her breath on very respectable occasions. She had a remarkable memory for details.

Emmeline's footsteps thudded faintly down the stairs, into the sitting room where the fire burned with sweet-scented apple logs. After a few moments she appeared at the kitchen door, looking round at the food arranged along the work tops, Henry busy at the table.

'Henry, I thought everywhere looked extra posh. You're entertaining.'

'In about an hour's time. Just people from round about. A lightning strike to repay all the invitations I get. Stay and be my hostess.'

'Oh, goody, yes. Who's coming?'

He told her while they sat drinking coffee. Emmeline was deeply interested in his neighbours, even those she had not met and, in spite of her vagueness, remembered everything he had ever said about them. When they had finished their coffee they set to work on the food. Emmeline said, 'Henry, *I'm* entertaining next Saturday. And you must come, say you will. I'm having a party at the hotel, and everyone's dressing up.'

'Next Saturday. All right. Shall I wear my fright wig and Dracula teeth?'

'No. You and I are going as beautiful people, 1930's style. I've got one of Mummy's marvellous crepe-de-chine dresses.'

'Sorry, Emmeline, I draw the line at drag.'

'Not for you, you fool. For me. I've altered it, so it fits, more or less. You can wear one of Daddy's suits, double breasted, chalk stripe.'

'But — ' Henry hesitated. 'Won't your mother mind?'

'No, I've asked her. She would if it was anyone else, I think, but not you. And his spats. *Spats*, Henry. Your hair's not right, it's too long. You wouldn't have it cut, would you? No,

I thought not. We'll part it in the centre and brush it flat. And we'll play all the old records and do proper dances. Foxtrot and waltz and quickstep.'

'I don't know why they went out of fashion, they're really sexy. I must brush up on my tango.' Picking up the Italian greyhound as a partner, Henry did a few practice steps round the kitchen.

Emmeline said, 'I've asked Gilbert. To cheer him up.'

'Have you seen him since he came to lunch?'

Emmeline arranged sausage rolls on a baking tray. She looked sheepish 'Not really.'

'That means you've been avoiding him. Jolly rotters of you. Offer to teach him to hang glide, then *he'll* avoid *you*.'

'I never thought of that,' she said seriously. 'Anyway, things must be a bit better for him. He's got a girlfriend.'

'*Gilbert* has? Are you sure?'

In general, Emmeline minded her own business, the only gossip that interested her centred on her photograph albums and was years out of date. But scraps of contemporary gossip attached themselves to her, inevitably, often inaccurately, as she was ready to point out, because she forgot, or wasn't listening properly in the first place. This time she removed any doubt by saying, 'Yes, Mummy told me, she heard it on the grapevine. Not who she is, just that they've been seen about together. So it might just be something casual, or maybe — ' Emmeline sat, chin in hand, pondering. 'Maybe she's Gilbert's type. Do you think?'

'Either that, or desperate. It comes to the same thing.' Henry put the little dog down and went to the kitchen table. 'Emmeline,' he sighed, 'you've got your elbow in the sausage rolls.'

The following Saturday night was cold, with a crystal moon.

Emmeline, transformed to a pre-war version of her mother, had done her best with the crepe-de-chine dress, but there was not quite enough of her to fill the beautifully draped bodice. More than usual, though. Henry studied her. 'What have you done?'

'Falsies. The only way I could get these folds to look right. Henry, you're marvellous, like something out of a silent film.' She gazed ecstatically at his feet. 'Two-tone co-respondent's shoes *and* spats. Did you show Mummy?'

Henry said yes, he had. Mrs Dash had gone out earlier. Emmeline put on her grandmother's fur coat. For Henry she had an overcoat with an astrakhan collar. It came almost down to his ankles. 'How the hell am I going to drive in this?'

'We'll walk. Then we can get drunk.'

'Good idea. I've never been drunk in spats.'

'I haven't in instant breasts. Come on.'

The old hotel accommodated the bizarre without effort. The shapes of creepers at the windows moved against moonlight; candles in bottles spread a wavering glow amongst high, strange shadows; fantastic figures, robed, masked, threaded through music and the smell of scent and dust.

Emmeline had sensibly locked up her workroom but there were plenty more rooms, filling and emptying as people ate and drank and danced. She had provided good wine and good food and left everything else to take care of itself while she tried to guess the identity of guests who had disguised themselves beyond recognition. Henry found some familiar faces and enjoyed Emmeline's good wine, heedless of a headache in the morning. He danced; some of the costumes were so effective the gender of his partners was occasionally in doubt; not that he minded if they did the right steps. Emmeline said that Gilbert was somewhere, but she was vague about his fancy dress, so Henry just hoped to avoid him. 'If he's recognizable I won't find myself asking him for a foxtrot.'

'He's brought his girlfriend. Ask me instead, while I'm still upright.'

'Stay that way, I'm not carrying you home.'

They danced until they came upon a group of young people from the hang gliding club who were in a heap on the floor, squirming and tussling like puppies. Emmeline stood watching without alarm, it was all evidently very good natured. 'They often do it,' she murmured.

'What exactly?' Henry asked.

'Get Richard's trousers off.'

The thresh of arms and legs permitted a glimpse of Richard's bearded face, valiant but resigned: he was losing. Henry wondered which bit of him would appear next. 'Emmeline, shouldn't you avert your eyes?'

Bystanders began to press round with cries of encouragement. In the noise and jostle a hand pressed Henry's shoulder, a voice he did not recognize said softly, urgently, 'I must speak to you. It's important. Follow me.'

He was turning before the words were finished, shouldering through the crowd after the small figure of a woman dressed as a cat, from head to foot in black. As she paused in a doorway to look back at him, then move on, he saw that with studied aplomb she was carrying her long tail over her arm. He laughed aloud. He had no idea who she was: in Dash's Hotel, on such an absurd night, anything could happen, and he was ready to meet it halfway, whatever it was. Keeping his eye on her, he paused to pick up his glass and, as an afterthought, a bottle of wine.

She kept ahead of him, slipping round groups of people, eventually turning a corner into a corridor. He knew the geography; they were at the rear of the hotel, there was only one place she could go, unless she went out by the side door off the corridor, which Emmeline always kept locked.

There was a widened area, cluttered with ancient furniture, then a round room, the ground floor of one of the hotel's insanely castellated turrets. The softest blur of light, the light of one candle, gleamed within the room. He went in and closed the door behind him.

She was standing before the lancet window, outlined by the silver radiance of the moon. Cold sober, he would still have been intrigued: the deliberate setting of the scene, the air of conspiracy, the silence she allowed to fall between them, orchestrating it with an elegant gesture.

She was average height, the soft contours of her body moulded by the black, furry material of her costume. Even her head was completely covered: two pricked ears, two slits for eyes, one for the mouth. As a disguise it was extremely effective. 'Alone at last,' Henry said. 'Who are you?'

'My name doesn't matter.'

It was like one of Emmeline's old films.

'Listen. I have a friend — she might need your help.'

'I don't suppose she has a name either,' he said. There was nothing about her voice he could place, he was sure he would have remembered if he had heard it before. 'Have a drink. I've only got one glass but I don't mind sharing. Will your friend bring her own?'

'Listen,' she said again, and began to prowl about, secretive, absorbed in herself.

He decided that, for the present at least, his function was defined. He settled himself on an enormous, half collapsed sofa that must have taken six men to lift. It was surprisingly comfortable. Or was he in that condition where alcohol turns the bones to rubber and anywhere was comfortable?

He stretched out, head propped on the arm of the sofa, wine glass balanced on his chest. The urgent, excitable voice looped round him out of the moonlight, everything became faintly surrealistic.

She was telling him about her friend: a rebel, a drifter. 'Life's not been easy for her but she's always believed the best of it, of people' — who had met this man, a mature business man. Two loners, sharing, caring. They had a future, or so it seemed. 'But you see, he'd been very close to his mother, and after she died he was grief stricken. My friend was doing her best, helping him through it, only he had this obsession that in some way he'd failed his mother. He had to put things right. So he began consulting a medium. My friend didn't see any harm in it, perhaps it was a way for him to reconcile himself to his mother's death. But there were things going on in his mind my friend never dreamt of. When tragedy struck she was completely unprepared. Suddenly, without warning, he took his own life.' Her small voice rushed to a halt on a sigh, heart-rending, lost; her neat little cat's head drooped.

Henry watched, fascinated. Did this barmy girl make a habit of contriving dramas for herself? From what compulsion?

'She tried to pick up the threads of her own life again. She moved back here — Did I tell you Avenridge was her home? Well, as much as anywhere was. She took an apartment close to where this medium lived. Chance? Or perhaps some subconscious motivation. She began to go to sittings there.'

'Of course,' Henry breathed.

'She was looking for consolation — and, something else. It was strange, but the dead man's obsession had transferred itself to her. She couldn't help wondering what had passed between him and the medium. She was in a position to observe the medium quite closely. She began to notice things. Gradually, it dawned on her there was something odd going on.' She stopped speaking abruptly, her body poised in an attitude of alarm. She was looking towards the door. 'Did you hear something?' she stage-whispered.

This was all of a piece with the drama, his participation. 'Shall I stride to the door and fling it open?' he whispered back.

To his amazement she nodded.

'You're not serious,' he said in a normal voice.

Her eyes glittered within the mask. 'Be quiet,' she hissed.

'Has Emmeline put you up to this?'

'Emmeline . . .' The whisper had a sharp edge, then Emmeline was dismissed as the cat's head turned once more towards the door, away again. 'You don't understand, do you? I could — I could be in danger, because of what my friend's told me.' The hesitation was beautifully timed, the statement underplayed.

'I must say, you're very good,' Henry said. 'Go on, what *has* she told you?'

'Something that could be . . . coincidence. Or could be a pattern. Her lover, grief-stricken after his mother's death, consults a medium. Now it's happening again, with another man.'

Henry decided it was time to be sensible, if only briefly. 'The grief-stricken consort with mediums. It's what they're for.'

'I know. In the general way of things. But this first man took his own life. Suppose she put the idea in his mind.'

'Why should she?'

'For gain. He left her money in his will.'

In the farthest reaches of Henry's mind a thought turned, faded. He picked up his glass. 'I think I've looked upon the wine when it was red.'

'D'you mean — d'you mean you're not taking any of this in?' Suddenly, she was an ordinary woman, exasperated, standing over him with her hands on her soft, round hips.

'Your act is slipping,' Henry said.

'I'm *not* acting.'

'Yes you are. But I'm enjoying it. Only I'd find the plot easier to follow if some of the cast had names.'

She allowed an effective pause. 'Hewitt.'

'Bloody Gilbert,' he muttered.

'What? aren't you listening? This is important. She's so difficult to pin down, she's deliberately . . . I don't know. And what's *he* doing with her? I'd have it on my conscience if it happened again. I had to tell . . . someone.' Her voice faltered, she spoke as if to herself, plaintively. 'No one ever believes me.'

Henry, confused, said, 'Can you blame them if you go through this performance every time?'

'But you . . . I didn't think you'd be drunk.' She sounded disgusted.

'I'm not very.' He held out his hand. 'Come on, little cat woman, come and share this sofa and my wine. I'm not up to chasing you round the room. I doubt I'm up to anything at all, so you're quite safe. Besides,' he considered her. 'I can't imagine how you got into that outfit but I don't think much of my chances of getting you out of it.'

She made a wild, impatient sound. He had succeeded in putting her off her set piece and wondered if it was worth it. 'Why me?' he asked.

'You're a policeman.'

'If you know that you know this isn't my patch. Why doesn't your friend go to the local police?'

'She has her reasons.'

'Ah. What's she done?'

'Nothing.' The answer came too sharply, too defensively.

I bet, Henry thought. Was any of this true?

'Besides, there's nothing — tangible. Nothing anyone can do, except watch.'

'Your friend seems to have turned herself into a one woman vigilante squad. I'm terribly confused,' Henry said peacefully. 'Stop being such a silly little feline and — '

'You're like all the rest,' she sounded plaintive again.

It occurred to him that whoever or whatever she was, this

was the only genuine note in her repertoire. He had heard it too often before, the misunderstood, the misjudged; and, too often, he had made the mistake of ignoring it. 'Why didn't your friend come to me herself?'

'If she's right — it could be dangerous for her to be seen with you. And for me.'

'You don't think anyone's going to recognize you in that get-up, do you?'

'They might.'

So people here knew her. He sensed in her not fear, but helplessness, a baffled appeal. If he was being made a fool of he was drunk enough not to mind. He said kindly, 'Look, if you think I can help you, I'm not going to do it at second hand. Let me talk to your friend — '

She padded swiftly across to him, standing just out of reach; the candlelight caught the glitter of her eyes within the mask, staring intently into his. 'Do you mean it? Will you do something? You can ask questions, find out. I can't, I mean my friend can't. You'll help? Promise?' She brought her hands together, her soft cat's paws, covered in black furry mittens; it was a gesture of decision. 'I'll get her. Wait — ' and she was gone.

The door opened, admitting from far away, fragile, the sound of music, then it closed. He was left to the weird room and its remnants of furniture, abandoned to the gothic light, the vibration of her uneasy presence.

Abandoned . . . By the time the thought had taken root in his mind it was too late. She was not coming back, she had taken whatever he said (what had he said?) as assent. Satisfied, she had gone about her own mad concerns.

He closed his eyes.

'Henry, are you all right?'

Emmeline was standing over him. She looked wrecked, a

process that had began early in the evening and obviously accelerated. Her hair was all over the place, she had lost her shoes and something had happened to the exquisite drapery of her bodice.

'Have your boobs slipped?' Henry asked.

'They started to. So I took them out and we played football with them. Henry, Gilbert's had some sort of fit.'

Gilbert again. 'Bugger him,' Henry said. 'But I'm not surprised if he suddenly found himself fielding your left tit.'

'No, it wasn't that. He was all weepy and lost. He couldn't find his girlfriend. It's all right, someone's taken him home. I suppose he's a bit edgy on social occasions when women disappear. After his mother, I mean. You haven't seen her, have you? His girlfriend?'

'I don't know her.' Henry had a thought. 'What was she dressed as?'

'I don't know half the people here. They've nearly all gone now, it's awfully late. He did say. I can't think. Was it a bat? Or a cat?'

Henry groaned and closed his eyes.

A couple Gilbert knew took him home. They were embarrassed by his tears and thought he must be drunk. He talked wildly, not knowing what he was saying, of his mother, or Veronica, wailing he had lost her, he must find her, she was all he had. The male half of the couple whispered, 'Who's Veronica? I never saw him with anyone, did you?' His wife shook her head, furtively put her finger to her brow and made a mad face. She asked, 'What was she dressed as?'

Gilbert made an effort. 'A sort of bat, all in black, with this horrible mask.'

'There were about seven of those.'

Gilbert began to wail again. He was dressed as a Spanish nobleman, a glamorous costume that would have suited his willowy frame, but he had gone to pieces inside it; his ruffled shirt was tear-stained, he had sat on his hat. Veronica had suggested he take off his spectacles to make the right kind of entrance; almost from that moment he had been lost, roaming the maze of rooms, barging into people.

The couple would have seen him into The Laurels, but in the porch he had a moment of apparent sanity and said he wanted to be left alone. Veronica might already be back, she disliked other people around her, she had only gone to the party because he persuaded her, promised her he would be all right. She would be angry. Mummy had always been angry when he'd got into squabbles at parties and been sick, it was no way for a little gentleman to behave.

They left him and went thankfully down the steps to their car. The wife said, 'I've never known one of Emmeline's parties actually destroy anyone before.' Her husband said, 'He was always a nervous wreck. His mother's death pushed him right round the bend.'

Lights had been left on in the house. Gilbert went about the ground floor, then upstairs. There was no sign of Veronica. Emptiness crept into him. Numb and shaking, he sat halfway down the stairs, watching the door. She came in soon, with the key that had been Mrs Blunt's. She wore a long cloak over her costume, she had removed her mask and was breathing quickly. 'There you are. Where on earth did you get to? I was looking for you, then someone told me you'd been brought home.' Her voice was sharp.

'I lost you. You left me. Don't be angry.' He began to cry.

She took off her cloak, talking more soothingly. 'I'm not angry. It's just that when I couldn't find you, I got in a panic.'

He gulped, stared. Veronica in a panic was something he could not believe.

'Well, your mother . . . I couldn't help thinking. She went out one evening and . . .'

He licked his lips, half whispered. 'Yes, that was what I . . .

You won't go away, like she did. You bring her so close to me.'

'I can bring her closer, I know I can. But only if you're good.'

He gripped the banister, staring down at her. 'I will be.'

She spoke carefully. 'But look at the state you get in, you're not safe to go anywhere without me. You're all right here, in the house —'

An unwilling thought obtruded. Was he? The voices in the night.

' — as long as you don't let anyone in.'

'Wilfred and Linda. I won't.'

'Anyone.'

'No, Veronica.'

'Good. Now go up to bed. I'll make you a hot drink and bring it up and you can take your pills.'

He went up quietly, like a tired child.

ELEVEN

In the morning, gently merciless, Emmeline woke Henry with the news that it was on for Windy Edge. He was beginning to understand the vocabulary: that meant another day pounding down the slopes of a bleak hillside. 'But I've got a hangover.'

'Just what you need, fresh air, blow it away.' Her recuperative powers were amazing; she looked, as always, vague and indestructible.

'But my head feels like an old dishcloth. Won't it interfere with my judgement?'

'What judgement? We shout instructions and you do as you're told.'

He did, and achieved three short flights, two stand-up landings and one acrobatic performance that whacked the breath from his body and threatened to dislocate his shoulder. 'You're doing awfully well,' Emmeline said. It was her judgement that went astray, she didn't work out a proper flight plan for herself and landed in a bog. She struggled out, plastered in slime, concerned for her kite, not herself.

Afterwards, they sat in her camper and drank tea before going home. The wind had freshened, carrying louring dark clouds across the hills. Around them, in the closing light, faces pinched with cold, people were de-rigging, loading kites on to roof racks. Emmeline observed them tranquilly. She had taken off her flying suit and boots but the slime had seeped through; she was filthy. 'Smashing day,' she murmured. 'What were you doing in the turret room last night?'

He had not had time to think of it. 'I had an interlude with a young woman.'

'Who?'

'I've no idea.'

'Isn't that a bit permissive, even for you? Don't you usually ask their names first?'

'Not that sort of interlude. Of course I do, I don't believe in anonymous congress.'

'Congress . . .' she repeated, reflectively.

He was trying to remember. The episode had become unreal. 'She was telling me about Gilbert going to a medium. I think.'

'Well, he's unhinged enough. I understand he's behaving very oddly. Ask Mummy, I think she knows.'

Henry was staring out through the window of the camper. A series of clicks occurred in his brain. Something was engaging, but he could not quite grasp what it was. Hang gliders. A man walking into the sea. A grief-stricken man who had left money to a medium. He needed to think. 'Oh, God, Emmeline, you do stink.'

'I know,' she agreed. 'I think it's sheep shit.'

Making himself presentable was not the major undertaking it was for Emmeline. He was in the sitting room with Mrs Dash, scones and tea on the small table, the dogs squashed together on his lap. Mrs Dash was busy with a report she had to make to one of her committees. She was usually busy with something. He told her about his day, asked her about Gilbert.

She made a note neatly, forcefully, in a margin and looked

up from her papers. 'It would seem he's had some kind of breakdown. I've tried telephoning but he doesn't reply. I'm surprised he went last night. But didn't someone take him, some woman friend he goes around with now? When he goes anywhere. Perhaps she thought it would cheer him up.'

'Would he be likely to consult a medium? About his mother's death.'

'In his present state he might. I suppose you mean that extraordinary creature on Inkerman Road.' Mrs Dash knew everything. 'And what did you think of Gilbert's young lady? I must say, I can't imagine anyone choosing his company, she must be very kind.'

Another kind woman, befriending an unbalanced, bereaved man. With money. 'What? Oh, I didn't meet her. At least, I don't know if I did, there were a lot of people there.'

'I can imagine,' Mrs Dash said dryly, making another note. 'Has Emmeline done anything about clearing up the mess?'

You could lose mess in that place and not find it for years and it wouldn't matter. Mrs Dash wouldn't see it that way, though. 'No, she was too keen to get out today. She says she'll ask Mrs Blunt to give her a hand tomorrow.'

'That's another strange thing. Gilbert sacking Mrs Blunt, after all these years.'

'Sacking . . . but last time he was here he was howling about her not doing enough.'

'It seems he's made other arrangements. Of course, Mrs Blunt is not a woman to waste words, but she did tell me . . .' Mrs Dash recounted what she had been told, about the letter, the request for the return of the key. Then Linda going and making a scene. 'It's too bad, as if any of it is Mrs Blunt's fault. It was sheer hysterical spite, because she'd been round to The Laurels and Gilbert didn't answer the door, although she was sure he was in. He need not have been, though.'

'Wasn't he at the firm?'

'They never see him there now. Of course, his cousin

Wilfred manages very well, and they have a most efficient staff, Midred saw to that. Gilbert never had an effective role, anyway.'

'No,' Henry murmured, absently distributing caresses between the two dogs. 'So he doesn't answer the phone or the door. He's isolated himself.'

'Except for his — friend.'

The smallest dog tried furtively to get at the plate balanced on the arm of Henry's chair, where there was a piece of scone left. Henry removed him, gently. 'Gilbert's very well off, isn't he?'

'Comfortable,' Mrs Dash murmured. Money was vulgar. She picked up her papers again.

Henry stared into the fire, thinking. Then he grew impatient with himself. It was a small drama. Gothic moonlight. Coincidences. He put the matter from his mind.

The following Thursday Mrs Carter was early. If he had not seen her, Henry would not have asked, 'Has Mrs Blore been behaving herself since that business, when was it, last autumn?'

'Oh, yes, she just refuses to speak to me, and I can't honestly say I'm sorry. She never did do anything about contesting the will. Whatever you said to her — '

'I can't take the credit for that. I think she just saw she wouldn't get anywhere. Or perhaps she went to a solicitor and he advised against it.' Henry put on his overcoat, it was freezing outside. 'Mrs Carter, make yourself a cup of tea, you need one after cycling here in this weather. What became of Arnold's girl, did she ever turn up again?'

'I did see her once or twice, just afterwards. Not to speak to.'

'So she lives round here?' This is ridiculous, he told himself, leave it alone.

'She must have done, then, I don't know where. I haven't seen her for ages. I daresay she moved away, rather than run into Mrs Blore. I can't say I blame her, I know what I went through. Of course, Mrs Blore had seen her off before — before poor Arnold . . . I don't know why she took against her. Nice young woman. She was kind to him, helped him with his shopping and gave him a bit of companionship. He was very lonely, you know.' Mrs Carter followed Henry into the hall, her voice musing. 'I suppose she went back to Avenridge, where you go. Wouldn't it be funny if you knew her.'

'Very,' Henry said. 'Did she have a name?'

'Mmm. Funny one. Unusual. Meena.'

In the garage he sat in his car, gathering together the thoughts that Mrs Carter, unknowingly, had scattered like startled hares.

Meena.

Meena?

When she was a child, Emmeline sang to herself a silly chant she had made up about her name. Emmelina — Lena — Meena.

Sometimes she had called herself Meena; the family teased her about it for years, long after she'd grown up.

'Don't be ridiculous,' Henry said to himself.

At the end of the day, during which his mind had displaced everything except work, he returned to his flat and his thoughts and found some perverse demon embedded there.

Once, Emmeline had made up a photograph album for him. He could not remember if he had taken it to Marchstearn but after he had searched methodically for a while, he found it. He went out, taking it with him, and drove round to Mrs Carter's. He had to know, he'd lie awake all night otherwise, being driven mad.

Mrs Carter was flustered. He apologized for calling on her out of the blue. 'If you could spare me a few minutes. What we were talking about this morning . . . I have a feeling I might know Arnold's young lady, and as I'm going to Avenridge this weekend . . .' He had not planned to, he was guiltily aware of taking advantage of Mrs Carter and her readiness to be charmed by him.

She asked him in. Through the half open door of the front room he glimpsed her ancient invalid parents, motionless as two stranded wrecks before the television. Mrs Carter spoke to them loudly, reassuringly, then shut the door on them and the raucous sound of a quiz show. 'We'll go in the kitchen, they have to have the telly up loud and we won't be able to hear ourselves speak. I'll make a cup of tea.' The unforeseen occasion gave her a faintly festive air.

In the kitchen, the only other room on the ground floor, nothing had been modernized. There was still a concrete floor, a square porcelain sink with crazily poised taps; the walls were half tiled, like a lavatory, white tiles crazed with age; everything was bright with Mrs Carter's care. When she had made the tea they sat at the kitchen table together and Henry opened the album. 'Just look through, see if you can pick her out.'

It was not so simple. Extracted from the monotony of an evening like countless other evenings, Mrs Carter responded to the album as a child to a picture book. *Who's that? Where's that? Isn't it lovely?* she kept saying softly. Unexpectedly, he had given her a treat. Her delight touched him, he saw it all through her eyes: the faraway place where the sun always shone, where ladies like Mrs Dash wore pearls and had tea on the lawn.

The album began during the war, Emmeline had compiled it as his personal record, placing him firmly in the family context. Mrs Carter did not fail to notice he was in every photograph. 'You were a nice looking little boy, weren't you?

And that's the house where you were evacuated. It's very grand.'

'Not really — ' Aware of how this must sound, remembering his own home at the time, he added, 'Well, I was overwhelmed at first, but I soon settled down and found it was just a very happy home. Kids finished up in some surprising places then.'

'I was on the buses,' Mrs Carter said nostalgically. 'I was only a bit of a girl. It was grand.'

He coaxed her on to the more recent photographs. People grew unrecognizable with the passage of time, except Emmeline, whose orphaned look and big dreamy eyes had simply grown up with her. There were certainly enough photographs of her, and a bewildering array of Dash relatives and friends. Mrs Carter gave no flicker of recognition. What did I expect, he asked himself, exasperated.

'Oh, I know *her*,' Mrs Carter said. She had picked out Olivia. Henry explained she was a daughter of the family. 'But she's that actress on telly. I love her in that series. Well, fancy that — fancy you — fancy — ' Overcome, Mrs Carter revived herself with tea. 'She's lovely, isn't she? And they say she's not a bit like that part she plays, all stuck up. Mind you, she's marvellous. They say she's *really* nice — '

Henry could not disappoint Mrs Carter by admitting that the first-class bitch Olivia portrayed was Olivia to the life, which was why she was so marvellous. He said tactful things, homely details Mrs Carter drank in. All the while his mind supplied the lift of Olivia's brows, the self-assured gaze, the disdain of her beautifully pitched voice: *The proletariat adore me. I'm such a snob. All those mechanics and factory workers have fantasies about screwing me.* To say nothing of policemen, Henry thought.

Mesmerized, Mrs Carter looked only for Olivia, enchanted to find her in everyday surroundings. Henry was patient, but they were getting near the end of the album. They came to a photograph taken almost three years before, during Aven-ridge Arts Week. It had been a Victorian evening and everyone was dressed up, more a crowd than a group. Even Mrs Blunt was there and had been coaxed to glare at the camera. She had helped with the costumes, Henry recalled.

Emmeline looked like an exquisite doll in her crinoline; her hair, which she'd worn long then and generally looked like a birds nest, coaxed into ringlets. Olivia had seen to that, she was very tender with her sister. In order not to steal the limelight, and achieving it to perfection, Olivia had dressed herself as a skivvy, bedraggled and downtrodden. 'Just look,' Mrs Carter said rapturously. 'fancy her getting herself up like that — '

'She did a monologue, it was very funny. I sang *Come into the garden, Maud*,' Henry said, diverted by recollection.

('Maud. Predictable. Trite,' Olivia drawled.

'Trite? It's passion, held down in a half-nelson and squirming. Listen — *My heart would hear her and beat, Were it earth in an earthy bed; My dust would hear her and beat, Had I lain for a century dead; Would start and tremble under her feet, And blossom in purple and red.*'

Emmeline, listening, all eyes, had gone away and read the whole of *Maud*. 'Henry, it positively throbs.'

Quite . . .)

Mrs Carter made a small sound of recognition and triumph. 'There she is. Well I never. Arnold's young lady. I'd know her anywhere. There.'

Henry looked. Frilled cap and maid's neat gown. An attractive face, with more than a hint of mischief to her smile. He had no idea who she was.

He had intended going to Marchstearn, but on Friday evening there were reports of heavy snow in the Midlands, with warnings of more to come; so he waited, knowing from experience the hazards of the rolling Cotswold plateau. Saturday morning he listened to the weather report: half the motorway was closed. There was no point in struggling to get through on the minor roads and back again the next day, that's if he wasn't cut off. There were only scattered snow showers forecast for the Avenridge area; the wind was north easterly. Emmeline wouldn't be flying. He knew the only north east site; access was difficult. Emmeline said that by the time she'd carried her glider all the way to the top she was too exhausted to take off. He decided to go to Avenridge.

When he arrived Mrs Dash and a friend were sorting boxes and bundles for an afternoon Bring-and-Buy. They were vigorous ladies but glad of his help. Emmeline was at the hotel, working. Mrs Dash seemed a little distracted. 'Is there anything else I can do for you?' Henry asked, after he had loaded the boxes in the friend's car.

'Would you like to take the dogs out? They haven't had a decent walk for days, Emmeline's been so busy.'

Henry loved taking the dogs out, they circled him excitedly, knowing he did. 'Are you all right?' he asked.

'Oh, it's just — ' The friend hovered in the hall with a reminder they were running behind time. 'I'll see you at supper, Henry. You're staying tonight, aren't you?'

He said yes, if it was all right. 'All right? Of course it's all right,' Mrs Dash said briskly, disappearing through the door.

Henry took the two leads and the spare key from the kitchen and walked the dogs through the quiet roads to the river. He joined the path behind the houses, the ever-steepening banks of the Aven to his left and beyond them, great vistas of stark, sombre hills. On his right lay the gardens, small openings leading to side entrances between the houses: frosted ivy glittered on grey stone walls, the backs of the houses were visible between naked trees. One of them was the Hewitts'. He strolled down the narrow opening, the dogs charging ahead of him.

The door in the wall stood ajar, giving a glimpse of a path and cleared ground, once the vegetable garden. The sight unlocked lost memories: a sunlit party on the lawn. He'd been the oldest child, in charge of Olivia, that tiny, vivid show-off: give her a collection of people and she turned them into an audience, even then, commanding attention while she danced, or recited. The Hewitts could produce food no one ever saw during rationing. Gilbert had been sick, but so had several other children.

The memories blurred and fractured. A game of hide and seek. He'd trespassed round here. Out of bounds. Discovered and hauled back: little gentlemen stayed away from the servants' quarters. 'He's only an evacuee, he's too common to know,' Gilbert sneered. Was that the source of his untraceable dislike for the pallid, overwrought creature? But his attention had fastened on that amazing domestic circumstance, accepted without thought then. Servants. Everyone had them: a maid, or a cook, or a housekeeper. It didn't seem possible that within his lifespan the props had been pulled away and an entire social structure had collapsed.

The door stood ajar to the vanished past. The present crept back: his numbed fingers and toes, the dogs impatient for him to move on. Before he turned away he noticed that the top of the back door, visible above some shielding bushes, was also open, and on the upper storey there was a light behind frosted glass.

He returned to the path, tangled and tortuous, climbing. Eventually, it led all the way to the Ridge, but he turned off before he was halfway there and went by side roads down into the Saturday morning bustle of the town.

In the unfocused state of extreme concentration, Emmeline was delighted to see him. She had wood shavings in her hair and was sucking a cut on her finger from which blood oozed. He put a plaster on the cut, went out and bought sandwiches and made her stop, briefly, to eat lunch. He had the photograph in his pocket, she was sure to have her own copy, but he had brought it, just the same.

'Aah,' she murmured, all her photographs gave her pleasure. It was odd, he thought, how she lived in them, and in her weird and beautiful models, attached to reality only insecurely, and occasionally.

He asked: who's this, and this? Then he pointed to the young woman.

Emmeline's dreamy, happy voice changed. 'It's so sad, isn't it? Rosa — Mrs Blunt's niece. You know.'

'I don't. I don't remember her that night. Or any other time,' he said. Mrs Blunt's niece.

'Well, there was a tremendous crowd for that Victorian evening. I think she came in at the last minute, someone had dropped out. And now she has. Well, she always did, for years, but now it's permanent. Poor Rosa.'

'What are you telling me?' Henry asked carefully.

'Didn't Mummy say? Mrs Blunt's so upset. It was awful. Rosa drowned, the other day.'

Words fell through Henry's mind: *I could be in danger . . . my friend could be in danger . . .* Her friend Rosa. Who was dead.

'How did it happen?'

'Her body was found in the canal, early Thursday morning. A policeman on his beat. At the end of Millers Lane, there's a lock you can walk across — '

He knew the place, a shabby corner of Avenridge, shut in by the backs of warehouses, used sometimes during the day as a short cut across the northern edge of town. At night it was completely deserted.

' — but it had happened late the night before. They think she must have been walking over the lock, it was very icy, and she'd had a bit to drink. She'd been to see Mrs Blunt and taken her a bottle of port. Mrs Blunt's partial to it, although she doesn't like to admit it. She had a couple of glasses, Rosa had several.'

'What do you mean? Been to see her? Didn't she live with her?'

'No, they couldn't get on at close quarters. And Rosa . . . always drifting off somewhere, which was the best thing, but then she'd turn up again. She had a flat in town.'

'Would she go that way home to it? Where does Mrs Blunt live?'

Kitchener Terrace, Emmeline told him. He knew that, too; also on the north side of Avenridge. It was not far from the canal. But Emmeline didn't know where Rosa's flat was.

He cleared up the coffee cups and sandwich wrappings while Emmeline sat brooding, smoking a cigarette. He imagined her thoughts must be on Rosa. Once she murmured, 'Kitchener Terrace,' in a puzzled voice.

Before he left he asked, 'Was Rosa at your party last Saturday?'

'Um? Yes. I saw her some days before and told her about it, I knew she'd come, she loved anything like that. She came quite late, I was a bit pissed. She didn't want me to recognize her, but she said something and I knew her voice. She was a bit put out, she adored being mysterious.'

'You blew her cover,' Henry murmured.

'What? Well, I said was a bit — '

'What was she dressed as?'

'It was awfully good. A cat.'

He had a great deal to think of as he walked the dogs back. He put them in their baskets, then went out again, taking his car.

The old cinema, converted to a bingo hall, stood at the corner of Kitchener Terrace. He parked there and walked down the short road. They had once been workmen's houses, a privy outside the back door and long, long back gardens. Now, as the old people who rented them died or moved away, they were coming up for sale, being converted into bijou residences; in the frosty, hanging air the street had a dilapidated charm, like a television advert for a place that never was.

He went into the corner shop; it was tiny, crammed with stock. The woman who was serving, in turban and curlers, balanced her cigarette on the edge of the counter and cut bacon for a customer. Henry felt the tug of nostalgia: once it was always like this, and what was wrong with it? We survived, didn't we? Sodding supermarkets.

He bought cigarettes and a packet of washing powder, the bachelor who had to do his own washing — which did she recommend, he wasn't very good at choosing. He also bought a bottle of port. And could anyone tell him Mrs Blunt's number? He knew her through Mrs Dash, he'd come to offer his condolences.

The three women shoppers edged closer. Ethel put her cigarette in her mouth and folded her arms on the counter, the immemorial posture for a good gossip.

By the time he left the shop he knew a great deal about Rosa.

He had to wait for Mrs Blunt to answer the door. He was there to offer his sympathy, but that was not the only reason; shreds of uneasiness attached him to the girl in the turret room. He wished to rid himself of them, this was the only way he could go about it.

On one matter his thoughts had clarified: there had never been a 'friend'. That was a fiction Rosa needed to shield herself — because she was a compulsive fantasist, and because she had had a considerable amount of money out of poor little Arnold Peabody. For all she knew, Edith Blore had told the police she'd stolen it. So, in her heedless fashion, she had come back to Avenridge and lived off it. It had probably all gone by now, leaving her with no hope of offering to pay it back.

There were lumbering sounds from within, then Mrs Blunt

opened the door. Perhaps she had been lying down, resting that bulky, hardworking body, that iron grief. She would not admit to a nap, she was of tougher stuff; she would not admit to the grief, either, but it was there.

She said, 'Young Henry Beaumont,' unwelcomingly. She had known him since he was a boy, although they'd rarely spoken, and not come face to face for years. He had no doubt that locked in her memory were all the sins of the rough little evacuee. After that she called him Mr Beaumont; she had her own scale of assessment: he had grown up, he belonged to the Dashes, they had polished him to their lustre.

He told her he had heard about Rosa and come to say how sorry he was. She regarded him impassively for a moment, then invited him in. The front door opened directly into the parlour. She took him through to the back room where she lived. It was a dark little house, every corner, every surface in a state of petrified cleanliness. The kitchen had a black-leaded hob, a ceiling rack draped with drying underwear, a table with a dark red chenille cloth, a crocheted doily, laundered, starched, placed exactly in the centre.

Henry diffidently offered the port. 'I thought, perhaps, something to keep the cold out.' A gleam, rapidly extinguished, appeared in Mrs Blunt's eye. Emmeline had been right about the one weakness of this uncompromising woman.

She took glasses from the sideboard, poured drinks, and they sat before the fire in worn, comfortable chairs. Mrs Blunt took up an immense, mud-coloured piece of knitting; Henry wondered what it could be.

He said, 'This is a sad time for you, and a difficult one, too. In cases like this there are all sorts of formalities, are you coping all right? Is there anything I can help you with, or explain to you?'

'Formalities,' she repeated, concealing distress beneath scorn. She had had to identify Rosa, make a statement, there was the inquest to face, and the police had been round, causing talk. This last circumstance was hard for her to bear. Her own life was blameless, Rosa's ramshackle ways had threatened but never invaded it; now, in death, Rosa had made her final assault.

Henry murmured that he was sure the neighbours were sympathetic. Mrs Blunt made a grudging assent and glared at him. But the glare was half-hearted, something wavered, hidden.

He coaxed her to talk. She was naturally taciturn and her vocabulary limited, the port helped a little; Henry watched the knitting and glass put down and taken up in turn.

. . . To end like that, a silly accident. If she'd had sense she'd never have gone that way. Death trap that lock, always had been, Rosa knew that well enough. Different in daylight, when there were people about to fish you out. But that time of night, who'd hear her shout . . .

'And,' Mrs Blunt finished vigorously, 'I'm not having no one saying she did herself in. Not her.' Suicide was a dreadful shame to those left to do the explaining, Mrs Blunt had had enough of explaining Rosa, she would settle for an accident.

Almost absently, Henry said he felt sure the authorities would, too. A silly girl dramatized herself and a few days later she was dead, it happened in the natural course of things. Why had she chosen to give him that rambling account, only half of which he could remember, about Arnold and Gilbert . . .? Because she knew who he was, because he had provided the reassurance of officialdom without its threat. And no one else believed anything she said. From what he had learnt of Rosa that was the least puzzling aspect of the business.

'But they searched her flat. Why'd they do that?'

'To eliminate the possibility of suicide. If she'd left any indication . . .' He was sure this had been explained to Mrs Blunt and in the confusion of events she had forgotten. She listened to him, sipping her port. When he had finished she nodded, satisfied; but still he had a sense of waiting. He said,

'Her flat. It was on her way home? That was why she was at the canal?'

Mrs Blunt picked up her knitting. 'Park Road. Posh place, so she said. Invited me. I never went.'

'Nice houses on Park Road.' He thought about the flat for a moment. 'She must have had a good job. What did she do?'

'Nothing.' The grey head was bent, the needles stabbed furiously. Henry knew what he was waiting for.

Suddenly she was still. 'Who paid for it? She'd been spending, spending. She'd never had tuppence in her life. Where'd she get the money from?'

Gently, he told her about Arnold. She listened immovably. She could not be shocked by anything Rosa did, she could be ashamed, avoided his eyes, muttered, 'Taking money off a feller . . .'

'He was an unhappy, lonely man, he needed a friend. Rosa was kind to him, that was all. He was grateful.'

'There was never no real harm in her. She could be kind. Fool to herself sometimes. I don't reckon she was ever right in the head. Her mother wasn't, in a madhouse now. Rosa's been spared that, any rate: it's where she'd have finished up. Took things. Right from a girl. Told lies. Many's the hiding I give her. Did no good.'

Henry looked at the brawny arms; as a young woman Mrs Blunt would have had a heavy hand. He could understand the outraged respectability, the baffled love. And no matter what had happened, Rosa had never deserted her, she kept coming back. Perhaps because she had nowhere else to go, perhaps because she knew this was the one person who cared for her, and would never be able to say so.

'Yes, I know, Mrs Dash told me. When she was small you used to take her there with you sometimes. She took the girls' things.' He was on safe ground here, they both knew that what was spoken of in that household was not spoken of elsewhere.

'I always knew. Made her return them. Mrs Dash was very understanding. And never a word from the girls.'

'Still, you couldn't blame her, they always had so much. She wanted to be like them. Sometimes she pretended to be Emmeline, didn't she? Called herself Meena.'

Mrs Blunt attacked her knitting. 'That's what I mean. Mad.'

'No, a harmless fantasy. When she was Meena she wasn't in a mess, or hard up. She could escape.'

Mrs Blunt looked at him as if he, too, was mad. Primitive as this psychology was, it was beyond her. 'Don't know what you mean about escape. Landed herself in more than one mess. Had to own up, apologize.' To Mrs Blunt the sin was not merely impersonation, it was Rosa setting herself above her station, sabotaging all Mrs Blunt's notions of class. She stared at him, puzzled, angry, her pain close to the surface. 'She'd have had a good home here, she knew that. If only she'd behaved normal. She used to come and visit. Oh, she'd tell me all her lies, what she'd been doing. I didn't listen. But we'd talk. She used to go through the local paper, reading bits out to me, and we'd talk. She loved a gossip. I kept them — ' The pain receded, the defences shut down. 'Well, I kept them to light the fire.'

They were there, *The Avenridge Journal*, in an orderly pile. She would have read them herself, ploddingly, over lonely cups of tea, put them aside, perhaps for weeks. No, not to light the fire, but for that bright, unstable girl whose chatter filled the room where the evenings were long and silent.

Rosa loved a gossip . . . Mrs Blunt had the reticence of a tombstone; shut in her mind was a store of knowledge of the families she had worked for, conversations overheard, private matters touching her by chance. Nothing would induce her to part with other people's secrets — under normal circumstances. But Rosa was one of her own, if not to be trusted at least to be at ease with, over a glass of port, in their easy chairs by the fire. These thoughts came to Henry at random, and faded almost as they occurred.

'That money then. It was what she'd got from him, what she was living off?'

He was surprised that she should return to a subject that distressed her; but as he was the only one who knew about it then, logically, if she had something to say, he was the only one she could say it to. He said, 'Had it all gone? You can't be made responsible for paying it back, you know. It was a gift, not a debt, there wouldn't be anything . . .'

'I wouldn't want folks knowing. There's enough being said about her as it is.'

'I give you my word, I won't —' That was not the assurance she wanted; he had lost track somewhere.

'If there was anything in that flat of hers.'

'Would you like to make sure? Do you want me to go with you? But haven't the police got the keys?'

'They give them me back. I couldn't go, I've no mind to. Yet.' She put down her knitting and stared at him with a dumb expectancy. She had run out of words.

'Would you like me to go?'

She got up, took a key ring from the sideboard drawer and handed it to him. Well, he had asked if there was anything he could do for her; it would set her mind at rest. And his.

He should have pointed out to her that he could not tamper with any evidence that had a bearing on Rosa's death; but if the keys had been returned to her then the local police were satisfied there was nothing left to find. All the same, he decided it was time to pay them a call.

He introduced himself and explained his interest — on personal terms of his connection with Mrs Blunt — to smart Sergeant Smith, whose mother lived round the corner from Mrs Blunt. 'Fine woman. I wouldn't like to have to get on with her, though. My Ma can't.'

'No. And Rosa was a cross she had to bear.' They exchanged glances. They understood each other.

'Perhaps you'd like to look at the file, sir.' The sergeant handed it to him. 'She was never in trouble with us but, by hell, it was touch and go sometimes. Well, you know, sir, no harm in her, she just lived a world of her own.'

'Yes,' Henry agreed again. He was not going to admit that the only occasion he had encountered Rosa she was disguised as a cat, although he had a feeling the sergeant would not be altogether surprised. And he wasn't going to admit he'd been too drunk to remember half she'd said, which wouldn't surprise the sergeant, either; chief inspectors got drunk just like other human beings. It was just that Henry felt a fool about the whole thing.

He glanced quickly through the contents of the file, read the recommendation of the investigating officer: In my opinion, there is nothing to suggest that this death was anything but an accident. 'So, it was an accident.'

The sergeant nodded. 'Not first time there's been one on that lock. And you can see for yourself, the conditions, she'd had a bit to drink. She couldn't swim.'

'She was taking a short cut on her way home.'

'Anyone with any sense would have gone round by the road. But Rosa —' he shrugged expressively.

'Mrs Blunt's very distressed by the suggestion of suicide.'

'I know, relatives always are, aren't they? There was no note in her bag, we fished that out. It was one of those with a shoulder strap, she had the strap wrapped round her arm, she could even have been fiddling with it as she walked across, lost her footing. But we had to search her flat, just in case, and we did explain to Mrs Blunt — '

'Mmm, I did, too, but she's a difficult woman to get through to. You know, sergeant, it's not uncommon, this initial resentment of authority. Mrs Blunt doesn't mean to be obstructive and in a way her attitude's understandable. Rosa's caused her enough heartache. She wants it to be decently over, finished. What's this? This letter?' He knew what it was, he had been reading it, his mind disengaged from what he was saying to the sergeant, a jolt occurring in his system.

'Ah, yes. Rosa *might* have been meeting someone there, although Mrs Blunt was adamant Rosa hadn't so much as hinted at it. But she needn't have told her aunt, there was a lot she didn't want her to know. That was the only thing we found in her flat — '

Henry had read it through again, to himself. The jolt had settled.

Cat Woman,
I've found out what you mean. Phone me tonight at 10 p.m.

There was a telephone number. No signature, just one initial. H.

'Of course, we had to follow it up. That's a Manchester exchange.'

'I know. Whose?'

'No one's. It's a call box on the corner of the Longford Road and Barlow Street — that's your patch, isn't it? Would you know where it is?'

Henry did. Within reasonable walking distance of his flat. 'There's no envelope.'

'No. So she could have had it days, weeks. We had to treat it as a possibility that someone might have made a date with her for Wednesday here, but as a lead it was hopeless. You see, sir, there's no date on the note, it could have been written any time, nothing to do with her death.'

Wasn't it?

Henry sat in his car outside the police station, anger in his dark eyes. This girl had left a trail of hints, threads too fine to stand any strain — but now, one attached him to the mystery of her death.

Sergeant Smith's bland assumption was wrong: that note could not have been written at any time — unless Rosa made a habit of going about dressed as a cat, which was too unlikely to be considered. She had received it after the party on Saturday. There was no collection on Sunday, so assuming it went through the post on Monday, she would have got it on Tuesday. Or was it delivered by hand? Had there never been an envelope? Had she simply found the note on her mat? An interval of one or two days to lend credibility to the fiction that Henry had spent some time following up her hints. H. And a Manchester telephone number. 'Shit,' Henry said disgustedly.

Either the whole thing was a random series of events, or someone hidden moved with great subtlety towards an unknown purpose. Using him — not implicating him — oh, no, that would be much too risky. There was nothing to connect him with that note, he would never have known of its existence if his curiosity hadn't impelled him to go to the police station, look at the file. He was being manipulated by someone who knew a great deal about him, about Rosa, someone who had been at the hotel that night and known Rosa had spoken to him about Arnold — and Gilbert. The implications multiplied, racing beyond him. He was much too angry to think straight, he had to settle his mind. He started the Stag and drove to Park Road.

The entrance to Rosa's flat was at the side of a grey stone Victorian house. There was a small lobby, a narrow staircase up to the first floor landing with doors opening off: a bathroom, kitchen-dining room, bedroom and living room.

It was like so many houses in Avenridge, like Henry's flat in Manchester: space to move about, large sash windows, moulded ceilings; but it had its individual quality, which he felt as he stood for a moment in the silence: a sense of loneliness and impermanence.

He began to explore, going through each room slowly, carefully. It did not take long, Rosa, always on the move, accumulated little in the way of possessions. Clothes, make-up, bits of jewellery, a few odds and ends that might have been her own or come with the flat. There were plenty of bills, Rosa owed money everywhere; a receipt for her car, which she had sold some months previously, no doubt to meet more bills. She liked to read, she had a small collection of paperbacks, a few hardbacks, well used by her or bought second hand. He looked through them until he came to one entitled 'The Eternal Beyond', murmuring 'ugh' at the photographs of the mediums, who looked like their own ectoplasm. Was this the inspiration of the charade into which Rosa had written herself a part?

There was an address on the flyleaf, crossed out but readable. A Manchester district. He knew it, pulled down for development some years ago, all the old roads had disappeared. A second address, underneath the first, stared out at him. 37 Inkerman Road.

That extraordinary creature on Inkerman Road, Mrs Dash had said.

The room was cold. He went to sit on the window seat, scarcely noticing the chill striking at him from the large pane of glass. The short winter day would soon draw in, but it was still light; he stared out, immersed in thought, until his gaze began to focus.

He was at the back of the house, near the end of Park Road where the neighbourhood, geographically as well as socially, began to go downhill. Some of the gardens, with their old coach houses and stables, remained; beyond them spread a network of steep, narrow streets. He knew the area well enough to identify some of the streets. One of them would be

Inkerman Road, but he couldn't see it, the roofs of the tall terraces were in the way.

He went to the other window seat and sat in its farthest corner. He could see it now: the backs of the houses at the very end of Inkerman Road, the waste ground at the corner, the alley behind the houses, the wooden door in the wall that opened into the yard of the last house.

She was in a position to observe . . . Could that daft girl have meant literally observe? If that last house was 37, then this position afforded an angled view of it so freakish and exact it was possible to see what could not be seen even by the next door neighbours or the houses backing on to it. It was possible to see who went in and out of that back entrance.

So Rosa sat here and watched. Did it matter who she saw? If it *was* number 37. There was only one way to find out. But still he sat, gazing out, the book in his hands, mentally changing gear until his thoughts engaged slowly.

Rosa had involved herself with Arnold Peabody, recently bereaved. He had committed suicide and left a sum of money to a medium he had been consulting. In Avenridge. Rosa returned to Avenridge and pursued Arnold's connection with the medium. Discovered Gilbert Hewitt, recently bereaved, was associating with the same medium. Rosa was drowned.

Full stop?

No. There was another death, sudden and unexplained. Mildred Hewitt. Another sequence. Gilbert, alone and defenceless, half demented, extremely well off, summarily dismissing the woman who had served the Hewitts so faithfully, for so many years. Mrs Blunt. Rosa's aunt.

It was like a mass of snarled threads in which, un-wittingly, he had become entwined. It was, if nothing worse, his sense of order that was outraged. He had to pick out a single strand, tease it loose, follow it, unravel the tangle.

Follow it where?

Inkerman Road.

TWELVE

He left his car outside Rosa's flat and walked. Halfway down Inkerman Road he went into a newsagent and bought a paper, then went on more slowly, reading it. When he reached the waste ground at the end he paused. Number 37. The end house. Yes.

Engrossed in his paper, he continued along the tall, blank side of the house and turned sharp left into the alley. The high brick walls swallowed him up, he was invisible to anyone in the houses on either side. No one, seeing him enter the alley, would know which house he was going to. He paused again at the door to the back yard of 37 and looked up and to the right. Between the rise and fall of rooftops there was that one, freak angle shot — the corner of the upper floor of the house in Park Road, the window of Rosa's flat. A few steps backwards or forwards and the view was lost.

He tucked the paper under his arm and walked briskly the length of the alley. When he emerged at the other end he glanced back, then went on, thinking.

Mrs Dash was in the kitchen, she looked tired. 'I can't think what to do about supper.' Henry said don't do anything, he would take them out. 'That is nice of you, Henry, but I'm rather frayed. I think I'll just have something in front of the fire and watch television. You and Emmeline go and enjoy yourselves. You went to see Mrs Blunt, that was thoughtful of you.' But there was a question in her eyes.

Henry stroked the dogs, who had come to make a fuss of him. 'Well, I happened to be near there, and Emmeline had told me. I wondered if there was anything I could help her with, the enquiries bothered her a bit.'

'Indeed. I popped in myself on the way home. She told me you'd been round. You don't think there's anything questionable about Rosa's death, do you?'

Suddenly he was eleven years old again and she was about to ask him if he'd washed his neck. 'The police are satisfied it was an accident.'

'I shouldn't like her bothered unnecessarily at a time like this. Such a good woman. Everything about Rosa was questionable, I'm afraid. *De mortuis* and all that, but she was a wretch.'

'Yes, Mrs Dash,' Henry said, and escaped.

Emmeline was in the conservatory, watering the plants, a concert tape playing to keep her company. When Henry went in she waved a hand at the foliage and said in her Katherine Hepburn voice, 'Part of Sebastian's war against the herbaceous border.'

'*Suddenly Last Summer*,' Henry said.

She returned to her watering. Henry sat on a cushioned cane sofa and watched her, listening to the music. They shared the same tastes, Vivaldi, Purcell, Telemann: delicate, vibrant music that stirred the soul and pierced the heart. In cascades of green, the air smelt of damp loam; outside, the garden was beginning to fade into the approach of dusk. The second movement of Vivaldi's Concerto in C was so tenderly exquisite that Emmeline stopped what she was doing and sat beside Henry till the piece was finished.

He said, 'I'm taking you out to supper.'

'Nice.' She looked down at herself. 'Will I have to change?'

'Yes, please, Emmeline.' She looked as if she hadn't for a week. 'I want you to tell me something.'

'What?'

'I'm not sure yet. Would you like to go to that new place? Ferdinand's?'

'Oh, yes. The one where Gilbert made a scene.'

'Did he?'

'Well, I think it was there. A couple of weeks ago . . . I think. Everyone was talking about it, but I can't remember.' Her sweet little voice was apologetic. 'Mummy will know.'

Henry said he was avoiding her mother at present. She looked interested and asked why.

'I haven't washed my neck. Emmeline, I know this sounds daft, but will you put your coat on, take the dogs and walk round to Gilbert's.'

'Now?'

'Yes. You haven't seen him since he was carried away in a fit from your party, have you?'

'No. I did phone, in the week, but no one answered. He might be away, he was going on holiday.'

'Holiday? He doesn't sound in any state to go anywhere. Are you sure?'

'Well, I thought that's what he said.' A faint note of anguish entered her voice. 'I told you, I was pretty plastered and he wasn't making a great deal of sense. He was rambling on about this holiday, I think we all passed it off as his general pottiness because he seemed to think he was going away with his mother. And I must say, Henry,' she sounded hurt, 'it's all very well asking me what was going on when you'd passed out in the turret room.'

'I hadn't. I went to sleep. He isn't away, he was there this morning, the back door was open.'

She didn't ask what he had been doing there. Instead she asked, 'Why are you concerned?'

Henry hesitated. It had become his nature to keep a guard on himself, but Emmeline was so much like a part of himself he was scarcely aware there were thoughts on his face she could read. The turns of her mind were subtle, not a great deal surprised her, she seemed to know by instinct when to question him, when to leave him to himself. He said, 'I feel uneasy, but I'm not sure why, yet. Go round to Gilbert's and knock on the door. If he answers say you were just passing with the dogs and called to see if he's all right. Don't go in. Promise. On no account go in. Say your mother's waiting at the end of the drive, anything. She won't be, but I will. I don't want him to know that, though.' He thought of Rosa concerning herself with Gilbert, talking to him in the turret room. Of Rosa drowned. 'Just see if he's there. If you can get a clue if anyone else is. If no one answers, see if there are any lights on, a car round the side. Anything.'

'Ah. The mysterious lady friend. Do you want me to look through the letter box and see if they're having it off in the hall?'

He took her face in his hand, held it for a moment. 'Emmeline, this is serious.'

'Yes. So I see. God, you're beautiful when you're angry.'

He sat back with a reluctant half laugh, realizing how intense he had been. She did not often tease him, when she did she was enchanting — the genderless Emmeline unexpectedly replaced by a mischievous, provocative woman, and he was susceptible to such women. He caught the shine of her dreaming eyes as she looked at him sideways, through her lashes.

'Cut it out,' he said. She would be flirting with him next, or he would with her, and it was all too unthinkable.

He waited for her at the end of the driveway of The Laurels. It was not possible to see the front door from there, and he could not be seen. Once he strained, listening, thinking he heard something. Just as he decided she had been gone too long the dogs ran towards him, pale woolly blurs in the fading light, and she followed. He took her arm in his and they walked away.

She said, 'No answer. Their curtains are thick, like ours, they don't let any light out. I *did* look through the letter box.'

'No scene of unbridled lust?'

'Nothing so interesting. I don't know, though. Interesting? Gilbert? I bet he never has.'

If Henry had ever asked himself the same question about Emmeline he would have come up with the same answer. For the first time, fleetingly, it occurred to him he could be wrong.

'Go on.'

'There was a faint light from under a door onto the hall, I couldn't tell which one, though. Garage all locked up. Mildred's car will be there, I don't suppose it's been out since she died. I went round the side.'

'Emmeline, I told you — '

'Listen, I was awfully clever. I called out, you wait there, Mummy, I'll just see if he's in the kitchen.'

So that was the sound he had heard.

'Well, maybe I wasn't so clever. I think a light snapped off as I went round, in this half light it's hard to tell. The kitchen door was locked. But I had that feeling — you know — someone's standing there, waiting for you to go away.'

'Yes.'

Gilbert sat on the stairs, wiping his tears. He'd had his hands smacked, Mummy had to be very angry to do that. But she had always liked Emmeline, she always let nice children come in and play. He said so, whining.

'Of course. And Emmeline can come back when you're feeling better,' Veronica said, gently now. She had replaced the curtain he'd pulled back from the landing window.

'Promise,' he muttered. He was never sure now when he was well, or when he had a headache, or a fever, not unless Veronica told him.

'Mummy wants us to be quiet, doesn't she? So she can come and see us. And she never let you run downstairs and open the door in your dressing gown, did she?'

Why was he in his dressing gown? He'd been having his afternoon nap. Was it afternoon? With the short, dark days and the curtains so often pulled together, time was something he could no longer be sure of. Not that it mattered, there was always a place he could go where nothing mattered, where he was safe, and happy.

'Back to your room,' Veronica said briskly. 'Tea's ready, I'll bring it up.'

The fire burned brightly and the light was soft on the blue painted furniture of his old nursery room. His toys were in a muddle, but Veronica never told him to put them away: she helped create the muddle, sitting on the floor, joining in games. Or she told stories, or read to him. She wasn't always Veronica, sometimes she was a fragment of someone's memory, a whispering creature with no name, who enchanted and terrorized him with her wickedness, who came and went by stealth.

He never slept in the nursery at night. It was next to the door of the back staircase, therefore dangerous. Night times he spent in his grownup room and if terror disturbed the darkness, Veronica kept it from him.

At Ferdinand's Henry bought a bottle of wine and went to sit at a table while Emmeline talked to some friends. It was quiet, there would be few customers on such a freezing night.

Emmeline materialized out of the cave-like darkness and slid into the booth opposite him. He said, 'Of all the bars in all the world and you have to choose this one.'

'Aah. *Casablanca.* You're better looking than Humphrey Bogart, though.'

'I'm glad.' They smoked cigarettes and drank wine, waiting for the meal they'd ordered. 'Emmeline, Grandmother Dash used to tell you all the old scandals, didn't she? Was there ever anything about the Hewitts?'

She hesitated, said, 'Well, yes,' then fell silent.

'Hey, what's this?' The past was Emmeline's passion, a word was enough to set her off, she could talk all evening in her wandering voice, her eyes on distant landscapes. But she sat, saying nothing, trying to look detached.

'Come on. Tell.' Henry said.

'What?' She made an unsuccessful attempt at innocence. Then, catching his gaze on her. 'Hell. It's a secret. I promised Grandmother I wouldn't tell anyone.'

'I'm not anyone.'

'No,' she sighed. He waited. He wasn't going to let go, and she knew it. 'Not even Mummy knows all of it. Well, I don't suppose anyone does now, even if they did then. Just talk, suspicion, and it's past, there's no one left from that time. Except Gilbert, and he never . . . Henry, you look as if you're about to give me a thick ear.'

'Any minute.'

'All right.'

She was silent, ordering her thoughts. A look of tenderness crossed her face, a silent apology to the shadow of her Grandmother. They must have talked over the same incidents many times — the old lady whose damaged speech patterns no one else could understand and Emmeline, rapt, encouraging. It was all there in her memory, a coherent narrative, evolved through long hours of slow and painful listening, prompting and interpreting.

'It begins when Gilbert's father married Mildred; they lived at The Laurels, with his parents. My Grandmother was best friends with Grandma Hewitt, so they shared confidences — the kind of things that wouldn't be said, or admitted — to outsiders. Gilbert's father had something of a reputation, in those days you only had to pinch a girl's bottom to get one. Waitresses, shop girls. People of his own sort turned a blind eye, including Mildred. She was probably too refined to give him any fun, anyway. Middle class ladies didn't have fun then, they had duty. Mildred must have done hers but it didn't result in Gilbert for years. Well, Mr Hewitt went too far, he fell in love with a local girl. Wildly unsuitable, wrong class, *and* she had a child. It was a great crime to be an unmarried mother then, in the late 1930's. But he quite lost his head, wrote her letters — that's how Mildred found out. Called her his little lily, and it seems she was a pale, drooping creature, ready to be pushed around by anyone. Sad, isn't it, these echoes of a lost passion. Unlikely, too, if you'd seen Gilbert's father.'

'I did,' Henry said, glimpsing in the detritus of memory a colourless, fussy man, occasionally pompous. Even at the time something must have registered, although only now could Henry define it: a man worn down to the marrow of himself. By what? His excesses with shop girls? Mildred's genteel tyranny, more like.

'Yes . . . Yes, of course you did.' Concerned with events that preceded her birth, Emmeline had to relocate herself: the principals in the story overlapped Henry's lifetime. 'The saga continues. It would even have happened, some of it, while you were with us. But you wouldn't have known, it was all hushed up, a few whispers here and there, nothing more.'

The waitress arrived with their meal but Emmeline could talk and eat at the same time. She was wearing a tortoiseshell hairslide that could have belonged to her mother when she was a girl, and no doubt had. She was so engrossed in what she was saying she didn't notice the slide fall into her paella and would have eaten it if Henry hadn't fished it out for her. She did not notice that, either.

'He must have been mad to think he could keep up the affair, everyone here knew everyone else, and especially they knew the Hewitts. And this, it seems, had all the signs of being more serious than his other furtive fumblings. Anyway, Mildred found out. The Laurels was in a ferment. Something had to be done before it all became common gossip. So the family settled things their own way. They took the young woman into the house. As a servant.'

Henry stopped eating, drank some wine. Emmeline had deliberately given him pause for thought. 'Not,' he said at last, 'as Gilbert's father's bit of extra on the premises.'

'Certainly not.'

'As his punishment.'

'Can you think of anything more calculated to turn the knife in the wound?'

'Who did think of it? Mildred?'

'Maybe. Maybe the older Hewitts. They could call it charity, there could even, genuinely, have been an element of that. Things must have been difficult for her, no social security in those days. Obligation? A Hewitt had taken advantage of an unfortunate creature, family honour was satisfied by seeing her situation didn't get worse. Gilbert's father would never dare to get up to anything under his own roof, and, anyway, what a passion crusher, that atmosphere of moral disapproval and his secret love nothing but a menial behind the scenes.'

'They really kept her behind the scenes?'

'Very much. After all, it was her place, and she was more of a shrinking violet than anything else, the kind who makes a mess of her life simply by doing nothing. Her official designation was housekeeper. She didn't exactly have to blacklead grates and unblock drains — although she might have occasionally and probably would have let herself be taken on on those terms anyway. But then, she did have a roof for herself and her child, she was well fed, in a respectable occupation. In the social structure of the time an arrangement like that worked without any trouble.'

'Of course it did.' Those big houses, the uncompromising demarcation of territory, the regulation of domestic routine. And what would she have in the outside world but hardship and slights? The Hewitts, for all their repellent altruism, were not cruel, she would never have been insulted, she would simply have been ignored — apart from her function. And that was, really, Henry reflected, a truly sublime form of insult.

He said something of the sort. Emmeline pushed her glass forward for more wine and murmured, 'Mmm. To us, now.' She did not need to qualify this: she had no notion of snobbery herself, but she could tune her mind to the distinctions and privileges of class that were outside her experience, that existed like shadows on the edge of Henry's.

'So she stayed?'

'She stayed. And not long after she'd been installed, Gilbert came along. Grandmother said it was sheer rage that stimulated Mildred into conceiving, she could have been right. Mildred had desperately longed for a child. He was her fulfilment.'

'And another weapon of her high-minded revenge.'

'Henry,' she said, sounding lost for a moment. 'How cruel. How true. Gilbert, pampered and coddled from the minute he was born. And the other child never allowed beyond the back stairs. Do you believe this — it was years before Gilbert even *knew* another child lived in the house.'

'I'd believe owt of that great girl's blouse.' When he wanted, Henry could speak in the authentic tones of the broad north.

Emmeline choked and recovered. 'Do the one about the ferrets in the privy.'

'Later. I want to hear what happened.'

'Time went by. The elder Hewitts were failing. Grandpa Hewitt had some kind of heart condition. Grandma became senile. She had her lucid moments, and they coped, but it put the household under a strain. She slept separately from Grandpa, they used to lock her in her room at night, to stop her wandering about. But one night she got out and fell downstairs and died on the way to hospital. No one said anything openly about her being locked in her room, it was Grandpa Hewitt who talked to my Grandmother afterwards. He was dreadfully cut up about the whole thing. It wasn't just that someone had forgotten to lock her door, or let her out by mistake. It was a wild business no one ever really sorted out — or maybe they did, but that really was kept in the family. Gilbert, hysterical on the landing. Not in his pyjamas but dressed, most oddly, in girl's clothes. They belonged to the housekeeper's child.'

Emmeline paused to finish the last of her paella. 'That was super. Can I have some chocolate gateau?'

'Have the whole sweet trolley. Where was the housekeeper's child?'

'In bed. Fast asleep. She shared her mother's room — and *she* was asleep, heard nothing of the commotion until she was woken up. But the child? Mmmm . . . She had some of Gilbert's clothes by her bed. She could have just flung them off and got in or she could, as she claimed, have taken them off hours before. What did come out was that she'd been sneaking off in the night to Gilbert's room. They'd play with his toys, tell stories, dress up — the normal sort of mischief children get up to. Only when there was this accident, and the great scene, Gilbert was screaming that *she'd* let Grandma out, guided her to the stairs and pushed her. *She* was screaming he'd done it, because he'd been boasting he'd murder his grannie after she'd caught them together one night and said she'd tell.'

Henry sat staring at her. After a while he said quietly. 'Wow.'

The waitress interrupted them, coming to take their order for pudding. When she had gone, Emmeline said, 'You see what a tangle it was. The only person who knew what had really happened — Grandma — was dead. Two frantic children, accusing each other. The housekeeper, kept firmly in the background for so long, suddenly in the midst of the family. Not that any of that came out, I believe, even in the hysteria of the moment. But when the shock had passed they had to do something. They kept the public facade intact, well, why not?'

'Yes . . . a feeble old lady falls downstairs. It happens often enough.'

'Of course. And whatever else happened was no one's business but their own. The idea that little Gilbert had been contaminated by association with a servant's child was appalling to Mildred. In spite of her regulations and her discipline and her power, that child had got the better of her. She could never feel safe again with her and her mother in the house, they had to go. She never for one moment believed that Gilbert was responsible, that was unthinkable, and she was strong enough to use Grandma's death to her own advantage.'

'She used it as a threat to hold over the other woman. Keep your mouth shut or I'll say it was your child.'

'Yes.'

'But had she — the housekeeper — really never known what was going on? You said her daughter slept in her room.'

'Who can tell? She said not, but my Grandmother always had her doubts — and so, I daresay, had Mildred. It would have been a marvellous way for her to get her own back on them all for pushing her around: she need do nothing, just let the child sneak off in the night, then deny all knowledge of it. Of course, nobody could know it would end as it did. Grandma Hewitt had said before that there was trouble brewing, the mother had no control over the child. They all seemed to despise her as thoroughly ineffectual, although she must have had something about her to enslave Gilbert's father. And, before that, get herself a child by another man.'

'That hardly takes initiative. A few minutes up against the park railings is enough.'

'Yes, I suppose so. She must have been a very passive creature, allowing herself to be paid off and packed off. Where, no one knows, certainly a long way from Avenridge. And it was wartime by then, people were always coming and going. She had no friends or relatives, no one to ask about her — no one ever had, that was how the arrangement managed to work as long as it did.'

'So she just disappeared. For good. But the family must have talked it all over, among themselves.' He hesitated. If the truth was something they could not accept, they would not want to discover it.

'I suppose so. But Grandpa Hewitt didn't live long after that, and Gilbert's mother and father never spoke to my grandmother about it, they didn't even know that she knew. I suppose they thought, with it all safely over, no one did.'

'Gilbert did.'

Emmeline shook her head. 'He was dreadfully ill shortly afterwards. Meningitis. He nearly died. Everyone said it was Mildred's sheer willpower that pulled him through. Whatever else, she was always a devoted mother. He was a wreck, though, and his memory was impaired, he had to learn to read and write all over again, it put him years behind everyone else. They were lucky it wasn't worse, though, it can be.'

'I see.' He retired into his thoughts and they finished their meal in silence. Afterwards, they had coffee and a cigarette and Emmeline said softly, plaintively, 'Henry, I've sung for my supper.'

He smiled. 'I know. You're a splendid chap, young Dash, there's no one I'd rather have with me in a tight corner.'

'Oh, God,' she said, fed up. 'You mean you're not going to tell me.'

'Not yet. Later.'

'Promises,' she sighed.

He took her hand and lightly kissed the palm. When he released her she drew back, closed her hand, and said nothing more.

It was snowing when they went back, lightening their hearts like children, the world transformed into a whirling, white silence. Emmeline was tired and went to bed. Restless, Henry took the dogs out.

His walk took him round by The Laurels. He turned into the alley beside the drive and walked along in the shelter of the high garden wall until he came to the door of the side entrance. It was shut, and he stood for a while, memories forming and fragmenting. There was something he searched for, not knowing what it was.

He made a small sound of exasperation. The dogs, standing beside him, looked up. 'What I could do with, chaps,' he said to them softly, 'is a little madelaine. Come on. Home.'

He slept for only a little while, then woke, breaking free of some untraceable urgency, his mind working remorselessly, down blind alleys. He tried all the sleep inducements he knew, none of them worked. He lay staring into the dark, then put on the beside lamp and reached for his cigarettes. Emmeline had thoughtfully placed her cassette player on his beside table; he switched it on to play very softly. Telemann. Concerto in E. Sublime. But when the last notes died away he was still wide awake.

He got up, put on his dressing gown and slippers and went down to the kitchen to make tea. The dogs, who had gone back to their baskets after greeting him, got out again and stood stock still, gazing towards the door. Emmeline came in, barefoot, in her bedlam nightshirt. She stood beside him, without speaking, while he made tea for them both, then she said quietly, 'Can't you tell me? Don't you trust me?'

'Of course I do. Yes.' But it was cold in the kitchen, in the dead hours of the night, and she had begun to shiver. They went into the sitting room; Henry switched on one table lamp. The air was just as chill but they could keep warm by sitting close together on the big settee, cushions round them. The dogs had gone with them, finding it all very interesting, and climbed up, too.

They gathered together in a heap, with some adjustment so they could drink their tea without spilling it; when they were settled Henry began to talk.

He told Emmeline about Arnold Peabody and his visits to the medium; Rosa's friendship with him; his suicide and Rosa's return to Avenridge. He made no speculations but spoke only of what he knew. When he told her that Rosa had called herself Meena, Emmeline looked resigned but said nothing. Then, he said, Mildred Hewitt had died her strange death, Gilbert had become involved with a woman no one seemed to know. Rosa had spoken to him in the turret room about Gilbert visiting the same medium. Rosa had been drowned. He spoke of his visit to Mrs Blunt, to Rosa's flat, his brief excursion to Inkerman Road. Again, he made no speculations.

When he had finished, she said, 'There are oddities, aren't there? And they're sinister. Mildred's death. Rosa's death. The rest is the kind of general crises and tragedies and commonplaces of people's lives and needn't have any significance. But . . . that note in Rosa's file . . .' She thought for a moment. 'It wouldn't have entered Rosa's head that that note came from anyone except you. It wouldn't occur to her to look up your number — even if she was sensible enough to do that it really wouldn't matter because she knew the exchange was in your area. It could have been your office, anywhere, somewhere you expected to be that night, at that time in order to speak to her. She couldn't possibly know it was a phone box. She spoke to someone she had confidence in, enough confidence to arrange a meeting with. She'd scarcely spoken to you, so she didn't really know your voice on the phone, people often sound different. And then, it needn't even have been you, it could have been someone you trusted, with a message for her.'

'Yes, that's how I worked it out. It doesn't get me far.'

'Gilbert's very vulnerable. You think he might be in danger?'

'Of some kind. But I don't know. I might just be having a fit of the vapours, and I don't want to make a silly ass of myself.'

'You only have Rosa's word for it that Gilbert consulted the medium.'

'I know. But why would she say it if it wasn't true?'

'Scarcely anything Rosa said was true. You had to pick your way through the lies — like walking through a minefield.'

'Mmm. You knew her, I didn't. But I'd say I knew enough about her to get the impression she lied to get herself out of trouble, to make herself important, to gain something. None of those things applies here. I think she was telling me the truth. Let's assume she was. It still doesn't mean that the medium Gilbert saw was the one in Inkerman Road.'

'No, there must be others. But the odds are for it, aren't they? What Rosa said about observing her — and Rosa's watching post from her flat. Do you think that's why she ·chose it?'

'I doubt it. She chose somewhere near — and it was one of

those happy chances she took advantage of.'

Emmeline said, 'And it would have to be during the day, wouldn't it? She couldn't see a thing at night, there's no lighting round the back there.'

'I was thinking about that when I was walking along there. Listen. I park my car on the waste ground, close to the entrance of the alley; the light from the street lamps along the pavement of Inkerman Road doesn't reach there, so I might as well be invisible. I get out. A few paces along the alley, the first door I come to is number 37. I go in, cross the yard.'

Emmeline frowned, picturing it. 'Still more or less invisible — from any distance.'

'Yes. Those houses are set high. Three or four steps up to the back door. When that opens, the light from inside picks me out. Like a spotlight.'

'Of course.'

He made an exasperated sound. 'Who could she have seen, though, going in? Not Gilbert, I'm damn sure.'

'Not at the back door, no. Front doors only for Gilbert, shown in and announced if possible. That's it, he's such a snob, the idea of mixing himself up in anything seedy . . . Still, he is in a precarious state of mind. Could you go and ask her? This Mrs Mountain?'

'Mountmain,' Henry corrected automatically.

'Have you *seen* her?'

'No. Have you?'

'I was in Inkerman Road once with Mummy, one of her second hand clothes sales for some charity, and this woman went surging past. So people talked. She's held in great awe there.'

'It's surprising how those people often are. Not least by themselves. I doubt that she'd tell me if Gilbert had been to see her, and I can't lean on her officially. I think it's the wrong moment, too. No, I don't think. It's what my instincts tell me.'

Emmeline didn't question the working of instinct, she lived too close to her own. For a while there was silence in the shadowy room, then she said. 'Listen, let's stop beating about the bush. If Rosa discovered something she shouldn't, someone could have shoved her in the canal to shut her up. Dotty, fantasizing Rosa wasn't much of a threat, but if she was going to go round approaching people like you, who *might* believe her, then she was. So you want to stay in the background, because you don't know who that someone is, and what else you might accidentally — nudge.' She gave a shudder, a long, deep tremor that startled the dogs, who had abandoned themselves to attitudes of sublime comfort.

'You're cold,' Henry said. 'I'm not gallant enough to give you my dressing gown — haven't you got one? Keep warm against me.' He put his arm round her and held her close. Even in the absorption of his thoughts he was surprised how tense she was; he expected her, so small and weightless, to lie against him easily. 'You're like a bunch of splinters. Relax. There's nothing for you to be afraid of so long as you stay out of this. There's probably nothing anyway, but steer clear of mediums or Gilbert's mystery woman at The Laurels and anyone else who might occur to you; just in case.' He thought of her hang gliding, of the near lethal motorbike she'd once owned, of the time she'd tobogganed down the Cricket Club roof on a tray, testing some theory that broke her collar bone. But these were physical risks she took on her own account: Olivia had always been able to terrify her with creepy stories.

'Now, promise, young Dash.' He gathered her and the dogs together in a hug, to warm her, and as a general gesture of reassurance. Her yes was slightly breathless. 'Sorry, did I hurt you? There are too many of us on here. Fourteen of you will have to go.'

She gave a muffled laugh. 'Tony Curtis. *Some Like it Hot.*'

'I thought it was Jack Lemmon. Dammit, how can I find out

what's going on at The Laurels. I need to talk to someone, without being obvious.'

'Desperately casually.'

'Mmm. Who and how? It's like chipping bits off granite with Mrs Blunt, and I don't think she knows much, anyway.'

'Wilfred. Gilbert's cousin.' When Henry protested he didn't know him, Emmeline said neither did she. 'But he's always in the Conservative Club, it's the watering hole for half the men in Avenridge, he's bound to be there tomorrow lunchtime. I can get someone to take you for a drink.' She brooded for a while. 'I know. Jazz Wood, lives over the road. You know him.'

'Do I? Oh, yes, vaguely.'

'He's a bank manager now, they don't come any more discreet. You could tell him why you want him to take you — no, I don't mean tell him, I mean say you have a reason for wanting to talk to Wilfred and he'll leave you a clear field. He won't ask why. Then . . . then when you're in the club, you can scrape acquaintance with Wilfred, spill his beer over him or something.'

'Emmeline, you see too many films,' he murmured. 'But it's worth a try.'

THIRTEEN

Henry got up early and breakfasted alone. The house was full of snow light, beckoning to him. Only children and irredeemable romantics responded to that pulse-quickening promise of the world made new. 'I'll never grow up,' he whispered to the dogs. Bright-eyed, they watched him pull on his boots. Neither would they.

Out in the sparkling, blanketed hush of Sunday morning he went down to the river and on to the path, but this time climbed all the way to the Ridge. It was a risky business in such weather, the path was slippery and in the clearings snow concealed tree roots and hollows. There were one or two early dog-walkers about and children playing, as children would, anywhere in snow.

Eventually he came to the fringe of trees on the sharp incline below the Ridge. There, tracks led up from the main path through the stripped and shivering larches; the climb was awkward, he slid back several times, losing firm ground beneath the drifts of unmarked snow. The dogs thought it was a game and scampered round him, giving little yelps. He made it to the top, dusted himself free of powdery snow, walked the short way to where the road switchbacked, and stood on the lip of the Ridge.

The landscape had the soaring quality of wild, unpeopled places, rolling and rising away into the distance; below him the rock face cut down, sheer, a giddying drop to the river. This was where Mildred Hewitt had fallen to her death that night when she had no reason to be there.

Unless it was to meet someone.

He turned away and looked down the road, picturing it in the dark: hazardous and deserted, the trees crowding in, a place of concealment. What had brought Mildred Hewitt up here? Something to be kept from prying eyes, eavesdroppers. But there were other places, assignations could be discreet without being uncomfortable. She was an arrogant woman, accustomed to putting her own wishes first. She was elderly, too, and no elderly woman he knew would choose to drive up a difficult road, at night, in the beginnings of a snowstorm.

He grew cold, standing there, whistled for the dogs and began to make his way back by the road. On his left the wooded ground rose and dipped to helter-skelter paths that led to the outskirts of Avenridge. He kept to the road that followed the descending Ridge; after a while the houses began. High garden walls where scarlet berries of firethorn glowed and the flowers of winter jasmine shone like yellow stars; behind these walls, set far apart and deep in their snowbound gardens, stood the big grey stone houses. Nobody would see or hear anything from within such fastnesses, whoever chose that rendezvous could be sure of that. And he couldn't believe the choice had been Mildred Hewitt's.

He tramped on, his boots gripping the crunched snow. Houses occurred more frequently, street lamps appeared; the wild region, softening, transforming, became the elegant, wide-verged roads of the residential area. He knew the way too well to register his surroundings with more than the edge of his mind, his thoughts remained stubbornly centred.

So if Mildred Hewitt had not chosen the Ridge, then

urgency had taken her up there, secretly, at night; urgency that overwhelmed not only personal convenience but all sense of danger. And whoever had lured her up there knew that.

As Emmeline had promised, James Wood was discreet. He asked no questions, conveyed Henry to the Conservative Club, and once there said dryly, 'Well, you can't miss him.' Wilfred's loud, equable voice, his rumbles of laughter, filled the Gentlemen Only bar. He had responded to the weather by wearing violent plaids and flamboyantly decorated boots.

'He looks like a lumberjack,' Henry murmured, wondering about a man who dressed as if he was ready to fell a forest in an outfit that would have disintegrated in a shower of rain. But it was the idea of the clothes, of himself in them, that mattered to Wilfred; his naively show-off air disarmed, no one would tell him he looked ridiculous. Every club, Henry reflected, had its Wilfred: reliably good humoured, interested in everyone, up to all the gossip and well ahead with the latest dirty story. There was no point of resemblance between Wilfred and Gilbert.

After a while Wilfred left the bar to make progress through the lounge, chatting here and there. In the snooker room he stood, pint in hand, watching a game. Henry drifted after him and, coming to rest beside him as if by chance, also stood watching.

'The red over the middle pocket would have given him a better position.'

Wilfred nodded. 'Maybe, but it would have been a hell of a shot, too much for John.'

'Bit of a check-side on the blue will put him back where he wants to be,' Henry said, feeling Wilfred's measuring, sideways gaze; from such relentless good fellowship he had expected something less guarded. 'There, he's only got one more red and the colours are on their spots as well.'

'I've not seen you here before, have I?'

'No, I'm just visiting. James Wood signed me in.'

'Ah, Jazz, our friendly bank manager,' Wilfred said. He knew everyone. 'I'm Wilfred Hewitt,' He thrust out a large, thick hand.

'Henry Beaumont. Hewitt . . . Are you related to Gilbert?' Henry injected a suggestion of grievance into the question.

'Know him, do you?'

'Not very well. Is he all right now, after last week?'

Wilfred looked ponderously puzzled. 'Last week?'

'Weren't you at — ' Deliberately, Henry got in the way of one of the snooker players lining up on the blue who said, 'Do you mind, old man?' Henry apologized, adding a silent apology for ruining his shot. 'We seem to be rather in the way here,' he said to Wilfred.

'Let's sit down a bit,' Wilfred suggested.

They went into the lounge and took a seat on one of the long leather settles. Wilfred looked over his pint at Henry, he had the easy air of a man always ready to give and receive information. 'Last week?'

'Weren't you at the party at Dash's Hotel? Saturday.'

'Oh, that. No. I heard about it.' Wilfred did not specify what he had heard. 'Good party, was it?'

'I'd say yes if I could remember. Gilbert was a bit — well, under the weather. It wasn't drink with him, though, he seemed to be — well, hysterical. Someone had to take him home. Is he all right now?'

'As right as he'll ever be, I suppose. He's never managed to pull himself together after his mother's death.'

'Oh, yes . . .'

'I was with her, that night. Well, not when it happened, but before . . .' Wilfred's account was fluent, it was evident he had given it many times, he would have been much in demand since the event.

Henry made the fidgeting motions of the unappreciative listener; before Wilfred had finished he said, 'Well, I'm sorry for Gilbert and all that.' He did not even try to sound sincere. 'And I know you're his cousin, but quite frankly, he gets up my nose.'

'He has that effect on some people,' Wilfred said, unoffended.

'I don't care about other people, I just wish he'd stop bothering Emmeline Dash.'

Wilfred raised his eyebrows, his voice was friendly. 'Little Emmeline.'

'You know her?'

'Not to speak to. By sight. Looks like a little lad.'

'The thing is — I'm interested in Emmeline, and I think I'm getting somewhere.' Henry sensed resistance behind the attentiveness; if Wilfred knew anything about him he was not giving any of it away. Like all gossips, he was relentlessly nosey, he could know of Henry's connection with the Dash's and think it strange if it went unmentioned. Henry leaned forward confidentially. 'I've known the family for years, of course, and I stay there, but it's tricky, I have to watch my step. I'm not a free agent.'

'Ah,' Wilfred nodded. Hunting males understood each other.

'But your bloody cousin keeps putting his oar in, keeps ringing her up.'

Wilfred was bemused. 'Does he?'

'Yes. Keeps trying to see her. Who does he think he is?'

The momentary hardening of Wilfred's face suggested he might have an answer, but he shrugged, making an attempt to explain Gilbert. There was no pretence it was anything except half-hearted. 'It's just that he's getting on everyone's nerves at the moment. Lonely. Mildred was never short of friends but as far as I know Gilbert hasn't got one. It's not really his fault'

'He *fancies* her,' Henry interrupted, peeved that Wilfred had missed the point.

Wilfred's expression dissolved. He gave a bellow of laughter, muted it. 'Bloody hell, man, you can't take Gilbert seriously. He doesn't know what it's for.'

'You've only got to look at him to realize that. But he doesn't think so. And Emmeline's a nice girl, soft-hearted, I don't want him getting round her, cutting me out.'

'You're a lucky sod to be in with a chance. My wife never lets me off the leash long enough to get a sniff at anything.'

'You have to train them right,' Henry said, with the appropriate touch of obnoxious conceit.

Wilfred stared gloomily into his beer. 'Tell me how.'

'The thing is, if he doesn't pack it in I'm going to go round and push his face in. You can warn him if you like, that's up to you, I don't care. But . . .' He looked round furtively. Emmeline would forgive his fantasy, if he ever got round to telling her, she would never forgive him hamming up his performance; but with Wilfred subtlety was a waste of time, it took a pile-driver to get through to him. 'You won't go talking to anyone else about this, will you? I told you, I've got to watch my step.'

'Oh, sure, mum's the word, old man,' Wilfred said. He would tell everyone, whether he believed it himself or not. His gaze went beyond Henry's shoulder, towards the entrance. He made the beginning of a movement to get up, but the movement came to nothing; he subsided, nodded a greeting.

Damn, Henry thought.

'Well, hello,' Linda said breathily.

Henry stood up to be introduced, regretted he could not offer to buy her a drink. 'No, members only at the bar,'

Wilfred said. 'Another?' Henry refused, he had most of his first pint left. Wilfred drained his tankard with the long swallow of the dedicated drinker and went off to the bar.

Linda remained standing, slowly taking off her elaborately fur-trimmed coat. Her voluptuous body bounced free of it and came to rest beside Henry, in the place where Wilfred had been sitting. She wore a straining jersey, low cut enough to give her pneumonia outdoors on such a day. She gave a little wriggle that set her splendid breasts in motion (God, if I fall into those, they'll be hours finding me, Henry thought) and said, 'I've not seen you around before.'

'No, just visiting.'

'I have to come for Wilfred, otherwise he'd be all day in here. Anyone would think he hadn't got a good home to go to.' She chattered on, the conscientious wife, the devoted mother, and Henry let her talk. He wasn't sure he'd got the measure of Wilfred; there was no doubt about Linda. Her eyes lingered on him, she was assessing his response, entirely in terms of what was necessary to her vanity. She was accustomed to being admired, lusted after, and no small measure of her satisfaction was that this should occur behind Wilfred's back. Henry had met too many women like her, the air of sexual generosity was a fraud, the connivances and deceptions of clandestine conquest were her thrill, she had nothing left over from them to give anyone.

'We were talking about your cousin Gilbert,' he said, when there was a pause for him to fill.

She looked faintly put out. She had not expected to be ousted as the subject of conversation, certainly not by Gilbert. She shook back her glossy black curls. 'Oh, him, who'd want to talk about him.' But she did. She told Henry how well she and Wilfred had behaved after Mildred's death, how they had put themselves to endless trouble, for no thanks, how Wilfred was carrying the entire burden of the firm, to no benefit to himself. Wilfred came back with his pint and Linda's fussy cocktail. He took a chair at the table opposite them.

'He should have been made a partner, that was what Mildred fully intended, if she hadn't popped off like that,' Linda said, as if Wilfred was invisible.

'Lin,' he protested. 'She never actually —'

'You know she would have done, she'd never let you work the way you do without some recognition. You're never home,' Linda said firmly, determined not to forego the nobility of suffering or the oblique hint to Henry that she had time to fill. 'And the way Gilbert's behaved to poor Mrs Blunt. I did my level best to patch things up.' While she gave her version of how she had gone about this, Wilfred shifted uncomfortably; he knew the truth, he could not know that Henry did as well.

'You never honestly liked her,' he said heavily when she had finished.

'I still can't see injustice and not try to do something about it. That's typical of you, Wilfred, avoid unpleasantness at all costs. He'd run a mile rather than face up to things. At least I get in there and sort things out,' she said to Henry, inviting admiration at the cost of humiliating her husband. 'Not that I'm like that as a rule, I'm really quite shy, and very easy-going.'

'Oh, but women have the ability to grasp the realities of a situation,' Henry said, with equal amounts of insincerity and charm.

It was the kind of meaningless remark that appealed to her. She gave him her devastating smile and Wilfred a deliberate look, brandishing the compliment. 'That's exactly what I say to Will, but he can't see it. You can't, Wilfred, what about that business with Gilbert and me?' She wore the secret look of her own uniqueness; her suddenly confidential tone hinted at amazing improprieties.

Henry took up the cue, suitable wolfish. 'Gilbert — and you?'

'He was upset,' Wilfred found it necessary to explain to Henry. 'It was just after Mildred's death. He wasn't — '

'That's what I said. Once she'd gone, there was nothing to stop him. He's probably some sort of deviant.'

He'd have to be, Henry thought, with an anguished mental vision. Would this preening, prattling woman ever shut up or stop admiring herself long enough for anyone to make it with her? Certainly not Gilbert, he wouldn't have the staying power.

Linda said, 'Wilfred, get me some crisps.'

Wilfred got up without a word. As soon as he'd moved away, Henry said quietly, 'What's so surprising about Gilbert fancying you? I'd say his responses were in all the right places.'

She gave him a smouldering look. Deliberately, he gave her one back. Her full lips parted, the red tip of her tongue came out delicately, wetting them. 'I'm not going to tell you what he did. I don't know you well enough.'

'That can be arranged.'

'What can you mean? I've got a husband.'

'I've got a wife and four kids,' Henry said, recklessly inventing them and casting them aside.

She looked pleased. He was someone else's property, which would count with her, and there were enough obstacles to ensure an affair of endless delays and evasions.

Henry took out his diary and pen. 'If I had a phone number, for instance . . .' He could easily get it out of the directory, but she expected to establish some small part of herself in his private life, even if it was only a number in his diary. And he was doing it to gain time, uncertain how long he could keep going. The bar was crowded, Wilfred had to wait. He had left the table with a mixture of relief and resignation, he knew exactly how his wife would behave the minute he had gone.

Henry could understand the resignation; the relief gave him momentary pause.

She murmured her number, adding the times when Wilfred and the children would not be in. She leaned closer. Henry felt as if a sofa was falling on him.

'I think your husband's about to come back,' he said, gazing into her beautiful eyes. The bar was behind her, Wilfred was still there.

'What if he is,' she breathed, sultry.

'You'd better edge off a bit. He's a big fellow. I couldn't take him on the state I'm in now.'

The tip of her tongue came out again, caressing her lips. 'And what sort of state is that?'

'My knees have gone like tripe,' Henry said, with complete honesty.

She sat back, satisfied, smiling her secret smile.

'You know, you could be right about Gilbert running amok,' Henry said. 'I've heard some funny stories.'

She understood the conventions: they must be talking of a neutral subject when her husband rejoined them. 'Well, he's got himself this girlfriend. And he's never had one in his life. Wilfred says he doesn't know what it's for, but I wouldn't understand what he meant by that.' She made her eyes round and innocent.

'I'll explain it to you sometime.' Almost light-headed with relief, Henry saw Wilfred approaching. 'What's she like?'

'I've no idea. I wouldn't demean myself finding out. He's welcome to her. If he gets trapped by some gold digger it's his own fault. Wilfred knows her, he would, he's got his nose in everyone's affairs.'

Wilfred sat down, putting the packet of crisps on the table before Linda. She ignored them. 'Knows who?'

'That female Gilbert picked up in Ferdinand's. I want nothing to do with it.' Linda held her head high to establish the necessary distance between herself and any creature of mercenary motivation.

'I don't know her. I just saw them there. And I didn't say he picked her up there. He might have done for all I know, the lighting's so bad even Gilbert could have passed for human.'

Henry, meanwhile, with clumsy concealment, was stowing away his diary and pen. Wilfred's eye caught the movement, turned away. He knew what it was all about. His manner to Henry did not change; but it had begun to change from the moment Linda entered the club. His heartiness had evaporated, there was now a dead look in his eyes; he sat over his pint, the droop of his face reflecting all the endurance of one permanently in the wrong, the surrender made, long ago, to whatever Linda's idea of their marriage should be. But was this surrender complete? Henry sensed a core of resistance. Perhaps Wilfred cultivated his own deceptions; if he did, Linda would be too intent on hers to guess they even existed.

Linda said that, anyway, people were talking about Gilbert; she managed to imply this was Wilfred's fault. He said were they, and what about?

Henry intervened. 'People make things up even when there's nothing to say. I heard — ' He took a sip of his pint, aware their attention had fastened on him. Avid gossips themselves, they could not bear to be uninformed. 'I heard Gilbert's been going to seances. You know, trying to get in touch with his mother.'

There was a pause while they digested this. Then Wilfred gave a half laugh, disbelieving. 'Not him. He'd have said.'

Linda protested at once. 'Not to you, he wouldn't. He won't tell you anything.'

Henry had no doubt she was right. No one could have sat through that Sunday lunch at the Dash's without being aware of where this couple stood in Gilbert's opinion. Did they know, he wondered, the sort of things Gilbert said about them?

Linda looked pleased with herself, scoring off Wilfred. 'I'm not so sure there mightn't be something in it. After all, we talked about it.'

'You and Gilbert?' Wilfred said, puzzled.

'No. Us. When we were at The Laurels.'

'Did we?'

'Yes. I told you Mavis Elliott had been to this medium and she'd told her all sorts of things and she was talking about it when the girls came round to Gilbert's that morning, and you asked me what she'd said and who it was because it would be a good idea to send Gilbert there. Of course, it might have been one of your jokes.' She made them sound like offal.

'I don't remember any of this. And we couldn't have talked about it at The Laurels anyway, because we left the day after you had all those girls round there.' Wilfred had a dogged air.

Linda looked momentarily put out. It had already become apparent her memory was selective, and operated without much regard for accuracy. 'Well, it must have been before.'

'How could it have been if Mavis Elliot hadn't been round? How could — '

'Your trouble,' Linda changed her line of attack, 'is the only spirits you believe in come out of a bottle. There's a lot you're not capable of understanding.' She turned to Henry, dismissing Wilfred, and began to talk about the paranormal. It was plain she engaged herself eagerly on its fringes, knowing several people who knew people who'd had strange experiences.

Wilfred, refusing to be dismissed, returned to the point at dispute. Linda began to argue with him; the you-said-no-I-said exchange settling down to the slogging pace of long practice. Henry became a spectator, the sheer tedium of it, the pointlessness and repetition, numbed his mind; it was obvious they were going to keep it up for hours. As soon as he had an opportunity he made an excuse and left them, they scarcely noticed. Their voices followed him as he walked away.

Beyond the deep sash windows of the dining room the garden lay in soft folds of snow. There was not enough to cause Henry to change his plans about driving home later in the day, he would manage the journey without trouble unless there was another fall. It was not unusual for Avenridge to be cut off for several days, like a town under siege. The excitement of those times had survived from his childhood.

'May we share?' Mrs Dash enquired.

He had not realized he was smiling. 'Oh, I was just thinking. During the war, when we were snowed in, congratulating ourselves we were safe from invasion. Then someone set up an alarm about parachutists — *they* could get in. So we organized parachute patrols after school.'

'You did, you mean,' Mrs Dash said, with an answering smile. 'You could be an awfully bossy little boy.'

He had caught it from her, the imperious sense that he knew best and, being young enough for naked emotion, had experienced the glorious self-righteousness of acting for everyone else's good. He must have been insufferable. But where Mr Dash had taught him the beginnings of love, Mrs Dash had activated his sense of responsibility.

'I was defending the women and children.'

'Of course you were. Quite right, too.' She asked him how he had enjoyed the Conservative Club.

'Fine.' They talked of it for a while. Once, his eyes met Emmeline's; they had agreed to keep the purpose of his visit from Mrs Dash, to prevent her worrying. And really, Henry thought, what could he say except that the suspicions breeding in him might be nothing more than the reflexes of that submerged, interfering small boy.

To change the subject he said that after lunch he would be going round to Mrs Blunt's, to take her some papers from Rosa's flat. Both Mrs Dash and Emmeline were too polite to intrude into Mrs Blunt's private affairs by asking him what they were. But Mrs Dash was interested in Rosa's flat and did allow herself to speculate how Rosa could have afforded to live there.

After lunch, Mrs Dash read The Times in the sitting room while Henry and Emmeline tidied up the kitchen and made coffee. Henry gave Emmeline an account of his inconclusive talk with Wilfred and Linda; she was briefly amazed by his description of Linda. 'Crumbs, you were lucky to escape with your vitals.' But she spoke inattentively, her mind elsewhere; then she grew silent, busying herself. Eventually she became quite still, standing over the stacked dishwasher, gazing through the window at the garden in its soft dazzle of snow. 'The last time it snowed I had flu. There wasn't much. When I was better it had all gone. I hated to miss it. It was the day Mildred Hewitt died.'

Henry turned to her. He had caught a note of furtive apology: a child being told to go and play somewhere else and not bother the grownups.

She went on. 'I don't know if it matters. If I should have said. It was something I didn't quite remember. At the back of my mind.'

The back of Emmeline's mind must resemble a mammoth jumble sale, Henry thought. 'The snow reminded you?'

'Ye-es. And Mrs Blunt. Everything. It was Saturday. I'd been coming down with flu, trying to fight it off. Not a cold — that awful flu with pains in your head, and nausea. I went to the workshop early in the morning but I felt so dreadful I had to pack up. I had an errand on the way home, it took me past the end of Kitchener Terrace. Mildred Hewitt was walking down it, her car was parked on the Bingo car park at the end, you know.'

Henry thought about this. Emmeline in her senses was unreliable enough; with a high temperature and a splitting headache she could have got everything wrong. But he didn't want to discourage her. 'Are you sure it was that day?'

'It must have been. I never saw her again. I was feeling so ill I just, well, registered her, and then forgot. When I got home Mummy put me to bed and called Dr Mack. I was scarcely conscious for about four days, then when I'd really come round it was all over — the inquest, everything. Does it matter? Would the police have wanted to know?'

'Well, they'd certainly have tried to find out where she'd been that day, who she'd talked to. Kitchener Terrace. It must have been Mrs Blunt, mustn't it?'

'Yes. I am a fool. Could it be important?'

He shook his head, because she looked anxious. 'I shouldn't think so. Anyway, if it was, Mrs Blunt would have told them, wouldn't she?'

FOURTEEN

Gilbert drank a good deal with his Sunday lunch. He did not eat much, the meat was tough and the potatoes shrivelled; Veronica did not cook as well as Mummy. He would teach her, he said generously, it was only right that she should aspire to Mummy's high standards.

'I should think that's beyond me,' Veronica said in mild surprise. 'Mummy was unique.'

Gilbert's eyes misted with sudden tears. 'She was perfect.'

'She was unique, anyway.'

'But then, so are you,' Gilbert said, touched by a faraway warning that he might have put himself under her displeasure. It was possible for him to do this without knowing why, the causes of her displeasure were obscure, his anxiety centred on the rebound effect to himself. 'I've never known anyone like you,' he added placatingly.

Her gaze dwelt on him for some time before she answered, 'Haven't you, Gilbert?'

The telephone rang, stopped; after an interval it rang and stopped again. It often did that. Their only acknowledgement of it was the sly smile that passed between them, the wicked delight of children safe in their hiding place.

As soon as lunch was finished Veronica gave him his

tranquillizers and said he must lie down. He went obediently up to the nursery room; she came up after a while, sat with him until he was about to doze off, then went quietly away.

Muffled sounds of her movements slipped from his consciousness. There was always something to do about the house. Too much? He dared not say this, scarcely admitted it to himself, but in the sleep-opened gaps in his mind it was there . . . The film of dust on polished surfaces, flowers left to wilt, washbasins crusted. He would have to say something. Mummy had been so good at Saying Something. But Veronica was not a servant to whom one could.

In a far, time-deepened corner of his mind, something stirred; but he had neither the wish nor the will to disturb it and the forgiveness of sleep stole it away like a thief.

When he woke it was still light, the lustreless winter light of late afternoon. Veronica had drawn back the curtains and was standing before the window, looking down into the garden. She spoke his name without turning and he laboured, fuddled, resisting its sharpness. His tea tray was on the bedside table, the fire had burned low. He wanted to wash his face and brush his hair smooth, sit in his dressing gown playing with his toy farm, but she said, 'Come here,' and he obeyed, stumbling, pushing on his spectacles.

'Look . . .'

Down below, a line of footprints wound along the path of the kitchen garden to the open door in the wall.

For some moments they stood in silence. When they spoke it was in whispers. 'Somebody's been here. Gilbert, did you hear anything?'

'No, no . . .'

'Neither did I. Not a thing. Who would . . . Why?'

His mind was blank. 'I don't know.'

'The back door. Those footsteps lead to the back door.' She went away.

He had nothing to do but stand helpless, gazing at the garden, the backs of other gardens, the far prospect, everything transformed under the burden of snow. There was mist about. And beyond that, on the rim of the low sky, the distant message of darkness.

He began to shiver. He wanted to go and warm himself at the fire but dared not move without the safety of her presence, so he waited for her to return and tell him what to do.

When she came back she ignored his obvious trembling, did not tell him to put on his dressing gown; instead, she took her place beside him, the cold striking cruelly at them from the window pane. She said, 'The back door was open. Wide open. But I'd locked it. You didn't unlock it, did you?'

He shook his head. How could she imagine he would do such a thing. He could not bring himself to go near that mean little lobby and its sharp-angled, narrow staircase. In all his life it had been a place he did not go; now, with its shabbiness and its taunts it had forced itself on him like a living thing. In order to be at peace anywhere in the house he had to pretend it did not exist.

She knew that. He looked for the comfort of the knowledge in her face, waited for words of reassurance, but she continued to stare down and his gaze was dragged back to follow hers.

The alley that ran beside the house was obscured by the high garden wall. The gate, pushed inwards, had left a scraped section of dark earth, a segment like some mysteriously magical sign from which the line of indentations led, passing beneath his window, then lost to sight.

His nerves strained in the silence, growing unendurably taut. His breathing began to make swallowed whimpering sounds. She said, 'Go and sit down,' and he crept away, his limbs scarcely under control, and sat huddled on the side of the bed, not looking at her but terrifyingly aware of her stillness, her attention, as she continued to stare out of the window.

'Drink your tea,' she commanded without turning, and he obeyed, slopping it all over the tray, his lips juddering on the rim of the cup. When he had finished he wanted to replace the cup, wipe the dribbles of tea from his chin, but his limbs would no longer answer to his will and he sat limply, the cup dangling from his hand.

It was some time before she spoke, then it was in a low voice. 'You see, you see, it doesn't matter how we lock up, fasten the windows, draw the curtains, it can still find its way in.'

This was something he did not wish to hear, his mind grappled feebly against it — the open doors, the voices in the night. If they occurred, Veronica kept them from him, there was no need to speak of them.

She began to whisper, a dry rustling of words in which no single word was distinguishable. Intermittently the rustling died, then resumed. She was not speaking to him, she was communing with something beyond the window, something that held her, forced her response.

He did not know how long he sat there, incapable of movement, while this extraordinary and terrifying communion continued. The light changed, the room grew shadowy, only the shape of her figure remained distinct, urgent, solid against the darkening glass.

At last, she made a little choking sound, like a sob, and said, 'I see, I see,' wearily, with resignation. Then, more clearly, 'Gilbert, I can't protect you any more. I need help. Mummy is going to help. But she can't come here, it's too dangerous. We must go to her. Mummy wants us to go to her, Gilbert.'

Snowbound, Kitchener Terrace had more than ever the improbable look of a television advertisement.

Mrs Blunt did not ask Henry in, in spite of the bitter cold.

He stood hunched into his anorak while he told her of his visit to Rosa's flat. 'There were some bills, money she owed. I thought you'd want them.' He kept them in his pocket. There was resistance on her face: if the papers had been in his hand she would have taken them from him and sent him away. But even Mrs Blunt could not be so peremptory, and he had an air of expecting to be asked in. Their glances held for an instant.

She yielded, stepped back. 'You'd best come through.'

The fire burned furiously in the black-leaded grate. The room was stifling and depressing. She did not ask him to take off his coat but he unfastened it, as a precaution against heat exhaustion. He took out the bills, laid them on the chenille table cloth and, with them, the keys to Rosa's flat.

'I want to talk to you for a few moments, Mrs Blunt.'

Once again her eyes met his, then she turned away, took out the bottle of port and two glasses. He took a chair beside the table, as far as possible from the beating heat of the fire. When she had settled herself, sipped her drink and taken up her knitting (what *was* it? he wondered again), she spoke. 'I've said all there is to say about Rosa.'

'It's not about her. Something else. It won't take long.'

'Good,' she said ungraciously. A woman with nothing to do, who wanted to be bothered with no one.

'On the morning she died, a Saturday, Mildred Hewitt came here to see you.'

Mrs Blunt took this in, gave a slight shake of her head. 'Did she?'

'You know she did.'

'How would I know? I wasn't here. Went to my sister's in Ashbourne for the day. Caught the early bus. Mrs Hewitt never came here, not hardly ever.'

She was not questioning the fact — if he said it, it was true — but her ignorance was genuine, he had no doubt of that. Maddeningly, it took him into yet another dead end 'Do you have any idea what she might have wanted?'

'Must have been something to do with the house,' Mrs Blunt said, finality in her voice, disposing of it. Mildred Hewitt was no longer anything to do with her.

But she had been. Henry pondered, studying the wooden face. 'Mrs Dash tells me you've left the Hewitts.' He paused, but she did nothing to help him out. Her dismissal had been humiliating, she would not go into the circumstances of it. He chose his words carefully, to convey that he understood this and no more need be said on the matter. 'Well, you were just about due for retirement. You've been with them so long, since . . . since I first came here, during the war. Before that. A long time. There are some questions about that time you might be able to answer.'

'I've had enough of questions,' she said roughly. Meaning Rosa, and the slow gears of officialdom that had caught her up, moved her irresistibly to their own purpose and left her with a locked flat, shamefully searched, the pity and gossip of the neighbours. It was not Mrs Blunt's ingrained bloody-mindedness that was obstructing Henry, it was her very human desire to retrieve her self respect.

'I don't mean anything official, I mean just a quiet chat between the two of us. Whatever you tell me will help me and won't go beyond this room.' He put down his glass and, as if absently, touched the bills on the table. Mrs Blunt's eyes were on them. He had done her a favour, she was not unmindful of the necessity of some small return. Mildred Hewitt had left her a sum of money; Rosa would already have tried to get it out of her. She would have her way now. Mrs Blunt, who had never owed a penny in her life, would not let those bills remain unpaid. Rosa had stolen from the Hewitts just as she had stolen from the Dashes and Mrs Blunt knew that Henry was aware of this; she was in his debt for his discretion, too.

'Can't think what I know of any use to you.'

'We'll see. You remember when old Mrs Hewitt had her

accident — when she fell downstairs. You were with them then.'

There was a submerged but unmistakable tremor of surprise; this was the last thing she had expected. 'Aye, I was.'

'There was a housekeeper employed at the same time. She had a child.'

Mrs Blunt hesitated, Henry could almost see her mind plodding back through the years. 'Oh, her.'

'Did you know her well?'

'Keep myself to myself.' Sooner or later Mrs Blunt was sure to say that. What she did not need to say was that whatever she thought of the housekeeper, it wasn't much.

'She kept pretty much to herself, too, didn't she? There was some talk, though, about her and Gilbert's father.'

Mrs Blunt frowned. 'Never heard nothing about that.'

The faint emphasis on that gave her away. She was measuring Henry carefully, not quite meeting his eyes. She owed something to the Hewitts, if deeper secrets had come her way, there would be the last ditch of her defence. But this was trivia; if Henry knew, then any number of people would, and she was human enough to be intrigued.

'He had a reputation for it, hadn't he?'

She nodded. 'In his younger days. But I never heard *that*. Steer clear of her, he would, she'd trouble enough.'

'Trouble?'

'Called herself Mrs. She was no Mrs. Gave out that child's father had been killed in the war. Daresay he was. He might have been someone's husband, but he'd never been hers.'

That could have been common gossip at the time for anyone who cared to concern themselves. Not many would. Mrs Blunt, and women like her, had the herd instinct for picking up such scent. And Mrs Blunt applied the moral standard of the day. She was not, he suspected, without charity towards the unfortunate, her judgements might be severe, but they would tend to be unspecific. Not here, though, this was a simple matter of personal dislike.

'I see, the child was illegitimate. It was decent of the Hewitts to overlook that, not everyone would have then.'

'That they wouldn't.'

'Still, this housekeeper, whatever her past, she must have behaved herself, or they'd never have kept her on.'

'Knew which side her bread was buttered, that one. About all she did know. Wishy-washy creature. Lazy.'

Gently, Henry drew her on. There was not much to hear, but Mrs Blunt sipped her port, took her time and innocent pleasure in revisiting an old animosity. Not that they ever 'had words', came close to it over *that child*, but Mrs Mildred Hewitt kept a sharp eye on what was going on, always stepped in. *Mrs Blunt, I don't want you to be troubled with such matters, you have quite enough to do as it is. I shall see to it.* The unspoken accord between Mildred Hewitt and Mrs Blunt was based on their assessment of the housekeeper: a woman incapable of controlling her appetites could scarcely be expected to control the result of them. 'Fiend — that child was. Had a devil in her. Heading for the reformatory and no mistake, I heard Mrs Hewitt say that to her more than once. Then butter wouldn't melt in her mouth. Talk her way out of anything, little liar. Well, you should know that.'

Henry's jaw almost dropped. 'Me?'

Mrs Blunt made a curious guttural sound that might have been a laugh. 'That party of young Gilbert's. Got yourself into hot water there, my lad.'

'Well, I remember the party. I took Olivia — that one, you mean. In fact, it was the only one I ever went to, I was out of Gilbert's age group. I got a telling off for going into the vegetable garden. Out of bounds. I didn't do anything more dreadful than that, did I?'

'Bad enough. The Hewitts were particular about things like

that. And the two of you there. Bound to cause trouble.'

'Two of us?' Henry refilled Mrs Blunt's glass.

'You youngsters don't have memories these days.' Mrs Blunt eyed him with malicious satisfaction, 'D'you not recall?'

'No . . .' Henry began. But on the point of asking what they had been doing, he thought, oh Christ, and with lightning panic felt a shifting of the log-jam of guilt behind which lay his early sexual curiosity in all its indiscriminate experimentation: willing girls, himself, older boys who could be relied on to know a thing or two.

He swallowed the panic before it did more than cause him a momentary inward gasp. Mrs Blunt would scarcely have relished the memory if it had been anything disgusting.

'Some toy of Gilbert's. She said you'd stole it. Broke it.'

Relief swept over him. Then a fragment, no more, moved in his memory: a child's voice calling from behind a hedge, and he had assumed (or was his adult mind supplying this?) that she was part of the game of hide and seek. But the child, when he followed her voice and found her, was unknown to him: what she looked like, what had passed between them, was blanked out. As he tried to force the images nothing came but the understanding of hindsight: excluded, she had found some vantage point to watch the party, envying the other children, hating them, too, perhaps. Who could blame her?

'. . . one of his special toys . . .'

What toy? He knew he couldn't have taken it, only because he hated Gilbert too much to want anything of his.

'. . . but she was like that. Getting others into trouble.'

'Did she do it with Gilbert?'

'Oh no.' Mrs Blunt was decisive. 'He wasn't allowed to have nothing to do with her.'

'But it must have been difficult, living in the same house.'

Mrs Blunt, after a moment's concentration, rejected whatever implications this might contain by simply shaking her head and muttering, 'Big house like that.'

And the invisible lines of demarcation firmly drawn, everyone knew what they were, where they were entitled to be. No one trespassed. Except by stealth.

He studied Mrs Blunt. She would have accepted the situation unthinkingly, but she must have had some contact with the housekeeper, they must have spoken about something. 'Didn't she — give you orders?'

'Took my orders from Mrs Hewitt, not from the likes of her.'

'Do you remember her name?'

Mrs Blunt looked grudging. Remembering the name of someone so thoroughly disliked conferred undeserved status. But she was honest. 'Funny sort of name. Yeend. That child was called Vera, or some such.'

Yeend was an unusual name, it meant nothing to him. 'They left, didn't they, just after old Mrs Hewitt had her accident.'

If there was any connection Mrs Blunt did not make it. She nodded, knitted, no more than the normal uncommunicativeness on her face.

'That must have been quite a shock, all that happening in the middle of the night. Did they ever talk about it?'

'Only as folks do.'

She knew no more, he was sure of that when he tried to draw her out. She had been told what it was necessary for her to know, then they had closed ranks. Of course. An increase of stubbornness in her attitude warned him off: these were family matters, not scandalous or discreditable, just intimate, no business of his. One more word and she would slam down her defences altogether.

'You don't know what became of them after they left?'

She shook her head.

'You never saw them again?'

'Saw them?'

'I mean, did they ever come back to Avenridge?'

'How would I know?'

He persisted. 'If they did, would you recognize them?'

But this was asking Mrs Blunt to make an act of imagination so much beyond her she could merely look blank. He let it go. It was time to leave. There was just one more thing.

'Did you ever talk to Rosa about any of this? What we've been talking about?'

'Why should I? I'd no call to.'

'No . . . But just sitting here, chatting by the fire. Was she interested?'

'Interested in herself, not things long gone.'

'But she liked to read the newspaper, have a gossip about what was in it.'

Mrs Blunt's brow creased in the effort to convey a complicated thought. 'That's different. About what's going on now.'

'Yes. Did she say anything to you about having anything to do with a clairvoyant. A medium.'

The terms confused Mrs Blunt. She gazed at him, uncomprehending. He explained.

She said, 'She'd be daft enough for that sort of thing. Said nothing to me. Or if she did, I'd not listen to her nonsense.' She paused and then added, as if to herself, 'I'd not listen.'

He stood up to go, aware of sadness lying under the surface of the hot little room. There would be so many evenings now, and no Rosa to listen to. 'Don't get up, I'll see myself out,' he said. 'Thank you for talking to me.'

As he closed the door behind him he thought of another woman alone in another ugly room. Edith Blore. But where Edith Blore's inner being was nourished on anger, for Mrs Blunt there was stoicism and a guarded grief. It was just the few points of comparison that had brought that other visit to mind. The surroundings. The sudden, bewildering death of a relative. Rosa.

It was as if there was a pause at the far edge of his attention; something lingering. He looked back at the small house he had just left, what he needed to know had never been there, it was in that pause, waiting. It had been there all the time.

Edith Blore saying *Madame Lily*. Lily.

And when he got into his car and sat smoking a cigarette, there was something else . . . The incident of Gilbert's party remained maddeningly inexact, he would probably now never recover its details, but his memory had been stimulated, and he found in it the impress of a central moment: everything around it was blurred, but the moment itself came back to him in all its startling clarity.

A girl, perhaps a little younger than himself, fair-haired, skinny, dressed in the sort of clothes he was not used to seeing children wearing in Avenridge. She was not a product of the dancing classes and riding lessons any more than he was. They had come from the same place, if not geographically, then elementally, there was in her the child he had so recently been: shabby, bold, knowing. His ferocity had been smoothed away, she still wore hers, not defiantly, as he had, but with a terrifying, adult containment.

Their confrontation had been brief. He, taken by surprise; she, never surprised, with the coiled, dangerous air of an animal who knows when to strike. There had been some words, a broken toy put into his hands . . . then footsteps, a voice . . . and she had flashed a look of loathing at the world that contained him in his party suit and Mildred Hewitt and her commands. There had been more words, then she had been dismissed and disappeared into the house with the swiftness of long practice, closing the back door soundlessly.

He had time now, in the tremor of this brief reprise, to wonder what on earth her effect on Gilbert had been.

FIFTEEN

Emmeline must have heard his car, she came out on to the porch as he drew up. He went up the steps to meet her: the dogs sensed tension in the air and ranged about, looking furtive. 'Emmeline, I ought to see Gilbert. Will you come with me?'

'Of course.' She turned to go in for her coat. He followed, shooing the dogs in. While Emmeline was pulling on sheepskin and boots, he glanced at the phone book. Yeend was an unusual name. There were none in Avenridge, but then, there wouldn't be. Lily had married and become Mountmain. Vera? His suspicions were taking direction, if it was the right one then Vera wouldn't advertise her presence; Gilbert didn't recognize her, but the name was unusual enough to strike a chord in his memory.

Emmeline was beside him. 'Is it something Mrs Blunt told you?'

'She had nothing to tell me I didn't already know. I'd forgotten. I didn't make the connection. That medium is called Madame Lily.'

'Lily. Gilbert's father used to call his lady friend . . . It's her. The housekeeper.'

'I think so.'

They went out quietly, down the drive.

Emmeline said, 'If Gilbert went to see her he wouldn't know her. She's sort of bloated, some thyroid condition, I should think. And after he'd had meningitis his memory was impaired. By the time he recovered she'd gone, not that he would have seen much of her, anyway.'

'She isn't the only one he wouldn't know. That mystery woman of his. I think it's her daughter. Vera.'

Emmeline's step faltered. He had to slow his long stride to look down at her. Her face had the slow look of recollection. 'Veronica. That's what Gilbert called her. I'd quite forgotten.'

They walked on briskly again, in silence for a while. Henry knew what Emmeline was thinking. Of all those years when one child was despised, pushed out of sight, an inferior being. While on the other child the gifts, the treats, the cossettings were lavished. Nothing had equipped Gilbert to defend himself. Then, she had found her way to him in secret. Now, with the armoury of the adult, she had returned. And he was still defenceless.

There was nothing destructive in Emmeline, but she could understand the terms on which destruction could be applied, with hatred at its source. She said unwillingly, 'She's got a hell of a score to settle.'

'He can't know. And he should. It's only since she's been on the scene that the state of his mind's deteriorated. If she's pushing him halfway to hell, at least he should be on his guard. It might help.'

An occasional car passed, otherwise the tree-lined roads were deserted. It was not an evening to be out, there was a strange glimmer to the cold air and the enfolding silence of the weight of snow on rooftops, walls and bushes.

Emmeline said, 'And she'd know things — things that were precious to him in the past. She could get through to him . . . In a way she's always been there, hasn't she? In the background, behind the family, behind Gilbert. Like that thing of Coleridge's about someone on a lonesome road — "and having once turned round walks on, and turns no more his head, because he knows a frightful fiend doth close behind him tread".'

'Stop getting imaginative, Emmeline, leave that to me. Vera. Veronica. Lily. Madame Lily. I could be putting all this together and making an ass of myself. It's only my interfering nature that won't let me leave it alone.'

'It isn't,' she said, her small voice stubborn. 'It's your tracker's instinct. And experience. And imagination. And all those things that make you the guardian of those who can't protect themselves.'

'That's got to be a line from an old film, but I can't think which one. I have to talk to Gilbert — shout through the door if necessary. But I'd rather get in. If you're with me he might listen. He likes you.'

'Does he?' Emmeline said wonderingly. Gilbert had never been known to like anyone, except himself. 'Did Mrs Blunt remember the housekeeper's name?'

He told her. She repeated it, shook her head, asked him was that why he'd looked in the directory. He said yes. 'Just a thought. There wasn't one.'

'No. And she's Mountmain now. She'd have married after they moved away. Where did they go?'

'First of all? I don't know. But at some time, just before she moved back here, she was living in Manchester.' He told her about the address on the flyleaf of the book he had found in Rosa's flat. 'I've been thinking about that book. Rosa could have got it from poor little Arnold Peabody. Either he lent it to her, or she helped herself to it. There are enough women of Madame Lily's type in Manchester, God knows, but Arnold wouldn't have the initiative to seek anyone out. He'd have to have the idea presented to him, maybe his mother consulted

her when she lived over there, that'd be recommendation
enough for him.'

The Laurels stood ahead of them, where the road curved,
the two dark columns of its gateposts capped with snow.
Emmeline said, 'I wonder why she came back here?'

'Well, the area where she lived was flattened and
redeveloped, about five years ago, she'd have had to move,
anyway. Why not drift back to her origins? She seems to have
drifted, or been pushed, all her — ' He stopped speaking,
halted and looked down. They were at the drive of The
Laurels; the lamplight showed tyre tracks along it, cutting
through the snow, they did not look as if they had been there
long.

They spoke in lowered voices. Henry said, 'We'll do it the
sneaky way, round to the kitchen door in case it's unlocked.
You're a friend, you can just walk in. We can always say we
tried the front door and they didn't hear.'

'You're assuming she's there.'

'If she's not, we stand a chance.'

They walked silently between the dense, snow-sculptured
shrubs. At a turn of the drive the bulk of the house loomed into
sight, its windows blind and lightless. At the front steps
Emmeline put her hand on his arm, leaving him standing,
waiting, while she went up the steps and was swallowed in the
cavern of the porch. Returning, she said softly, 'I looked
through the letter box. No lights.'

They went round the side. The double garage was set back
from the frontage of the house, its doors stood open, it was
empty. 'Someone's out in Mildred's Rover,' Emmeline
whispered. 'Gilbert can't drive.'

'They could both be out. Damn. Come on, let's try.'

The side of the house was in darkness. Softly, Henry tried
the kitchen door, it was locked. He turned at once and made
his way quietly round the back. He had got his night sight and

the snow gave back its own soft illumination to the moon. 'There's another door,' he whispered to Emmeline.

'Is there?' She would have no reason to know of it, certainly never to use it. If she wondered how Henry knew she did not trouble him with questions. A cluster of fruit trees, a low hedge and a gate marked the boundary of the old vegetable garden. Without pausing, Henry stepped over the gate, leaving Emmeline, too small to do the same, to find the catch and let herself in. She did it swiftly, the only sound he heard behind him was the faint, squeaking crunch of the gathered snow as it was pushed forward by the lower edge of the gate.

At the corner of the house he halted. The back door stood open, pale light seeping from it. He saw the footmarks printed down the steps, along the path to the door in the garden wall — the door that opened to the alleyway.

He went up the steps and into the hallway at a run, no longer caring how much noise he made. He was too late, he knew it, they had gone, but he had to make sure. He shouted, 'Gilbert — ' as he went rapidly through the few rooms, switching lights on and off again; shadeless bulbs revealed it all without pity: threadbare carpets, cheap curtains, shoddy furniture.

Emmeline followed, her face bemused. She had known the Hewitts all her life, known the show and grace with which they lived. This place was like a guilty secret; uncovered, it betrayed their contempt for the people who had occupied it.

Henry took the angled stairs three at a time, went into the first room he came to. Embers still glowed in the small grate, the bed was rumpled, a dressing gown thrown across it. Toys, books, games, were scattered about. A child's room, where a child had recently been playing, absorbed, forgetful of the adult world.

Emmeline, catching up, made a little sound. Her gaze went round the room, taking it all in. She looked at Henry. They had no need to speak, her face held the painful awareness of it all: this is where he was loved and tended, this is where he was safe. And Henry shook his head, meaning: he only thought he was, he hasn't been safe since that other child crept up the stairs in the dark.

He said, 'They've only just gone. But we must make sure.'

They ran through the house, it did not take long. Downstairs again, in the lobby, Henry did not pause. Emmeline was running full tilt to keep up with him on the path through the vegetable garden to the door in the wall. He said, 'She's taken Gilbert to the Ridge.'

'*What* — '

'Where else — ' They were in the alleyway, halted momentarily, the cold clamped down around them. 'Go to the nearest phone — '

Automatically, Emmeline turned back towards the house; Henry grabbed her arm. 'No. Not back in there. She might come back, and she's dangerous. The phone box on the corner. Dial 999, ask for the police. Tell them to send a car to the Ridge, straight away, you have reason to believe a crime is about to be committed there.'

'Shall I say who I am?'

'God, no, we don't want your house surrounded by patrol cars, your mother would never forgive me. Go on — ' He sent her off, running down the alleyway while he took the opposite direction, sprinting to the river path at the back of the house.

He could see well enough, but it was hard going. He slipped, grabbed tree trunks to steady himself. Gilbert would not move nearly so fast. She would urge him on, oh yes, but those fumbling, ill co-ordinated limbs would slow them up — He tripped and went sprawling, picked himself up at a run. Would Gilbert know where he was going? To Mother — that was all that mattered. She would find a reason, she had wrung out his grief, he was helpless in her hands, he wouldn't look beyond to what she really was, all he cared was that she was the only person who concerned herself with him. Henry was working out how she had gone about it as he raced along; he lost his footing and pitched sideways, half buried in a bush, scrambled out, shaking off the snow. Even the weather had obliged her, it had been snowing the night of Mildred's death, too. *I'll get you, you bitch.*

The tree trunks thickened, paths threading through them in all directions. He skidded to a halt, panting, and began to move warily, peering through the columns of the trees. His boot kicked something. He bent down. A pair of spectacles. So the poor sod was half blind as well.

There was the faintest movement to his left. He went quickly, noiseless as a cat. In the gloom of bushes and trees a pale oval hovered: a face. He made for it.

Gilbert stood, his back to a tree, his teeth chattering. His eyes had a terrible intensity in his white face.

'Gilbert . . .' Henry said softly. 'It's me, Henry Beaumont. Here, put on your spectacles.'

Gilbert gaped at him without recognition — he was someone to talk to, that was all. 'I'm frightened. Veronica says I have to wait — '

'She isn't Veronica. She's Vera. Don't you remember Vera? When you were — '

Gilbert was wearing leather gloves, he was clumsy with his spectacles, dropped them. Henry bent to pick them up.

'Mummy's here. She's gone to get Mummy for me. I have to wait.'

'Gilbert, your mother isn't here, pull yourself together.' Henry wiped the wet lenses, pushed the spectacles on to Gilbert's face. There was the possibility that if he could see Henry he would know him.

But Gilbert babbled, in a high, faint voice broken by bewilderment, and the possibility fled. 'Mummy's going to tell me why she came here. Mummy's coming back to me. I have to be good, and wait. But I'm frightened by myself—'

'Come with me, I'll see you're all right.' It was no good being gentle, nothing except force would get through to Gilbert. Henry took his arm; Gilbert drew back, flailed feebly for a moment, then they both halted, shocked into stillness. A clear, sweet voice called through the night, 'Gilbert . . .'

Gilbert's mouth dropped open, he peered beyond Henry's shoulder. Henry kept hold of his arm, turned.

Above them, to their left, on the jutting lip of the Ridge, stood the figure of a woman. Moonlight outlined her clearly, distance and darkness obscured detail. She wore a fur coat, a full length skirt beneath it. She lifted her arm, the sleeve of her coat fell back, a moonbeam touched a glitter of diamonds at her wrist. 'Gilbert . . .'

Gilbert called 'Mummy . . .' in the pleading, uncertain voice of a child waking in the dark.

She had turned in his direction, the outstretched arm was a gesture to draw him on, up to her side. Henry, aware of this, was also aware of something else. She was looking toward Gilbert, to where she had left him to wait, but she was looking into the concealing backdrop of the trees — and could not know that he was no longer alone.

'Right, you bitch,' Henry muttered. He kept hold of Gilbert's wrist, pulling him along. It did not matter how much noise they made, they had cover and she would expect Gilbert to scrabble and thrash about. It did not matter what he called out, either, she would expect no sense from him.

He was making whimpering sounds, broken sentences, full of yearning, of terrified appeal. Henry ignored him, yanking him along as they scrambled up the steep banking to the road. He kept his eyes on the woman. She was too far away, her features indistinct: dressed in Mildred's fur coat she could have been Mildred, standing there. Then, as he made it to a higher level and more of the road was revealed, he saw the dark bulk of the Rover drawn up into the lay-by.

Gilbert cried, 'Mummy's car. Mummy's come in her car . . .' The scene was set, it made sense to him, as much as anything in his toppled world.

Henry said nothing. He was thinking. She didn't bring Gilbert along the path *and* drive the car up. And she would have been wearing ordinary clothes, not the fur coat and long skirt — even Gilbert would have wondered about that. She could have gone out earlier, driven them up there in the car and left it there; but he did not think so. An idea that had planted itself in his mind when he was running along the path began to take shape. He had time to examine it, fit it to the ragged edges of his imperfect understanding — then they broke the cover of the trees and were out in the moonlight. He tried to shake free of Gilbert, but now Gilbert clutched him, dragging at him on the final, snow-churned, acute rise. Suddenly, they were all in the open, the stark, white, waiting space.

The woman acted instantly, tore off the fur coat and threw it over the Ridge, at the same moment turning, running, cutting behind the car and crossing the road into the shelter of the wood on the opposite side.

Gilbert gave a great, sobbing cry and stumbled towards the void where the coat was floating down. Henry snatched him in time, hung on. If he let go Gilbert would lurch blindly to the edge of the Ridge and that woman's job would be done for her.

This distracted him. Tugging at Gilbert he had only a glimpse of the movement in the trees. But it was enough. Two figures. Two, running, swallowed into shadow. Yes, he had been right.

He dared not release Gilbert and was too hampered by him to give chase. He pulled him to the driver's side of the car and glanced through at the dash. No keys. He turned and set off at once, down the road. It was slippery on the sharp descent, but easier going. Gilbert twisted in his grip, looking back.

'Mummy was there . . .'

Henry swore briefly, but comprehensively, it relieved his feelings. 'Mummy wasn't there. That was Vera, Gilbert. Where's Vera gone? Where does she live?'

But Gilbert had begun to cry, hiccupping. Mummy was angry. So was Veronica. He'd been good, played nicely with his toys . . .

'Oh, Christ.' Knowing it was hopeless, Henry tried again. 'Where can we find Veronica?'

'Mummy talked to her, Mummy told her things, about when I was little.'

'Did Mummy talk to her at Madame Lily's? Is that where you met, at Madame Lily's?'

Gilbert jerked to a stop, stamped, yelled, 'Stupid woman. Stupid-fat-smelly old woman.'

'Who told you to go to her, Gilbert?'

But Gilbert was sagging, his body loose and angled like a discarded marionette. He began talking to himself, he wanted to go home, he was tired, Mummy would tuck him into bed.

Henry heard the sound of a car and the next moment lights dazzled ahead of him. Only lunatics would drive up this road in this weather, or people with something to attend to.

The two stolid constables gave him a hard look. He had his warrant card out before either of them could speak, then he was pushing Gilbert in the back seat and getting in after him. He spoke without urgency, but leaving no room for argument. 'Back to town. Now. There's a woman on the way there, she tried to shove him over the Ridge. She got away through the trees before I could stop her.'

There was a passing place cut out of the woodland, the driver began to turn the car. 'Where can we pick her up?'

'I don't know. And never will unless you get moving. Get your foot down, constable. I haven't got a description of her, either.'

The second constable sat twisted in his seat, studying Gilbert. 'Who's he?'

'Gilbert Hewitt.'

'Hewitt — It was his mother — not long ago — The Ridge. An accident.'

'Same sort that was about to happen to him. Same woman. She's done it once, he was next in line.'

The driver had got the car moving, skilfully, making good time along the hazardous road. His partner said, 'He looks as if he needs a doctor.'

'He isn't hurt. Just don't turn him loose. He's off his head, with any luck it's temporary.' But he doubted it. Gilbert had fallen silent, huddled into the corner of the back seat. His face was blank, tear-streaked, smooth as a child's. 'Gilbert, you remember when you were little? The girl who used to come to you in the night, play with your toys. Vera, that's what you called her then. Didn't you know it was Vera? That was how she knew all about you.'

'Mummy talked to Veronica,' Gilbert quavered. 'You've taken me away from Mummy.'

'No, Mummy never talked to her. She was Vera, and now she's Veronica. Where does Veronica live, Gilbert? Where does Veronica live?'

When Gilbert had stared stupidy, and in silence, at Henry, the driver asked, 'Veronica who?'

'God knows. It used to be Vera Yeend, but that's not what she calls herself now,' Henry said.

'Doesn't he know?'

'I doubt it. I don't think he knew anything about her, she covered her tracks too well. And he's been like a zombie lately. You can try him though. Who's in charge of the station?' There were street lamps around them now, they were on the outskirts of Avenridge, the going was easier. Henry calculated: the police station was on the far side of town, he could make better time on foot, to get where he needed.

'Sergeant Smith.'

'Good. I spoke to him yesterday about Rosa Dawson's death. As soon as you're back at the station, five minutes, I'll phone him. There's something I've got to see to.' The car slowed to take a corner, Henry had the door open.

'Wait a minute, sir, do you need any help?'

'No, I'll handle it at this stage, the last thing I need is a police car and uniformed men all over the place. I'll tell Sergeant Smith why. Five minutes. And keep hold of him, he's a material witness. If he ever gets his marbles back.'

As he shut the door the driver's partner was on the radio, 'Alpha Seven to control. We're on our way back with a passenger . . .'

Within seconds, Henry was in a small courtyard, then running down steep, curving steps, on his way to cut through side alleys to the terraced north side. He heard the patter of footsteps behind him, at first ignoring the sound then, because he was so obviously being followed, turning to look back.

Emmeline. He kept moving. She caught him up and was swept beside him, trotting. 'I was waiting. You had to come down that way. I saw you get out of the police car. Was that Gilbert?'

'Yes. He's in one piece, more or less.'

They were going swiftly through quiet streets. Snow began to fall, fine flakes in the lamplight.

Emmeline said, 'Vera?'

'What do you think? Got away. She's good at it.'

'Is that why we're going to Madame Lily's? Is that where she is?'

'No, she won't take that chance.'

'She won't go back to The Laurels, will she? No one knows

she's ever been there — except Gilbert. I've known that house all my life, Henry, but when we were in it tonight, I've never seen it like that, scruffy, uncared for. Not as if a woman had been there, looking after everything, but as if Gilbert had just been making shift for himself, getting more and more unbalanced then, just wandering off to the Ridge on his own.'

'That was what it was supposed to look like.'

'Of course. She's invisible. No one knows anything about her.'

'Someone does. She hasn't fixed all this up on her own. I'll tell you what I want you to do when we get to Madame Lily's. Are you listening?'

She expended just enough breath to say yes, then she saved it to keep up with him.

They stood at the door of number 37, waiting for an answer. Emmeline panted, gulped, steadying down. Her cheeks were flushed. Henry's face betrayed nothing. He looked up and down the road. Several houses along, a knot of youths scuffled on the pavement. Two ancient men, defying the weather, made their way carefully across the road to the pub. There was no one else. It'll be the back door, if anything, Henry thought.

A light snapped on behind coloured glass, the front door opened. 'Madame Lily? Good evening, I hope we're not late.'

Her bulk filled the doorway, but it was yielding. Henry's was solid, it had the pressure of determination, and years of experience had refined his technique of being polite and unstoppable. He was inside, Emmeline behind him, shutting the door firmly.

'Was it a reading?' Madame Lily retreated, looking dazed. She was blinking, half asleep, her wig askew. 'What's the time? Only on Sundays, I don't generally, I don't recall . . .'

'That's all right,' Henry said forgivingly. He glanced down

the hall, saw the open door of the back room and herded her towards it. Once there, he glanced round, nodded at Emmeline. 'If you'll excuse me, Madame Lily, I must make a phone call. Won't be a moment.' As he closed the door she was saying confusedly, 'Did you make a booking? Was it a booking for a reading — ' and Emmeline, sweetly inflexible, guided her towards the sofa, 'Why don't you sit down and make yourself comfortable. I'm sorry we woke you from your nap . . .'

The house was not large, he'd covered it in a matter of minutes. She must have heard his footsteps as he did it and he wondered how long it would take her to pull herself together, and get restive. From what he had seen of her she looked like a woman who had given up pulling herself together and Emmeline could cope, smoothing her down, talking about nothing.

In the hall he picked up the telephone. Sergeant Smith sounded as if he was hanging on to his patience with an effort. Henry talked rapidly, saying only what was necessary, combining tact, persuasion and authority; he got what he wanted, the Sergeant was accustomed to making decisions without delay. Henry put the phone down, deliberately leaving it off the rest.

In the close air of the back room the gas fire popped, the curtains were drawn across the window that overlooked the back yard. Surrounded by her jumble of furniture and ornaments, Madame Lily had subsided on to the sofa.

Henry saw he had been right. If she had ever in her life displayed restiveness then all memory of it was buried, unrecognizable now, in the sluggish body — along with Mr Hewitt's young, desired Lily. Because he knew her history, he saw what endured: the habit of passive survival that said as plainly as words she would do nothing until someone told her, know nothing if she could possibly avoid knowing.

He nodded to Emmeline and she went to stand beside the

window. It was doubtful if within the room he would hear the latch lift on the back gate, snow-deadened footsteps cross the yard. No one outside could see anything through those thick curtains, and voices would not carry. He had warned Emmeline to keep quiet and listen: he could only hope she did not become so engrossed in what was said she would miss any sound outside and not warn him in time.

He drew up a chair, sat down beside the sofa and gave his attention to Madame Lily. His manner was relaxed, inviting confidence. The willed blankness of her gaze slid about him; no question, no curiosity, disturbed her torpor. Here in her setting, in the clutter of her existence, he was absorbed: the dark, handsome stranger of the Tarot cards, so often predicted for others, had materialized for her. His physical presence was no more than an extension of the improbabilities by which she lived.

'Mrs Yeend,' he began pleasantly. She neither accepted nor rejected the name. 'No. It was Miss Yeend when you worked for the Hewitts. You married after you left them. They gave you a bit of money to tide you over. Still, that wouldn't last long and you had a child to look after.' Incapable of looking after anyone, least of all herself, Lily would fall into the hands of the first man who came along. Perhaps she had had some attractiveness then; if not, the money would make her attractive enough. 'Where does your daughter Vera live?'

'We lost touch,' she said at once, with evident relief to come in on cue and dispose of her part.

'What name does she use?'

'We lost touch,' she repeated, picking up a box of sugared jellies. 'He knocked me about. She left home. She'd be sixteen or so. He drank.' The whine was pronounced, a woman who had suffered much.

'Knocked her about, too?'

'Well, he drank.' This excused and explained everything,

none of the responsibility was hers.

'Worse than that? For Vera? He messed about with her?'

'She might have said, but girls say things.' And she would not listen; if it was true, what could she do? How Henry had come by his information was nothing to do with her; he was not shocked, not even surprised by any of it. His presence was powerful, and, insensibly, she was responding to it; his attitude managed to convey what she had always known: that her life was not a series of blunders but the remarkable workings of fate. 'She could have come back after he'd gone. He walked out of a pub under a bus. But she was looking out for herself, training to be a secretary, proper training, everything. She always looked out for herself, never mind me. We lost touch. Then I married Sid Mountmain. He's gone, too. It was his heart. Tragic. These things are meant.'

The faintest movement by the window made him glance at Emmeline. But it was only her reaction to this information: her eyes on Henry signalled amazement that this gross, ineffectual woman had gathered an illegitimate child and two husbands on her lethargic progress through life, to say nothing of the accumulation of emotional disorder. His gaze gave back to her the measure of her ignorance: Emmeline, you don't know how many people have this sort of tale to tell. It's nothing.

Emmeline looked shaken. Reality had obtruded into the cherished past of her black and white photographs; some truth behind the feuds and alliances and scandals was as squalid as this. She would rather not know.

'All alone I was. And my illness had come on. Thyroid. I have to take pills. Then I got my gift. Suffering, you see. I'd always been psychic, but suffering brought it out. It's a great comfort.'

Henry agreed gravely that it must be. 'And you had nothing else, they even started to pull down where you lived. Moss Side, wasn't it?'

'All demolition. I couldn't cope. Sid knew the people as rented this house, they'd been very good to me. Then they left and it came up for rent . . .' It was part of the pattern. She'd dumped herself on them, stayed. 'Well, there was nowhere else to go . . .'

'Vera didn't think much of you coming to live back here. She told you to keep quiet about the past. About her.'

The jowls sagged, there was no outrage, even in betrayal she was helpless. 'Ashamed. Too good for her own mother. After all I've done for her. None of it was my fault.'

'No. You mean when she got you thrown out of the Hewitts'. It wouldn't do to have that brought up again. She'd hated them so much she didn't care what she did — but you paid for it — threatened, sent away to fend for yourself. She still hates, but she's much more cunning now. You'll have to pay again, if you're not careful, you know that.'

A tremor moved the flabby, collapsed body; real fear glinted, like the eyes of an animal in the night. She had no resources, just reflexes. She looked across at Emmeline. 'Was it a reading, dear?'

Henry said, 'I'll give you a reading. If anyone ever asks, you're to say that the night Mildred Hewitt died Vera was here with you. She wasn't, she was up at the Ridge. If you provide her with an alibi, you'll be making yourself accessory to murder. She didn't tell you that.'

His manner had changed, calm and hard. Her stupidity broke against it as feebly as water spattering a rock. 'She never tells me things. I don't know anything.'

'And Wednesday evening. You're to say she was here, late. That was the night Rosa drowned. None of these things were to be your concern. They will be now it's all gone wrong. Like tonight. She'll blame you for it.'

He waited. The fat fingers scrabbled blindly for jellies in the box, her gaze wandered the room, seeking forgetfulness in the comfort of its familiarity.

He said softly, 'You're afraid of her, aren't you? She's a mad dog, your Vera, and she's running free. No one can save you from her, except me. She tried to kill Gilbert tonight.'

'Gilbert,' she repeated foolishly.

'You know who I mean. When he came here she told you what to say to him, then forget about it, leave everything else to her.' He was almost casual, easing the pressure, if her fear took hold of her she would collapse completely and be no use at all. He looked thoughtfully about the room. 'You'll be all right here. You can't take any more trouble, there's no reason why you should. If you're sensible.'

She had been waiting for a direction, adrift in her confusion. Her eyes fasted on him. 'She never tells me anything. I don't know anything about tonight.'

'I don't suppose you do. How long has she been back in Avenridge?'

'About two years. Her job . . . I don't know where it is. Like where she lives — said I didn't need to know. And I don't get about.'

'She came back here for a purpose. You were already here so she could use you. What did she say to you about that?'

'That everything had to be right. Well, she said it after. I've never seen her so angry. I daren't ask her what she meant. I was ill, and she was here, going through my things. I was that ill. Helpless. I could have died, not that she'd have cared. It was after that. I'd never been able to do anything with her, but it was worse, after she found out.' Her whining voice ran down. There was no self-preserving cunning in her, it was fear and sloth that made her scarcely intelligible. She pressed her fingers to her face, trying to think. When she removed them grains of sugar stuck to her wobbling cheeks. 'It's all mixed up, the beginning. I'd been so ill, nearly died,' she said pitifully.

Henry sat in silence, working out the muddle. He couldn't

say to himself that he'd known. The possibility had filtered into his mind the night before, at Ferdinand's, when Emmeline had told him the story. He had let his suspicion lead him on; but even the fact that Vera was Madame Lily's daughter still held the possibility too finely balanced against what could be proved, after so long. And what had puzzled him was why Vera had waited. She needed time, certainly, to work out her moves, set things up, play in her accomplice . . .

Now he knew why she had not acted before: she had been ignorant of the truth. Once she discovered it, the fatal spark had been struck from her hatred. He looked at Madame Lily. *Christ, you're lucky she didn't murder you with her bare hands.*

Madame Lily's eyes wandered away. Her body surged, as if his thought had touched it. 'I'd never have told her. I daren't. For what she'd do.'

'They knew. The Hewitts. That was why they took you in. To have you where they could keep an eye on you, give you a home. If you kept your mouth shut.'

She nodded.

'And you did. But — what? Two years ago? Vera found out. She found out that Gilbert's father was her father, too.'

Emmeline started, astonishment on her face, then enlightenment: of course. She gave a slight shake of her head at Henry and returned to listening at the window.

He said, 'What proof is there? His name's not on her birth certificate, or she'd have known all along.'

'Letters he wrote when he started courting me. I kept them. No one knew. He said always to keep them, in case.' Her brow creased. In case of what? She could never plan for the future: in this, as in everything else, she just did as she was told.

Long ago, his secret disclosed, Gilbert's father had no hope of standing up to his wife and his parents. His sins were small and sly, he could not live with disgrace, he settled for living with his punishment. Lily wouldn't make trouble, but she was a threat, at large, at the mercy of anyone who wanted to take advantage of her, and the Hewitts could not endure the thought of a by-blow openly paraded, under their eye they could make sure this would not happen.

And perhaps for Gilbert's father desire failed with discovery, there would be nothing left to fight for. What he had ever had of authority would be in shreds and would stay in shreds for the rest of his life — Mildred would see to that, it was her right, as the wronged wife. What he saved for his pride, what she never knew, was that he'd cheated her of a scrap of her vengeance: the letters that held proof of his paternity. It must have seemed to him that he'd paid dear for his pleasure; how could he know, poor fool, what the price of those letters would be?

'Who's got them?' Henry asked.

'She has. Took them. Said I wasn't to be trusted with them. Me, as kept them all these years, like he said. Tell the truth, I can't really remember what was in them. I was never one for reading.'

The irony, of which she was unaware, spread like small waves through the room, touching everything she had gathered about her to make her life secure. Speechless, Emmeline's gaze held Henry's, then she turned her head sharply, listening, and nodded to him.

He said to Madame Lily, 'Now. In a minute, you're going to answer the back door. No, it isn't Vera, don't be afraid. You know who it is. They met here, didn't they? Because it was the last place anyone would think of looking for them. You opened the door sometimes then, didn't you? Do it normally, but don't say anything, just point in here.'

For an instant the only sound was the agitation of Madame Lily's panting breath, then the door bell shrilled, harsh in the waiting emptiness.

'Come on, we're here, no one can hurt you.' Henry stood up as he spoke. Drawn by his authority, she heaved herself up; there was a tremor all about her, her eyes staring, but she did as he said. The bell rang again. She waddled out.

She had left the door wide open. Henry went to stand against the wall behind it, Emmeline stayed where she was. A waft of cold air from the unheated house invaded the stifling room.

There was the sound of a key turning, a bolt being drawn. No words, but a stir of movement, the door closing. Footsteps. Then the voice, breathless, and for once muted, but audible, 'Is she here?'

And Wilfred walked in.

SIXTEEN

Wilfred's impetus carried him to the centre of the room before he halted, staring at Emmeline. While his attention was on her, Madame Lily shuffled in, and Henry closed the door and leaned against it.

Wilfred turned round. The first instant of shock juddered through him, forcing his voice, 'What's this?'

Unmoving, Henry said quietly, 'Vera's thrown you to the wolves, Wilfred.'

Wilfred was breathing quickly, his heavy face flushed, his hair plastered to his head: he smelt rank. He had dressed himself for an evening indoors, for travel by car, his coat was smeared, torn across one sleeve, his trousers soaked almost to the knee. In his unyielding vanity, he had not even had the sense to wear decent shoes.

He took the full impact of Henry's hard, assessing gaze. One small ingredient of his desire to save himself was a sense of his destroyed showiness; he made an effort to draw himself together, smooth his hair, then he arranged his face into incomprehension. 'Who? I don't know who you're talking about.'

'Vera. Or do you call her Veronica?' Henry allowed himself a moment to look at Madame Lily, then back again at Wilfred. 'Her daughter.'

Wilfred burst out, 'What have you been saying, you stupid old — '

Madame Lily had submerged herself to a level where nothing could reach her. She made a fatigued progress to the sofa: she had exerted herself, she needed a rest, nothing else concerned her.

Wilfred's rage bounced off her and quivered back at him, he winced from it, recognizing how he had betrayed himself. He began talking quickly to Henry. 'All right, I've been having a bit on the side with her daughter, Vera. Meeting her here. You know how it is, my wife'd give me hell if she ever found out. I had to keep it quiet. If it's blown, I'll pull out, I've had my fun, I'm not wrecking my home life for it. I can't afford trouble.'

'You've got more trouble than you ever dreamed of when you started this. You were just what Vera was looking for — a vain, disappointed man with no prospects and a wife who'd been treating you like dirt for years. No wonder you were such a pushover. A secret affair, getting your own back on Linda, you could do it, Wilfred, you could do anything. Vera made you feel such a big man.'

The truth of this was written on Wilfred, in guilt and satisfaction. 'We all fall for it sometime or other,' he said, man to man.

'I suppose she told you how the Hewitts had treated her and her mother. You couldn't blame her for hating them. You hated them, too, you wanted what was theirs, but you'd never had the guts to do anything about it. Until Vera showed you how you could have the lot.'

'You're talking rubbish. I got nothing from Mildred, not a farthing, that's a fact.'

'You didn't expect anything. I suppose Vera told you it was an accident, up at the Ridge, and you told yourself you believed her. She was so clever, putting you in the clear. And it was easy, it worked. It gave you confidence. All you had to give her was information. You knew every arrangement of the Hewitt household, down to the last detail. You knew Gilbert hadn't made a will, if you moved fast enough you could get him into a state where he was incapable of making one. With him off his head, declared incompetent, the way was clear for you.'

Wilfred's face was turning the colour of clay. Overweight, out of condition, he could take neither the physical punishment nor the collapse of events: he began to barter. 'Look, I had an affair, I admit it, but if Vera was up to something I don't know anything about it, I'll swear that on oath. She wanted to talk to Mildred — well, give her a bit of a fright. I don't blame her, Mildred was an arrogant bitch, she needed — '

'How did she get her up to the Ridge?'

'Sent her a letter. I don't know what was in it, something to do with what happened years ago, I don't know. I saw it in Mildred's bag that morning, frightened her sick it had, served her right. Then Vera rang her up, arranged to meet her. I was nowhere near, I was at the Pavilion all evening, I've got a hundred witnesses — ' His voice strengthened, he was almost the old Wilfred — in the wrong again, but innocent of evil intent, innocent of any knowledge of it. 'Listen, I've got to get home. Lin's been a bit funny lately, I don't want her to start suspecting anything. I'll just cut out now and no more need be said. I know I've been a bit of a fool — '

'If it had stopped at Mildred that's all you'd have been. But then there was Rosa.'

'Rosa?' Wilfred made an effort, placing an inconsequential name, but his control was giving way, the effort was too painful.

'She saw you coming here, saw Vera opening the door to you. Saw Vera with Gilbert. And she knew something was going on at The Laurels — how could she not know, Mrs Blunt's niece. She started making a nuisance of herself, coming here, asking questions. Then she approached me at

Emmeline's party. Vera knew that. Vera was there.'

Wilfred shrugged this aside. 'She couldn't recognize her. No one could recognize Rosa the way she'd done herself up.' Too late, he saw the contradiction in this, but the words were spoken.

Henry said calmly, 'Christ, Wilfred, you can't have it all ways. That race down through the wood has shaken something loose inside your head. Vera knew very well it was Rosa, because Emmeline said so loud enough for everyone to hear.'

Emmeline shifted uncomfortably. Wilfred did not look at her: like a man on the edge of a precipice he needed time to think out the move that would save him, but Henry gave him no time. 'Vera's got so much staked on this she hasn't let a single thing slip past her. She put the fear of God into you about what Rosa might have told me, but she'd got it all worked out, exactly how to stop Rosa wrecking everything. She told you what to do, and you did it.' He paused. 'You killed Rosa.'

'Oh, my God,' Wilfred said. He felt blindly for the nearest chair and sagged into it. 'I didn't, I didn't, I didn't — '

'Vera said you did.'

'I was nowhere near — '

'Vera said you were.'

Wilfred began to swear in a hoarse, frantic voice, clinging to his innocence with a rage of obscenities directed at Henry, at Gilbert, at Linda, at Vera, at Madame Lily. They had all betrayed him, they were all guilty, they were all making him the scapegoat. For what? For his degraded marriage, his debts, his impotence . . .

For months he had sustained a double life, lived with suspense and improvisation, while underneath the strain stretched him to breaking point. The worst strain of all was the need to deceive himself, to keep going and, at the end, to come face to face with his own deception. Watching him,

Henry was not surprised his control had given way. He had kept up appearances for years under his wife's infidelities, the Hewitts' insulting treatment, appearances were all he had. He was not made of the stuff of desperate venture, without Vera he would have attempted nothing, take her away and he collapsed and the filth came out, snarling in the stuffy, listening room.

Madame Lily stared vacantly at the gas fire. Wilfred might just as well be talking to himself for all the effect it had on her. Emmeline had grown paler and paler until her eyes looked like bruises in her white face. She had heard bad language before but never anything as foul as this. Henry said, 'Go and stand in the hall if you want to.' She shook her head and looked away from him.

He had spoken in a hard, clear tone, not out of consideration for Emmeline but with the intention of pulling Wilfred up short. It worked. Wilfred glared at Emmeline, furious she had escaped his rage. 'What the fucking hell is she doing here?' Then, shouting, 'I never killed Rosa. I wasn't even in Avenridge.'

'Weren't you now?' Henry said, softly derisive.

Wilfred was bursting, but the voice that issued from him was muted, anguished, 'I *wasn't*. I swear.'

'That's not good enough.'

'I was — I was in Manchester. Miles away.'

Henry shook his head.

'There was — there was a phone box.'

'A phone box. Ah. Where?'

Wilfred struggled. He would have had his instructions that night, memorized them; in his present stress recollection was difficult, but he'd manage it, he knew he had to. 'On a corner. One road was Longford Road, the other Barlow Road — no, Street.'

Henry considered this. 'You'd better find someone who saw you there, or it's your word against Vera's.'

'Did she say . . .' He was slow taking it in. Then he yelled, 'It *had* to be me, I had to pretend to be you — give Rosa that message, she expected a man's voice. It was *Vera* met Rosa at the canal. She was going to bribe her, bribe her to shut up and go away.'

'And I suppose there was a struggle and another accident. Like Mildred's.'

'That's what she said. I had to believe her. There was nothing I could do then. It was too late.'

'It was always too late for you, Wilfred. You still can't see what Vera's done, can you? She's kept herself so much in the background she's almost invisible — but then, she had to learn to do that when she was very young. She engineered it so Gilbert came here, she got you to do that, didn't she? It didn't take much to set Linda and her silly friends chattering to Gilbert about this medium with remarkable gifts. Just at the right moment, too. You were walking out on him, he was desperate enough to turn anywhere.'

Wilfred could see the trap closing, he had the painful concentration of a man seeking the last way out.

'Just one visit was enough; Vera was ready, waiting. She knew exactly how to handle him, isolate him, prey on his nerves. But she wasn't going to send him mad. She was going to kill him. You've suspected that, more than once.'

'No — I swear it — '

'She made all the moves. You didn't have to do anything. Except take the Rover up to the Ridge tonight.'

'Well, it was — I only did what she told me, I didn't know *why*. If I admit it about the Rover, and the phone call, will you keep me out of all this?'

'Be your age.' Henry looked Wilfred up and down. 'You've gone to pieces and Vera's not here to put you together. When you made off from the Ridge she told you to hang around for a while. You daren't go home till you knew how things stood, but she needed you out of the way, in case we picked you up and you said too much. She wouldn't say that to you, though, she just said meet her here, didn't she?'

Wilfred stared at him, savagely mute.

'Meet her here and she'd fix things up. She has. For herself. If she hasn't left Avenridge by now she soon will.'

Wilfred's putty-coloured face flooded red. He shouted, 'You said — she'd said — you'd got her — '

'I did? Oh, no, you must have misunderstood me. We will get her, it'll be quicker if you help us. Give us her description. What's the make of her car? Its number, its colour. Where does she live? Come on, Wilfred, save yourself, she's not going to save you.'

Wilfred sat with his mouth clenched. The red was draining from his face, but he was saying nothing.

'Or she might still be there, at her flat. She had to go back for those letters.'

'Letters?'

'She daren't leave those. You know where she lives, don't you? She never let you go there, there was never going to be anything to link you with her. Can't you see what she was doing — '

'What letters?'

'They were her insurance, she's ruthless enough to think they will still be when all this has blown over. Nothing stops Vera, you should know that. You can tie her in with all this. What about it?'

Wilfred had fallen back into silence, his eyes on Henry, staring him out, holding himself together.

Henry said, 'You've never known who Vera is, have you? Why she's done this? For you? Because you're next in line to inherit and she was helping you towards it? You bloody fool, do you think any woman could love you enough to connive and kill for *your* benefit?'

The last, longed-for deception was tearing slowly from Wilfred, leaving a face that said nakedly *leave me that*. Not love, not a remnant of the will that had driven him, but a despairing glimpse of the effort itself: *at least if it had worked it would have been worth it.*

'There was never anything in it for you, Wilfred, there never would have been. You're not next in line. Vera is. She's Gilbert's half sister. They had the same father.'

It took Wilfred a moment to understand, then the shock hit him. His face collapsed in an agony of comprehension.

Henry nodded towards Madame Lily. 'Ask her. She'll tell you.'

Wilfred brought his gaze round to her slowly. His voice was scarcely more than a whisper. 'Why in Christ's name didn't you tell me?'

Madame Lily roused herself, returned his gaze dimly. 'You didn't ask.'

'Oh, Christ,' Wilfred whispered.

Would he still have done it if he had known? He was a foolish man, a hopeless man, tempted beyond himself. But if he had known . . . Yes, Henry thought, he'd still have done it. Now all he had left was revenge. 'Are you going to help us?'

Wilfred closed his eyes. After a moment he opened them, and nodded.

Henry said to Emmeline. 'Go to the front door. There's a plain clothes man out there in a shop doorway or something, or a uniformed man trying to look like one. If you can't see anyone, stand on the step and shout officer, that'll bring them all in.'

Emmeline went out thankfully, passing Wilfred, who did not even look up.

Henry and Emmeline walked home from the police station. They had been there some time, made statements, then, as they were about to leave, learnt that Vera had been picked up by a patrol car on the Ashbourne Road. They had been offered a lift home but Emmeline said, 'I'd like to walk, please.' So they set out, taking short cuts through the town which was going to sleep in the soft, enfolding silence of the snow.

Emmeline walked with her head bent, stray snowflakes glistening on her hair. 'Will they bring her back here?'

'For questioning, yes.'

Between pools of lamplight the shadow of shuttered buildings fell upon them. Across an untrodden sweep of snow the Pavilion glittered like an ice palace. 'I'd better not leave it too late to get off,' Henry said.

'Must you go tonight?'

'The weather might close in. If I leave it till morning I could be stuck.'

'I suppose so . . .' After a while she spoke again, her voice muted, not looking up. 'It was awful. Wilfred in that dreadful room, the things he said. He'd gone back there, trusting her, the way he'd trusted her all along.'

Henry said dryly, 'I don't think trust had much to do with it. Self-interest, confusion, greed — whatever she could exploit. He was as helpless in her hands as Gilbert was.'

'But you — how could you know that was what would happen?'

'I didn't know.'

'You mean you guessed?'

'Not quite. I thought like her.'

Emmeline made a muffled sound of amazement, as if she would reject this. 'You've never even seen her.'

He thought of the girl in the garden, all those years ago. She had hated him then, without reason: she had reason enough now. Hatred was what she lived by. And destruction, which they both knew about, although from opposite sides. He glanced down at the top of Emmeline's spangled hair. 'All in a day's work,' he said gently. He thought she must be tired and it had all rather shaken her, but he couldn't take away from her what she knew. He halted and she looked up at him, her face pale in the lamplight. 'Are you all right?'

She nodded, smiled her wisp of a smile. The falling snow glittered between them.

'Good.'

They walked on again. He took her hand and drew it through his arm. To cheer her up he teased her, softly, 'I always said I could rely on a splendid chap like you, young Dash.'

He thought she sighed.